TIGER LILY

Also Available from Noel-Anne Brennan:

Burning Bright (Tiger Lily 2)
The Sword of the Land
The Blood of the Land
Daughter of the Desert
A Changed World
Winter Reckoning Meow Cat Poems
Hurricane Warning (poems)
February's Country (poems)

TIGER LILY

NOEL ANNE BRENNAN

AUCTOREM
HOUSE

Auctorem House
276 5th Ave, Ste 704-2591
New York, NY 10001
www.auctoremhouse.com
Phone: 1 888-332-7718

Published by Auctorem House: 04/21/2024

ISBN: 978-1-965687-90-1(sc)
ISBN: 978-1-965687-91-8(e)

Library of Congress Control Number: 2025905434

TABLE OF CONTENTS

CHAPTER ONE

T HE SUN WAS NO LONGER as warm as it had been and the rock where she rested was starting to cool. Twilight had come all too soon. Lily stretched and yawned, baring her impressive canines, not wanting to leave yet. Dusk would not be a problem; she knew her way around these woods and could find her way out of them blindfolded. Besides, her night vision was excellent. But Beth was due home for dinner soon and then Beth's father, Lily's ex, would be picking Beth up, and she couldn't be late. Beth didn't know what her mom was and neither did her ex, fortunately.

Lily sniffed the air. She wanted to be sure no one had wandered close to her rock while she napped, even though it was unlikely. If anyone caught her here, it would mean disaster. She always kept an ear cocked for danger when she napped in the woods and she almost literally slept with her eyes open, or at least with only the third eyelid closed. But nothing substituted for smell, which some biologists claimed was the oldest sense.

Lily opened her mouth slightly, letting the forest-scented air roll into the back of her throat across her Jacobson's organ. A fox, which she knew about; the animal had given her rock a wide and startled berth earlier; a fisher, heading for the stream. Lily grimaced. Vicious little animals, fishers. Although they were no match for her, she preferred not to tangle with them. And rabbits. Now, she was hungry. She almost considered having dinner right there, al fresco, a nice rabbit for starters, but it would probably take too long. She needed to be home. The most important scent was the one she didn't find. There was no trace of humans on the wind. It was risky but she needed these little episodes alone in the woods, needed them desperately, and it was hard to find a safe place for them and getting harder. Too much development. She grimaced.

Lily rose to her feet in one fluid motion, the last red light of the sun burnishing the orange in her coat, making deep shadows of the dark stripes. She stretched, extending her claws, and then shuddered. Fur and muscles rippled, and the air shimmered. Tiger vanished and a naked, well-built and impressively muscled woman in her early thirties stood on the rock.

Lily ran a hand through her short red-brown hair and then looked around for her clothes. She shivered. It was late spring but not late enough, apparently. It was chilly now that the sun was almost down and her fur was gone. Her clothes were where she had left them, in a neatly folded pile. She reached for them, stretching again. This had been a peaceful time, and just what she had needed.

She was the only shape-shifting tiger she had ever heard of, even with the proliferation of "psi diseases". No one knew she existed. That fact kept her safe, that and the quiet place she had picked to call home. She had always protected her secret at all costs. She had no idea that not all that far away someone else with her abilities had been attacking children.

"Ow," she muttered as she stepped a sharp stone, a chipped piece of the ledge she had rested on. She hastily pulled on jeans and sweatshirt, and then checked her foot before pulling on socks and hiking boots. Blood oozed from a scrape but it wasn't bad. She had almost certainly stepped on a few sharp pebbles in her tiger form but they hadn't bothered her then. She didn't know why not but then there were a great many more important things that she did not understand about her ability to change form. Unfortunately, there was no one she could ask.

The sun had set by the time she got home. The tiny house had once been a summer cottage near the Rhode Island shore. Some enterprising owner had it winterized and rented it out to students from the university. When he grew tired of being a landlord who always had to pour money into repairs, he had put it on the market. It was small and it had been a "fixer-upper" when Lily bought it but that was the only reason she could afford it. Its relative isolation was another plus as far as Lily was concerned. It was on a dead end street near a wood patch. She had neighbors on her street but they weren't right on top of one another and they tended to mind their own business.

The phone was ringing as she closed the door behind her. She lunged for it and caught it just before it went to voicemail.

"Hey, Mom, I've been texting and trying your cell but all I got is voicemail. Sarah wants to know if I can stay for dinner. Can I? Please? Her mom says it's okay. She'll drive me home right after. Please?"

"You know your father is picking you up tonight, Beth. It's his weekend. And you know we can't make him wait." She had forgotten to turn on her cell when she left the woods or she might have headed this off earlier. Now her daughter would have her heart set on dinner with her best friend.

Beth had only the slightest of ideas what it meant to make her father wait for something he wanted, something he felt was his due. Even that slimmest of notions was too much, and Lily wanted to keep it from getting worse. A nine-year-old, no matter how precocious and intelligent, should not understand some things, not yet.

"Sarah and me - I mean, Sarah and I - are working on our science project.

We're making this awesome volcano; it smokes and everything, and then the computer tells it when to erupt, well not really erupt but you know, it looks like lava and I did most of the code for that."

Lily grinned. She was inordinately proud of her daughter. It was fortunate Beth couldn't see her right now or Beth would take advantage.

"I'm sorry, Beth, but you need to come right home."

"But mooom! Ms. Lattinger said I could have dinner! And it's mac and cheese! Here, she wants to talk to you."

"Elizabeth!" But it was too late. Before Lily could object she found herself on the phone with Sarah's mother.

"Lily, it's Deb Lattinger. I know your ex is picking Beth up later and I don't want to cause any trouble; I understand how he gets."

Deb thought she understood, at any rate, Lily mused. Deb was divorced, too and had occasional visitation "run-ins" with her ex. But nobody could really comprehend what John was like, not unless they had lived with him, lived through a marriage with him and come out the other side, maybe not intact, but at least out.

"I'll feed them dinner and bring Beth back within an hour, pretty much.

That should give enough time, shouldn't it? And no more science project tonight. You should see it, though; it's pretty dramatic. They're really getting it together. And having a great time of it. Those two are pretty hard to separate."

"That they are. Yes, an hour should do it. As long as Beth is back here and ready to go before John shows up it will be fine. Thank you. I was going to give her pea soup and salad; no way that can compete with mac and cheese. And Deb, I owe you one. I really appreciate this."

She did, too. It would give her a little extra time, badly needed time, to prepare herself for seeing John. It wasn't that she missed him and it certainly wasn't that she still loved him. Lily was, if anything, slightly afraid of him.

Actually, that wasn't quite true. She was a little afraid of him but more afraid of herself, something she would never admit to herself and she would certainly never admit it to him.

As the founder and CEO of Skyline Pharmaceuticals John had more than enough money and power to intimidate most people. He had government contracts and government connections that were, in this day and age, invaluable. She knew he had contracts with the new Psi Disease Center Special Unit which was enough by itself to frighten almost anyone. It should have frightened her more than it did.

Lily was not especially intimidated by any of this, however. It wasn't even that she had her secret to protect, a secret that John had not once come close to guessing, not in fifteen years of marriage. If he hadn't guessed then, he wouldn't now. But it was different when it came to Beth. Lily was terrified of what John might discover about their only child.

There might be nothing to worry about, nothing to discover. There was nothing to worry about; Lily murmured the oft-repeated mantra. Beth had never exhibited the remotest hint of any paranormal ability and Beth had watched her like the proverbial hawk. The problem was that not all the genetic markers for paranormal capacities were known yet. Certainly nothing like Lily's ability had ever been mapped.

Neither Lily nor Beth had ever shown any signs of the more common "psi diseases" which terrified the public and that the media loved to exploit: no telepathy, no precognition, nothing like that. But Lily knew her ex-husband well enough to realize that if he thought there was anything to find, he would have had Beth's DNA extensively tested and examined and that he would continue to examine it on a regular basis until he believed such scrutiny was no longer necessary. Lily's own ability had not appeared until her preteen years. There was nothing she could do to stop John from testing Beth, nothing, at least, without contesting John's court-mandated visitation rights, which she was not prepared to do. There was another thing that frightened her: how much she had loved John, or thought she had, and how close she had come to telling him her secret.

"It's only a couple of nights," Lily told herself as she packed Beth's bag. "What could possibly go wrong? There's nothing to worry about."

She finished just in time. Deborah's Prius pulled up and disgorged a chattering Beth, still giggling with her friend. Lily said her thanks, waved goodbye and managed to get Beth out of the shirt and jeans smudged with macaroni and God knew what else, and into cleaner clothes just as John's Lexus pulled into the small driveway.

"Did you pack Bunny-buns?" Beth was nine years old but completely unabashed by her attachment to the stuffed rabbit she had since she was an infant.

"Of course. Are you sure you don't need the book bag and the homework?"

"Homework's all done, mom; told you that. I am taking the American Poetry book, though. In case things get too intense with dad, I can pretend I've got that stuff to read. Okay, okay, I will read it. You don't have to give me that look. And yes, I have my cell, and no, don't worry, I won't drive up the bill by texting too much. I'll be back Sunday evening. You know dad. We won't be late." Lily helped her daughter into the car. She would have said, "Call me", except that she and Beth both knew that John would not permit this. Instead she whispered, "You can text me if you want."

"John," she said with a nod. "How are you?" It was courtesy, for her daughter's sake, for propriety.

"Well, and you're looking well, too, Lily."

John Belkner looked good and he knew it. He was approaching forty but he looked ten years younger. His hair was thick and black, and clipped short but not so short its natural wave didn't show. He had the lanky physique of a runner and in fact he did run every day, three miles rain or shine. He did it in the predawn hours so it wouldn't detract from his business day. He also lifted weights during his lunch hour, when he could, which wasn't often, and he bicycled for an hour in the evenings. Working hard, he liked to say, was no excuse to let yourself go to flab. He took a certain amount of pride in referring to himself, rather anachronistically, as a "babe magnet". Being rich and powerful, Lily thought, might have more to do with that, but the looks didn't hurt. She was not so far gone as to be bitter.

"We'll be back Sunday by four, four-thirty at the latest. We might fly. If we do, I'll let you know. We'll come into Quonset; can't put up with the hassle in Warwick."

"Right," said Lily. He said the same thing every time. He had his private company jet which almost never flew into T.F. Green in Warwick, the Providence airport, where they would have to deal with international as well as domestic air traffic. It was fine with her; Quonset was much more convenient as well as far less busy and more laid-back. Beth much preferred driving to flying but that was not a consideration if her father was in a hurry. Apparently he wasn't now. He was quite amenable to letting his daughter enjoy the scenery between Rhode Island and his rural getaway in upstate New York. They would not be stopping at a motel, however. Beth could doze in the comfortable back seat of the Lexus utility while the chauffeur drove through the night.

Lily gave her daughter a kiss and watched the Lexus pull out of the driveway. As usual, she fought back trepidation. John had the resources to give his daughter everything she could want or need. His money provided her with the private school that Lily otherwise could never have afforded and it also provided her with the after school activities that her friends enjoyed.

"I don't know why you don't get your lawyer to go after John for more than child support," Deborah had said to her on more than one occasion. "Not that he's shirking in that department but he can certainly afford more. You helped him build his company to where it is. He owes you."

That was how Deb managed her lifestyle. She was a Narragansett Indian, formerly married to a member of that tribe who had more than made good. Her ex-husband owned a small chain of restaurants. Since she had divorced him, Deborah had never had to work another day. She now spent her time volunteering for the tribe.

That approach did nothing for Lily. If she could have managed without the child support, she would have. She wanted nothing at all from John and considered it more than unfortunate that life dictated otherwise. Her position as an anthropology instructor at the university would never provide them with everything that they needed so she had to rely on John, at least for the foreseeable future.

It was definitely getting chilly now. Lily crossed her arms and stared off into the lilac-scented dusk. For the briefest of moments, she thought she smelled something on the wind. The scent of another tiger. But that couldn't be. Her human nose could not have picked that up; she was imagining things. The scent of lilac over-powered everything, anyway.

She loved spring and lilacs, and she loved the feeling of new beginnings, real or not. Spring did that to her but in some ways, it was more ending than beginning. Her semester, at least, was almost over. The desk in the corner of her bedroom was piling up with papers from her university students, and somewhere in the mess was the application for Beth's camp, the two-week summer sleep-over camp that Beth wanted so badly, the camp Sarah and some of the other girls were going to. She might as well get started with some of this.

For a moment she considered bringing in some firewood but getting the wood stove started was more trouble than it was worth at this time of year.

Easier to wear a sweater and if necessary turn up the thermostat on the oil furnace. She went inside to the kitchen, found a can of cat food and opened it.

"Monster!" she called, but it was hardly necessary. The big Maine Coon appeared from wherever he had been napping. He was a huge gray tiger-striped cat, almost the size of a small pony, with enormous white paws. He invariably intimidated unwary humans but in reality he was a timid thing who loved and trusted only Lily and Beth.

"Meep!" said the cat, in gratitude for dinner, and Lily headed upstairs to work.

It was almost eleven thirty when the sound registered: a knock on the door. Lily frowned, emerging from her work-trance, unable to imagine who it might be at this time of night. She pushed aside the stack of papers, grabbed the baseball bat from its place near the waste basket and headed for the door. She flicked on the outside light just in time. She didn't need it but most ordinary people would not understand how her night vision could be that good.

"Stan!"

"You forgot, didn't you. And you turned off your cell and the ringer on your landline, and you aren't checking your email. I assume the kid got off okay with her dad. And I assume you're starving and you forgot to eat." He held up a large pizza box, still emanating heat. "Now that you know it's just me, you can put down the bat. If we were under nuclear attack, you'd be the absolute last to know, babe." He managed to lean around the pizza box, not an easy feat, and give her a kiss.

"Right on all counts." Lily felt herself flushing. She ignored the fact that he had called Beth "the kid" and her "babe", something she hated, and took the box from him with one hand and with the other grabbed the front of his sweatshirt and pulled him into the kitchen. Stanley Brentworth was a postdoctoral student in biogenetics. They had met at a gathering for new faculty and that had been that.

At first glance they appeared completely mismatched, a fact which caused occasional remarks and speculation among their acquaintances. He was tall and geeky-looking. Lily was tall, curvaceous (a "hottie") as one of her students had written, anonymously, on the "GradeYourProfessors.com" site, and strong enough to have astonished more than her fair share colleagues who had asked for assistance in moving furniture. Stanley was heavily involved in work very few understood, not even his colleagues. Lily was an anthropologist. Anyone, she thought, could understand what she did, it was just that few cared to.

"Mmm, pizza. God, I'm starved." She started to open the box right there in the kitchen.

"Let's take it to the living room and eat it on the couch." Stan scooped up the box, a roll of paper towels that would substitute as napkins, and deposited it all on the battered coffee table.

"Damn, it's cold in here."

"I try to keep the heating bill down." Lily grinned and sidled next to him on the old couch. As long as she kept her feelings for Stan in the realm of attraction, liking, and sex, she should be okay. She needed to be careful. There were a few things about him that had been bothering her lately, but she chalked it up to end of semester stress.

"I got it half and half. The pizza. Broccoli, eggplant and olives on your half. Pepperoni, meatballs and sausage on mine."

"Thanks. One of these days, you won't have an artery left to your name." Lily had never figured out why, in her tiger form she was, like all cats, an obligate carnivore, but in her human form she was a vegetarian. Well, almost a vegetarian. She did still eat fish.

"Hey, isn't that that kid from your class?" Stan had turned on the tv and one of the local stations was doing its version of the evening's local interest news. "That Thai kid or Laotian or whatever?"

"Young woman," said Lily. "By the time they're freshmen they are young men and women. You should remember that. Hey, that does look like her. Mai Lee."

"The Laotian kid, right?" "Hmong."

"What?"

"She's Hmong. One of the old Hill Tribes. During the Vietnam War they fought on our side." She glanced at Stan but he wasn't paying attention to her. He was focused on the tv. "Oh, for God's sake, Stan, learn some history."

Stan turned up the volume.

"The family is denying it, of course." The tv reporter was an earnest young woman, blonde and good-looking, and from Lily's standpoint maybe twelve years old and very overly made-up. "Out of all the varieties of the current psi plagues, lycanthropy is the rarest. But no matter how unlikely, the PDC must investigate a report like this. A PDC Special Unit team is already on site."

The camera angle switched, zooming in now on the young woman Lily had identified as one of her students.

"I cannot understand why anyone would accuse any member of our family of this frightening disease. We are the victims here. All I can assume is that there is some ethnic or cultural discrimination in play here."

Stan reached over and hit the mute button. "She's right," he said. He looked tense, focused. "That Thai kid from your class. Good-looking kid, by the way, and good with the sound bite. There's something else going on here. Why would anyone accuse someone of being a werewolf? It's barely recognized as a psi disease. Hardly anybody knows about that; it's not on the radar. There've been what, three cases? And I should know. It's my research field." He grinned and then struck a pose and howled. "Hoooowwwwl! Werewolves of Providence! Hoooowwwl!"

"She's not Thai, she's Hmong. And you're not Warren Zevon so stop before you get all the neighborhood dogs barking. And lycanthropy is now being used as a catchall, to refer to any kind of shape shifting, I believe." She knew better than to point this out. It was hardly in her self-interest. But she couldn't help herself; it was undoubtedly the academic in her.

"Yeah, whatever. Like I said there's what, three cases? Anyway, I have something else in mind for us for the weekend other than following the local news, now that your kid is gone."

Lily never invited Stan to spend the night when Beth was home. Beth knew they were "dating", as she put it, and she wasn't stupid, but Lily had certain self- imposed limits and they were ironclad.

"Beth," she said. "Her name is Beth." "Right. Sorry."

That might have been the end of that discussion. Looking back on it later, Lily fervently wished that it had been, that she had done something to prevent later developments. Suggest, for example, that she and Stan go somewhere else. A motel, perhaps. A trip to the Cape. A tent down in Burlingame Park. The reason didn't matter. Where they went wouldn't have mattered, as long as it was away. As it was, they turned off the tv and went to bed.

Early on Saturday morning, far too early, there was a knock on the door. A knocking, a banging, really. Far too loud and far, far too early.

"Who the hell could that be?" grumbled Stan.

"Stay here," said Lily, trying to sensible. "Obviously it's for me."

Clutching her ratty old robe around her she went to the kitchen door and opened it. Standing on the cracked cement steps was a little girl with her dark hair in braids.

"Please help me, Ms. Mossberg. I didn't know where else to go. The cops have got all my family watched. But you know my sister. And I'm scared. He'll get me!"

As a reflex, Lily glanced behind the child but there was no sign of police or anyone else on the little dead-end road.

"Come in, Lucy." She took the girl gently by the shoulder and drew her in. "Lucy?" Stan had not taken her advice. He stood behind Lily in the kitchen, his only nod to decency being the t-shirt he had pulled on which almost covered his old boxer shorts.

"Lucinda. Lucinda Lee. Lucy. She's Beth's classmate, in Beth's school on a scholarship. And she's Mai's sister. Mai Lee. My student. You saw her on the news last night." Lily positioned herself between Stanley and the child. The evening's news cast was coming back to her and she was beginning to realize how serious it was. A PDC Special Unit, the reporter had said.

"Lucy, come in, you're shivering. Who is after you? They can't be watching your whole family." And why would they? Lucy's family was vast and as far as Lily knew extended through several states. "Can you tell us what happened? How can I help?"

Lucy allowed herself to be seated at the kitchen table while Lily went about making toast and hot cocoa. Lucy accepted both gratefully but glanced sideways at Stan.

"That's Stan. He's okay," said Lily. As she spoke she suddenly wondered if it were true. Stan worked in biogenetics, the same field that had made John so rich. It was a very hot field today due to the touted proliferation of psi "diseases" and the attempt to cure them. Stan had made no secret of his focus on that aspect of the discipline and on his hope for continued grant money and an eventual endowed chair at some university.

Since most of this was academic politics are outside her field, it had never bothered Lily. She didn't take his ambitions all that seriously and she had actually managed to pretty much ignore his research, so accustomed was she to successfully hiding her own secret. Lucy's situation might be another matter entirely but it was too late for any second thoughts. Stan pulled out a kitchen chair and sat down, helping himself to a piece of toast. Lucy took this an endorsement on Lily's part and relaxed a little.

"They've found kids who have been attacked." Lucy's eyes were big. "Their souls were stolen and even the shaman can't find the souls. The kids - they just lie there, they can't talk or anything. And now my little cousin - her soul, one of her souls, is lost and can't come home." Lucy's eyes welled with tears. "And they think maybe one of us did it! The government people think that!"

Stan caught Lily's glance over the top of Lucy's head. He rolled his eyes. "Stan, if you can't take it seriously, go back to bed." Lily surprised herself but her temper was frayed. Lucy was terrified, and she wouldn't have Stan make fun of the child, however ridiculous he found her story.

"Kids' souls got stolen, right." Stan pushed back his chair but he made no move to rise. "And somebody called the cops and the PDC Special Unit, of course the Special Unit, beloved of the media, and they decided it was what, werewolves. Because somebody has a feud going here or doesn't like Hmong or Asians or animists or something. I think Lucy's big sister is right about that. But the Specials, bless their over-funded rotten little souls, are responding, acting like there's real werewolves here, a psi infection. What would do more good would be the sacrifice of a chicken or a pig, more than one if possible, by a good shaman. There's gotta be at least one good Hmong shaman in the city."

Lily stared at him, openmouthed. This was the guy who last night didn't seem to know who the Hmong were, who couldn't tell a Hmong from a lowland Thai. Why had he pretended?

"What, you think you're the only one who ever learned any ethnology? Why don't I start some coffee? Hot cocoa is great stuff but it just doesn't do it for me."

"What we think," whispered Lucy, "what the shamans think, is that the souls might be eaten. One of the souls of all the six children." According to the beliefs of some Hmong, each person had four souls, all necessary. The loss of any one of them could cause a person to lapse into what a Westerner would probably call a coma.

"And my cousin, too." Lucy's eyes were spilling over with tears. "And I might be next. I thought maybe you could help. You're Beth's mom and you're Mai's professor, and you know something about these things."

"Not more than the shamans do, or the cops," said Lily. "And why does anybody think it's a werewolf anyway?"

"They don't," said Lucy. "It's not a wolf. They think it's a tiger. A were-tiger. That's what they called it. The shamans think it might be. And the doctor cops."

"The PDC agents," said Stan. He looked more interested and excited than contemptuous or amused. "A tiger, really." His fingers twitched. Lily knew what that meant. Stan wanted his laptop. He had some notes he wanted to make, something he was sure would lead to a profitable area of investigation. Good research potential. Lily did not want anything in her life to be research material, not even one of Beth's classmates.

CHAPTER TWO

Tᴴᴇʀᴇ ᴡᴀꜱɴ'ᴛ ᴛɪᴍᴇ ꜰᴏʀ ᴍᴜᴄʜ of anything, as it turned out. Stan made coffee, and he and Lily both had a cup. This was a good thing; without her morning coffee, Lily found it hard to function. But there was no time for even a second cup before the stream of visitors began arriving. First was Jen Lee, Lucy's mom. Apparently it hadn't taken much in the way of deductive reasoning to figure out where her daughter was.

"Lucinda will be more safe at home than here and we will not let harm come to her." Jen was in the process of tying a colored string around her daughter's wrist for supernatural protection.

Lily was a little taken aback. It had never occurred to her that Lucy had planned to actually stay with her.

"We have the ceremony prepared already, for this evening, so she will be fine. You might want to consider something like that for your Beth," Jen Lee suggested earnestly. "Where is she?" She looked around anxiously.

It was at this moment that Lily realized that Stan had made good escape, no doubt to find a little more socially acceptable attire for himself. This was a relief, and not just from a fashion standpoint, although Lily herself was still in her ancient robe.

"Beth is with her father," she said. "Spending the weekend in upstate New York. I doubt the were - the tige - the bad spirit - will find her there."

"Probably not," Jen agreed, "but when she gets back you might want her to be safe. We could do a ceremony for Beth."

Lily was touched. She doubted the Lees were well off. She realized that she didn't know much about them. She knew Lucy was in Beth's class on a scholarship and she knew Lucy's older sister Mai was a standout university student in her upper-level anthropology class, headed for grad school, but that was about it. She had a sudden desire to get Beth back home immediately.

"It sounds as though you think there really are spirits out to get children and not just someone with a grudge as Mai suggested last night." Spirits or more human predators, the result was the same. She wanted her child home with her.

"Yes, we talked to a shaman, my father," Jen Lee began, but she was interrupted by another knock on the door.

"Hello?" Lily called.

The knocker did not wait for more of an invitation but opened the door and stuck his head in.

"Excuse me, Ms. Mossberg? Dr. Mossberg? Professor? I'm not sure what to call you."

"Any of the above is fine." Lily knew she sounded as grumpy as she felt and she didn't care. She examined the identification and the badge the speaker extended toward her like some sort of peace offering. They identified him as Detective Wesley Martling, Providence Police.

"A bit out of your jurisdiction, aren't you, detective?" she said. "This is Narragansett, not Providence."

"Yes, I am out of my jurisdiction but I'm hoping to put out a fire, head off this thing at the pass - oh hell. I was never very good with figures of speech. What I would like to do is stop a bunch of damn fool media hysteria before it gets any worse and panics the public, jurisdiction or not. And I would like to stop some sick pervert from preying on children, if that's what this is. And no, before you ask, I am not a member of the PDC Specials although I now have to work with them. I wish they had stayed out of this. Hello again and good morning, Mrs. Lee. And you must be Lucy." He smiled at the girl, who did not smile back. "I'm glad your mom found you."

Detective Wesley Martling was short and slightly round. Anyone who thought his shape was due to lack of conditioning would have been due for a surprise, however. Lily could see the muscles ripple under his short-sleeved shirt. His dark hair was clipped close to his head in a military cut. Lily guessed his age as somewhere in the thirties.

"Detective." Jen Lee sounded much less than pleased to see him. Because he had been questioning her during the night or because he possibly did not take any supernatural aspects of this case seriously? Lily had no way to guess.

"Just what is this case, detective? Nobody, not even the media, seems to want to be clear about what's going on here." It was Stanley, returned so quietly that no one had noticed him, dressed now in faded jeans and a hooded sweatshirt that said "Watson University". He wasted no time but extended his hand.

"Dr. Stanley Brentworth, biogenetics post-doc at Watson University." "Ah. Good for you. In that nice new building you've got over there, courtesy of our taxes and - which referendum was it?" Detective Martling did not accept the offered hand. "I would be delighted to speak with you later but I'm actually here to see Dr. Mossberg. She, I believe, had or has, the oldest Lee daughter in her anthropology class?" He made it a question but there was absolutely no doubt he knew the answer.

"And I would like to talk with her before my esteemed colleague from the PDC Special Unit does. There is no 'team', by the way, as the media reported last night. Just this one PDC doctor." He intercepted the look between Stan and Lily. "The explanations can come later, when there is time. I would appreciate it, too, Mrs. Lee, if you and Lucinda would wait here until I get some of this cleared up. It might give the PDC guy less to build into his fairy tale.”

“He is right.” Jen Lee made an odd ally for the Providence detective. They all looked at her. “Lucy and I will wait here until you are finished. Go talk to him, Lily.”

“Do I have time to change my clothes?” asked Lily, looking down at her bathrobe.

“Later. Believe me, I’ve seen worse.”

“I’ll just go work on my notes,” said Stan, excusing himself, heading for the stairs.

Lily took the detective into the living room where he sat on the battered easy chair and she on the old couch. It occurred to her, suddenly but with a sense of inevitability, that Stan would be perched at the top of the stairs where he could overhear what they said.

“I’m sorry, I neglected to offer you coffee, detective.” He shook his head; it didn’t matter.

“I hope we’ll have time for much lengthier discussion later. But the reason I want to talk to you now, Doctor - Professor - uh Ms. Doctor Professor Mossberg -”

Lily grinned. “That sounds rather Germanically formal.” Despite herself, despite her preconceptions about police officers, she liked this one. “You can just call me Lily.”

“I will, Lily,” he grinned back at her, “if you call me Wes.” “Okay, Wes, what can I do for you?”

“You have probably deduced that so far, I don’t put much stock in the supernatural explanations for what’s going on here. At least I’m reluctant to; ordinary non-paranormal predators are more my line of work. And what is going on, by the way, is that there are six children, all of them Hmong, who have fallen into a coma within the last few days. Somebody mentioned a bad tiger spirit, a were tiger, a shape shifter, something like that, and mentioned it in connection with the Lees. As I understand it, the older Lee girl is a student of yours. The PDC guy will ask you about this.”

“Personally, I think it would be a better use of time to look into what they ate, or maybe mosquito bites and West Nile, things along those lines. Or, a worst case scenario, a predator who uses drugs to knock the kids out. I don't believe the Lees had anything to do with it; one of their kids was just one of the last victims. Be that as it may, the Hmong shamans are adamant about a tiger and then the media got hold of it and now the PDC. So tell me, since all of this did in fact happen in my jurisdiction, about Mai Lee's final paper for your anthropology class."

"What?"

"Exactly." Wes was expressionless. "I'm sorry - her paper?"

"I understand she turned it in early."

"She did. She's one of those super-motivated students. Always goes above and beyond. Final papers aren't due for another week but she got hers in already, along with a stamped, self-addressed envelope so I can mail it back to her, the whole nine yards."

"Mail it back to her?"

"Yes, some students do that; they want their papers back. Of course since hers was early, I can give it back in class. It was an 'A', by the way. And what does this matter?"

"She doesn't live on campus."

"No, detective." "Wes."

"No, Wes. As you well know, she lives with her family in Providence and commutes to class here. Sometimes she takes the bus."

"And her final paper was on - what?"

"A Hmong legend. I can't imagine what an anthropology term paper could have to do with any of this." But she could. As soon as Wes had mentioned the paper, she knew there was trouble and she knew one of the reasons behind it.

"The Special Unit doctor thinks it's got plenty to do with it. What Hmong legend?"

Lily hesitated. Finally, she sighed. "The legend of a tiger who eats the father of a family, takes over his appearance and then terrorizes and eats his family, one by one. Except for the youngest daughter. She outwits the tiger and eventually kills him."

Wes gave a long, low whistle. "Wow! Of course there's more to this term paper than just recounting a legend; am I right?"

"Quite right. This paper did several things. Well, one important thing really, other than recount a plot that Stephen King would be proud of. The most salient, ah, important thing was to deconstruct the legend in the light of changing gender expectations in a traditional society." Lily paused for a moment but Wes did not comment. "The course for which this paper was written is 'cultural aspects of gender in a postmodern world'. Anthropology 407, suitable for upper level undergrads or early graduate students."

"Um," said Wes. "Right." He was making notes. "Back to the deconstructing thing."

"Deconstructing means -"

"I know what it means. Took my share of theory; I was a late grad student.

Only got my master's a few years back. One thing I never understood is why academicians can't just say what they mean. Present company excluded. I hope."

Despite herself, Lily laughed. "Mai's paper deconstr - uh, took the old legend apart," she paused and grinned at Wes, who grinned back, "in the light of the new roles and aspirations of Hmong women in America. Some of the newer tellings of this tale have the father killing the tiger and taking on the tiger's appearance, then waiting to kill his family. The traditional patrilineal family, the foundation of Hmong culture, turned on its head, become evil."

"And so it is up to the daughter to save the family, and thereby society, from a toxic patriarchy and to perhaps restore a balance with the natural world as represented by the tiger," said Wes.

Lily stared at him. After a moment she realized that her mouth was open and shut it. "Yes," she finally managed to croak.

"This is quite interesting in the light of the domestic violence statistics in the Hmong community, which are approaching those of the mainstream," said Wes. "Although I doubt Doctor Fletcher will see it quite that way."

"Who?" Lily was still thinking of his analysis of Mai's paper.

"Our Psi Disease Center Special Unit friend. Domestic violence in society as a whole is one epidemic that he should perhaps investigate. Although it isn't usually paranormal."

"If you don't mind my asking, Wes, what did you get your master's in? Criminal justice?"

"No, that was my bachelor's. My master's is in Women's Studies." Lily stared. No way, she thought, but didn't say it. Wes grinned.

"Yes, way," he said. "And you can see why our Special Unit colleague might find Ms. Lee's paper interesting."

"Interesting, maybe, but not much more than coincidental."

"In the realm of psi disease, especially this newest aspect of shape shifting, there is no such animal. So to speak. Besides, wait till you meet this guy."

"I hope that's not until I at least change my clothes."

"Probably won't be for a while, but he will want to talk to you. What else do you know about the Lees? Anything that might give any weight to this bad tiger thing?"

"Nothing. Or rather, I don't know much about them at all. I met Mrs. Lee once or twice at some school thing. You know her younger daughter's in the same class and school with my daughter. On a scholarship. Bright kid, like her older sister. And Mai is in my class at the university. That's it."

"Good enough. Perhaps I could have some coffee now? Oh my God, look at the size of that cat! A Maine Coon, right? Come here, handsome!"

To Lily's surprise and annoyance, Monster did, approaching the detective hesitantly before retreating to Lily's side. For Monster that was high praise.

Not much later, Wes left, with Jen and Lucinda Lee close behind. Lily had been advised not to leave the state for the time being, since the PDC operative would certainly want to talk to her and the Providence police might have more questions, although Wes stressed he thought this unlikely.

She went upstairs, with Monster following her, to find Stan apparently packing. As soon as Monster saw Stan he turned and ran. The cat did not approve of the current man in Lily's life. Packing for

Stan didn't mean much more than throwing stuff into his backpack but Lily was surprised.

"I thought we were spending the weekend together," she said.

He was sliding what looked like a small hypodermic needle into his pack. Lily frowned. He wasn't diabetic; she had never known him to need injections of any kind. What was that? She opened her mouth to ask.

"Sorry, babe, so did I. But all this werewolf stuff has changed things. We'll have to take a rain check. I wanna run back to the lab, check some data."

"What do you mean, 'changed things'?" She no longer had any doubt that he had been listening at the top of the stairs.

"You know this is my field, my research. Not just psi disease, but lycanthropy. If there really is something going on in Providence, and it sounds like there is, I want to check it out. Maybe I'll go up there. There's hardly anybody else working this side of the problem."

"Maybe you should leave that to the PDC Specials. Or talk to them."

Stan snorted. "My opinion of the Psi Disease Center Special Unit is right up there with that detective's. In fact, it's probably worse. If anybody could screw things up it would be some guy from the PDC. But you're right. It's a waste of time to go up there."

Screw things up, Lily thought. More likely, Stan wanted to gather whatever information he could before the PDC found it and put a lid on it, allowing no access. Stan had his career to think of. She would bet good money that he was heading straight from her house to Providence. Then she smiled slightly. Good luck to Stan gaining any sort of entrance or acceptance into the Hmong community if he went about it as she thought he would. She would lay odds that even the PDC guy might have better luck in that department.

Stan interpreted her smile his own way.

"I'm glad there are no hard feelings," he said. "You know how I feel about you, babe." He only called her "babe" when he was being far less than sincere. "If I can, I'll come back when I'm done at the lab."

"We'll make it up," Lily assured him.

After he had left she went back downstairs to clean up her kitchen and to try to think. It was well after noon on Saturday. Beth wasn't due home until tomorrow later in the afternoon. She could grade papers and finish Beth's camp application, and wait for the call from the PDC doctor which she knew would come. Or she could try to work out the mystery for herself. Beth should be quite safe at her father's house but it didn't feel safe to Lily. Jen Lee had lit the fires of unease in her. Jumping in to find things out for herself had its appeal.

"What do you think, Monster?" She leaned down and gave the big cat a gentle scratch behind the ear. "I think I'd do better by taking a walk and thinking than washing dishes and grading papers."

"Meep!" said Monster. It had always struck her as ironically incongruous that such a tiny sound came from such a large animal.

"I'm glad you agree."

Lily grabbed her jacket - the late April afternoon had turned chilly - and her cell phone - and headed for the door.

"No," she told Monster, "you stay here. Somebody has to hold down the fort." In reality, the big Maine Coon never went outside. His predecessor Fluffball had, but when Fluffball was eaten by a coyote, Beth had been inconsolable and so had Lily. After that, the rule was that any pet stayed inside.

Beyond that, the unvarnished truth was that Lily did her best thinking by herself, when she was on one of her walks. She carefully locked the door behind her even though she had little to worry about. Although this neighborhood had once been a party neighborhood "down the line" as the university students referred to winter rentals, most of the houses had been bought by owners who now chose to live in them rather than rent them out. The neighborhood had become working class, quiet, and relatively safe.

One of the features of this area which had so appealed to Lily was the small pockets of woods and tangled wetlands which had been left alone and undeveloped. This was just the environment favored by a person wanting a solitary walk or by a tiger on the prowl. In a few places these areas ran together into larger tracts. That these larger tracts were intersected several times by the more recent, and popular bike path did not bother Lily at all. She was quite capable of staying away from what she privately considered a small road, complete with lane markings and traffic signs but the truth was that it was interesting. It was amusing to watch the different creatures that used the path, and used it in so many different ways.

The good thing about the bicycle path was that its human users rarely strayed from it. With her emphasis on protecting her secret, that was reassuring for Lily. Today, Lily decided to push her luck. In tiger form she made herself comfortable behind some dense azalea shrubs that closely lined the path. From this barely adequate cover, she surveyed the bike path's recreational travelers.

The inline skaters, the people with their dogs, leashed or unleashed, were completely unaware of the golden eyed feline that lurked just off their safe highway. Occasionally, a leashed dog would bark itself into a frenzy, to the confusion of its owner, or an off-leash dog, something completely forbidden by the bike path's posted rules, would run cowering to its owner.

It was the running of these small dogs and the scampering of small children that made Lily quiver and even, to her own disgust, salivate. There was something almost irresistible about the erratic movement of small creatures, but resist she did. In part, it was the memory of Fluffball but it was also a self- imposed moral imperative. Lily would never attack a human or the animal companion of a human while in her tiger form. She could never let down her guard. Self-control had become easier over the years but occasionally the desire to spring surprised her still.

Tiger form did not diminish her capacity for human thought, although it did affect her desires. Her mental mantra on these occasions was "I am not a wild animal". She was beginning to understand that other shape shifters were not so constrained but she did not understand why. Nor did she understand how it was possible to consume a human soul, or why a shape shifter of any sort would want to do this. Shape shifting was too new a phenomenon, too new a "psi disease" for there to be much information about any of its forms, and there were too few shape shifters known. As Stan had pointed out, there were only three.

Or had been until now.

She knew she was playing with fire by being so close to humans in her animal form, especially in the light of the current media hysteria. Part of the purpose of her walk today was to consider just what the rules were by which other shape shifters operated. This, obviously, was not the way to go about it.

Lily carefully backed away from the shrubs which lined the bike path. She made her way silently, a dappled form that rippled with the sunlight and shadow, until she came to a small stream. Although the stream was not all that far from the path, few people knew of its existence. Modern humans, apparently, preferred to stay on the known and well-used path. There was a cluster of rocks at this stream and it was a favorite place of hers in both tiger and human form. It was here that she had hidden her clothing. Certain that no one was watching, she shuddered, changing form rapidly from tiger to human and then pulling on her clothing. Once dressed, she turned on her cell phone and checked for messages. There were none. No text from Beth. She sighed.

Nothing was happening here. Things were obviously happening in Providence and that was where she needed to be. But first she needed a bit more information. It was time to check out Stan's notes. She had noticed that he had left his laptop behind. It was an odd thing to forget if you really were going to the lab but not if you planned on sleuthing around the streets of Providence and coming back later.

CHAPTER THREE

IT WAS AFTER THREE O'CLOCK when she got home. Stan was still out, the breakfast dishes were only partially washed up and Monster had eaten all his dry food. She poured more into his bowl, prompting his immediate appearance, and then checked for voicemail messages. There were none. Lucy, she noticed, had left her sweater on the back of the chair. Feeling guilty, she went upstairs to look for Stan's research notes.

She was still surprised that he had left his laptop here. Obviously he would be coming back before Monday's classes. She knew he had back-up notes on an external drive somewhere but this laptop was his main repository. It reinforced the notion that he meant to do more investigating than note-taking.

It was easy to access the files she wanted. Stan had no security lockouts, no passwords, and the reason was clear. His notes were written in a shorthand that made sense presumably to Stan but very little sense to anyone else. There were notations that she assumed made sense to a biogeneticist but were pretty technical. She could tell, however, that they had nothing much to do with the information she sought. There were plenty of references to shape-shifting and to lycanthropy, most of them coupled with terms like "gene activation" and information about alleles.

Lily sighed. In an odd way she felt better informed on shape-shifting than Stan. Anthropology was full of accounts and she had read many of them, from the stories of the Celts to the horrifying tales of Navajo skin-walkers. Being something of a science fiction fan didn't hurt, either, as that genre had its share of werewolves and others. Driven by her own secret condition, she had searched wherever she could.

Eventually she came to the conclusion that Stan had theories with nothing to tie them to. On the other side of the coin, she had an armory of tales with an equal amount of nothing behind them. But something was out there now. Lily felt it. It made the back of her neck prickle. Lucy was obviously upset about something and the Special Unit investigator had been called in. They didn't call the PDC in for nothing, despite what people said. Odd that there was no message from him yet. She had been sure he would want to interview her immediately.

The only piece of Stan's theory that truly disturbed her, and it disturbed her greatly, was the phrase that had been repeated throughout his notes: "initial attempts in a culturally primed population". The same idea had been rephrased a number of ways, for example, "Early attempts would best succeed where there is a bulwark of cultural support". Initial attempts? At what? And cultural support. As in a repository of cultural legends. Stan also mentioned the possibility of extending the "phenomenon". Extend it? There was a lot more here than was apparent. Stan was involved in some sort of research, the notes for which were not on this computer.

She had been taking care to try not to fall for Stan and she was in no danger of it. Stan was fun to be with, intelligent and witty. Maybe a little too possessive but so far she was handling that. She didn't believe either of them was thinking in terms of a commitment of any real sort. She didn't want to make that mistake again, not after John. She had deliberately kept things from Stan, of course, above and beyond her most closely held secret, and she knew had done the same with her, but not at this level. Whatever that level was.

She put Stan's laptop back exactly the way it had been. She wanted there to be no sign that she had accessed any of his files. Were the Hmong "culturally primed"? And for what, exactly? Stan was in Providence. Wes and the PDC Special Unit doctor were in Providence. And Beth's Hmong friend and her own student were in Providence. This did not seem like a good conjunction of happenstances.

Lily turned on the light in the living room. She checked again to make sure Monster had enough food. She got her cell phone, her jacket and her car keys, took Lucy's sweater from the back of the chair, on the theory that it never hurt to have an ostensible reason to be where you were going, locked the house, got into her silver VW beetle and headed out to Route 1 and from there to Route 4 and from there to Route 95. She had Lucy's address and a pretty good idea where the Lees lived.

As North Main Street made its way from Providence through North Providence, it encompassed many little neighborhoods that were in some ways their own small ethnic villages. Parking was never easy here, especially on the little streets that branched off of Main Street, angling uphill. Lily took another quick glance at the address the university had provided for Mai Lee and doing so almost missed her turn. She downshifted into second and took the hill slowly, looking for a good place to park. She found one between two triple-decker houses, probably the remnants of the old days when the Rhode Island economy was dominated by the textile mills and mill owners provided their own accommodation for some of their workers. Lily blessed the Beetle's small size, turned the wheels against the curb and yanked hard on the parking brake to make sure the car wouldn't roll.

She barely had the doors locked before the front door of one of the houses opened and a man came out on the concrete steps. It was difficult enough to see the steps, as they were almost covered with greenery. The tiny front yard was overflowing with plants, even in April: flowers, vines, things that Lily had no name for.

"You lookin' for Mai, right?" The man scratched at the stubble on his chin and hauled at his sagging jeans. Any more sag and he could have been arrested for indecent exposure. He could have been anywhere between thirty and sixty years of age; it was impossible to tell. He was white, and his most prominent feature was his brilliant blue eyes, sunk in a nest of lines.

"I'm Mason Lee, her dad. Everybody calls me Mase, so you might as well. Mai ain't here now."

Lily stared, literally unable to think of a thing to say.

"You think cause I'm white I can't be her dad. Well, I am. Lee's a Hmong clan, all right, but it's also a white name. English on my side." He grinned and Lily found herself grinning back.

"Mine, too, I mean the English," she said, and was rewarded with a broader smile. "I'm not looking for Mai, exactly." She paused for a brief second, then hurried on. No need to make it clear that she wasn't really sure why she had come. "I have Lucy's sweater in the car. She left it this morning. Just let me get it."

"You get it, that's fine. But whoever you come to see there's someone who wants to see you. Says it's real important. It's Lucy and Mai's granddad, on my wife's, their mom's side. If I were you, I'd come talk to him pronto. I've seen too much of what that old guy says come to pass and I've seen too much of what he can do. Granddad is a txiv neeb. You know what that means?"

Lily nodded. "Shaman. That's not really the right word but that's as close as most people come. Why would a shaman wants to see me?"

"You'll have to let him tell you. He's been waiting for you. Wants to see you before the relatives show up for the ceremony to call back the souls. Not that I think it's gonna work this time. Come on in."

Lily grabbed Lucy's sweater and followed Mason into the house.

The first thing she noticed was the smell of something cooking, and then the plants in the windows and then the beautiful hand-sewn tapestry on the wall, one of the fabled story cloths. And then there was Jen, smiling, ushering her in. "Here's Lucy's sweater," Lily said, feeling awkward.

"Thank you, that was most kind to bring it back. Would you like tea?" "She did not come for tea, or even to bring back the sweater. She came because I called her and she came because she must. Because of what depends upon her. And we have so little time." The speaker was apparently offering an apology for retracting the tea offer.

Jen actually jumped back a step. "This is my father," she said, looking down, not meeting his eyes. "Choua Lee."

"Pleased to meet you." Lily knew enough not to meet the glance of an elder male but she wracked her brain for other protocols. As she hesitated she felt her hand grasped in a strong grip. Surprised, she looked up, meeting the older man's amused glance after all.

"Americans call me George," he said. "And many people think it's funny to have Lee on both side of family."

His grin was infectious and Lily found herself shaking hands back.

"Have seat, please," said George. "We have some few important matters to discuss, and quickly."

What was going on here? Lily mentally shrugged. "Thank you," she said.

She looked around. There was an old easy chair, obviously somebody's favorite, she suspected George's, so she wouldn't take that, a straight-backed chair, a small bench in a corner, and a couch. She glanced at the bench and actually started toward it when she felt the hair rise along her arms. This was no ordinary bench. This was the magical horse upon which the shaman, the txiv neeb, rode between the worlds. She thought she could feel its power. She felt her eyes widen as she backed away, edging instead toward the couch. As she settled into it she looked up to find the old man's eyes on her. He nodded.

"You know what I am," he said. "Maybe not all what I am and what I can do, but you know some. And you feel some more, some here." He touched his chest. "And I know what you are." His eyes bored into her.

Lily was back up off the couch before she even realized it. She could admit to nothing and she would admit to nothing, but just by being here she was complicit in - whatever this was.

"Sit. Please, sit. I mean you no harm. You have a dab, one of your souls - it is a spirit, a very strong spirit from the other world. Most unusual for a white woman. You are white, yes?"

"I guess so. I mean, I think so." The variants of the out-of-Africa theories she taught her students tumbled through her mind, along with less popular out- of-Asia theories. And there were rumors about some of her far more recent ancestors - how far back did one go? "I mean, within recent memory, that I know of, more or less, mostly, probably - yes. I think."

The old man grinned at her. "Sometimes it can be harder than expected to know just who your ancestors are," he said sympathetically. "Look at us here. But however it came to you, you have this spirit. A tiger spirit. Sit!" He commanded, when Lily would have risen again.

"Most tiger spirits, or many, are not good. They can eat people, if they are real tigers, or sometimes even if they are tiger spirits. And if they are tiger spirits they also eat souls. They eat human souls. You - you do not. There are times when you wish to eat people, when you fight against this. Is it not so?"

Lily had a flash of the bike path, of the little dogs, of the children scampering. The children especially. Erratic movement, small prey, the almost but not quite overwhelming urge; she felt her muscles twitch.

"Yes," she admitted, despite herself, horrified.

"But you do not. You have taken a vow." His eyes were boring into hers. "How do you know that!" She was far too astonished to deny it.

The old man shook his head. "I have traveled far," he nodded at the bench, his horse, lest she think he meant only from another continent, "and I know things. I know there is evil abroad now. Much evil, a great deal of it springing from the greed of men. You must stop it."

"What?" Lily stared at him. "I don't know what you are talking about." There was always evil springing from the greed of men. That sort of "psychic" statement would normally make her roll her eyes.

"Yes, you do. You have learned that there are tiger spirits other than your own - that eat souls. You have never once done this. You do not understand why suddenly it seems there are more - what? - shape shifters - or at least stories of them. And those other things people are so afraid of, like seeing a thought within the mind of another. But I can tell you part of what is behind this. It is greed. Human greed. You are not part of this and yet you are part of this. You must stop it."

"How can I be part of it and not part of it at the same time? And how can I possibly stop it?" She had a flash vision of herself as a superhero. Tigerwoman. In a costume. With tights. Ridiculous.

"Grandfather!" It was Lucy. Lily had not even noticed the child come into the room. "I do not want to interrupt."

"But it is important," said George. "What is it?"

"It is that detective, the nice one. But he has that government doctor with him. They know Professor Lily is here. They asked for her. They saw her car, I think."

"You must leave now, Ms. Lily. I am sorry I cannot answer more of your questions but you must leave. It is dangerous. You perhaps can stop some of this evil of which we spoke, stop it tonight, if you are lucky. There is," he glanced at Lucy but then continued, "a soul-eating tiger dab nearby. Do you understand? An evil shape-shifting tiger here tonight in the city. If you stop to talk to the police you will not have time to hunt the evil shifter and to stop him. Especially if that doctor cop talks to you." He shook his head. "That doctor will take you away and lock you up, or try to. He try that with our Mai and she only write paper for your class, so no success for him. Be careful, please be careful. It is very dangerous for you. But if you go now perhaps you stop the evil tonight."

Before she had a chance to protest or to question, Lily found herself herded around through a room crammed with two beds and a desk with a laptop computer - Lucy's? or Lucy's and Mai's? - and then the kitchen and out the kitchen door.

"Thanks for bringing my sweater back," said Lucy. "Please, please stop the tiger man from eating anybody else. I'm scared."

Lily was in a short alley between houses. *Thanks for bringing my sweater back and please stop the tiger man from eating people,* she thought. That's what it had come to today; this was acceptable. And it was all so recent. The belief in psi powers: mind-reading, fire-starting, seeing the future, and now shape shifting, all this was so new in mainstream America. Until the genetic mutations had made some of this real, it was all the stuff of comic books. But then these traits had started showing up, for real, and they were supported by scientific research, the sort of thing her ex-husband John did. And Stan. She musn't forget Stan.

At first the CDC got involved, when the government claimed it was a sort of plague. Then the Psi Disease Center was created, an offshoot at first of the Centers for Disease Control. People started believing, and seeing this stuff everywhere, except for people like the Hmong and other groups, for whom it had always been real. The Psi Disease Center took on its own separate life, fueled by public belief and hysteria as much as by science. There was some phrase that she wanted, that she was looking for, something that was important, something she had forgotten.

But she couldn't find it now. She looked down the street. There was Wes, walking toward her car and there was a tall guy with him, brown-haired with streaks of gray. That must be the doctor from the PDC Special Unit. She turned and walked quickly to other end of the alley. She had no desire to sit in some room in the Providence police station - if that's where they would take her - answering whatever questions this Special Unit doctor could think up. The Special Unit was the Psi Disease Center combination investigative and SWAT team, with too many horror stories attached to it. He had the right to lock her up in a medical facility without a hearing for an indefinite period. In fact, one of the places they could lock her up was her ex-husband's facility.

Lily squeezed her way between a dumpster and a pile of cardboard boxes. Flattening herself as best she could to the side of the building she inched along, trying to find shelter behind the shrubs and plants, hoping the men wouldn't turn. If one of them did, they'd almost certainly spot her. She would have to leave her car and come back to it later. She was almost to the edge of the building where she could round the corner and be on the next street when the inevitable happened. Wes turned and saw her.

He said nothing, at least initially, which surprised Lily, but the direction of his glance caused the other man to turn. The Special Unit doctor. She felt his eyes on her, gray as rain, piercing. Wes knew his colleague had seen her.

"Lily!" Wes called. "We need to talk to you. Would you come here a minute?"

His colleague was not so polite.

"PDC Special Unit! Halt right there, Dr. Mossberg!"

She should go with them. She knew she should go. Reason said they would not lock her up in an institution. It would be unpleasant, certainly, to answer questions, but it would be temporary. They would put her in some room for hours and ask her questions about Mai's paper, about her knowledge of her ex-husband's business, which was next to none. They might even do something like draw blood, which didn't bother her; they had done it often enough before, with no useful results. It would probably take all night. Eventually they would be finished. Wes might buy her breakfast and she would get to go home, find out just how John was planning on returning Beth, help Stan get his laptop and whatever else he had left behind and get on with her life. Get ready for Monday morning classes. It would have been a hell of a weekend but bad weekends happened.

She knew this was what she should do. The worst possible thing she could do would be to run. If she ran, she would have to come up later with some very good reason for running. She could not begin to imagine what that reason might be. An old man told her to stop an evil spirit? Lily ran.

She heard shouts behind her. Wes, calling that they just needed to talk to her for a minute, then becoming more forceful, shouting

"Providence police". And the PDC doctor shouting, telling her to "halt" and to "put your hands in the air, now!" She ignored it all.

Then there was a crack and a whoosh of air by her cheek and a thud as something hit the side of the building. Lily glanced back. The Special Unit agent had drawn his gun. He was shooting at her! He couldn't mean to kill her, not if they wanted to question her, but that shot had been far too close. She put her hand up and felt her cheek. Nothing. Either he was not shooting to kill or he was a terrible shot. Armed doctors; the world was insane.

She flung herself around the corner, saw a crawl space under the house and rolled into it. It was nasty under there, dank and full of cobwebs and there were things - bugs - crawling on her, and it was hard to see. Was that a rat? Those glittering eyes?

Lily wasted no time. With maneuvers that would have made a circus contortionist proud she pulled off her shoes and socks, stuffed the socks into the sneakers and tied them around her neck. In almost no time flat she was nude.

Everything possible was crammed into her backpack, which she also strung around her neck. There was a brief shimmer in the darkness of the crawl space. Then a tiger flattened herself into the dirt beneath the house, the membrane of the tapetum lucidum in her eyes glowing, increasing her vision to six times that of a human. The rat squeaked and ran. The tiger slid through the darkness with a practiced ease.

The houses connected via a garage and the space beneath the garage, a fact the tiger considered a stroke of luck. Stealth and natural camouflage made her for practical purposes invisible as stripes blended with grass and darkness. In the crawl space under the house at the end of the street a squirrel quivered, impaled by a golden feline gaze. The tigress realized that she had not eaten all day and she was hungry. A squirrel wasn't much but it would take the edge off. The squirrel gazed back, frozen, incapable of moving. Lily crouched and quivered, preparing to pounce. The pack around her neck would not slow her down; she had had plenty of practice.

But then her head snapped up. She could smell the squirrel's fear but that wasn't what caught her attention. It was the scent of another tiger. It wasn't right here but it was close enough that she could smell it. She could smell that it had been here. Forgetting the squirrel, she concentrated on the signature scent of the other big cat, opening her mouth wide to pull in every scented air molecule to her Jacobsen's organ. The tiger was a male. She could tell that much. And there was something wrong about it, something she could tell even from here. It had passed this way recently, hunting, but not hunting large animal prey (what could be large enough in a city?) or small prey such as the squirrel, which had since made its escape. This tiger was after other prey. Human prey.

Lily eased forward, intent on finding where this other tiger had been, intent on trailing him. Grandfather Lee - she thought of him this way now - had been right. Little Lucy had been right to be afraid.

Fortunately, she looked before crept out from the crawl space. Wes was standing in the street looking around, as if expecting her - or someone - to be there. He seemed perfectly at ease and yet alert.

"Damn it!" Lily muttered. As she was still in tiger form her mutter came out as a growl. Wes turned his head, as if he had heard.

Lily backed deeper into the crawl space. There was a shimmer and then a naked woman, shuddering at the touch of bugs and cobwebs, was struggling into her clothes. She straightened herself as best she could, slipped the pack over her shoulder. Then, when Wes was turned away, she came out from under the crawl space into the tiger-scented dusk.

Wes turned back. "Lily!" he said, seeming not even slightly surprised. "I was hoping to have a little conversation with you." He smiled and then jumped as a man came crashing around the corner of the building.

"Halt! Don't move or I'll shoot!" The tall guy was out of breath, obviously struggling. One hand did indeed hold a gun, which wavered slightly due to his exertions. He needed a bit more time building his stamina, Lily thought. The other hand held a badge of some sort. Lily put her hands up.

"Doctor Fletcher of the PDC Special Unit, I presume?" she said.

"My temporary, ah, colleague, Doctor Clement Fletcher," said Wes. "Clem, put the gun down. You really don't want to shoot her. Lily, put your hands down."

She did, but she waited until Fletcher had reholstered his gun.

"Clem, let me introduce Doctor Lily Mosssberg, the authority and scholar you wish to interview."

"Please," said Lily, "I'm not that kind of doctor. Just call me Ms. Mossberg, Doctor Fletcher. And if this has anything to do with the were tiger scare I would be very happy to help." She looked at Wes. "I have gleaned a bit more information since we spoke earlier today." It was always best to go on the offensive, she thought.

CHAPTER FOUR

IT WAS NOT ALL THAT unpleasant, not what she had thought an interrogation room would be. A conference table, some astonishingly comfortable chairs, a window - barred, but with actual curtains. Lily wondered if there were different interrogation rooms for different kinds of interrogation. Even the inevitable two- way mirror was smaller than she expected. The door would be locked, she assumed, but they had a big pot of coffee, a real coffee maker, and cream, sugar, sugar substitute and a box that had contained a dozen doughnuts. It took great restraint to avoid a cops and doughnuts joke but Lily managed.

"So you went to the Lees to return Lucy's sweater." Wes leaned back in his chair.

"Yes." They had been over this territory a million times, it seemed, but Lily knew they had to do it again. Eventually, she figured, they would get tired of it. She wanted out of here. She was supposed to get Beth back tomorrow. She wanted Beth back home. "And to see if Lucy was okay. She was really upset this morning."

"About the shape shifting tiger." Clement Fletcher seemed to feel the need to assert himself, thus inadvertently reaffirming a stereotype of Special Unit agents.

"Yes. She's only nine years old, for God's sake. She asked me to be careful." Lily decided to keep some things private; there was no reason to tell this PDC doctor that Lucy had asked her to stop the tiger-man from eating people. "But I really didn't talk to her long. As I said, I spent very little time there, most of it with her grandfather, Choua Lee. He calls himself George. As he is the eldest male, it was only polite that I pay my respects to him."

"Maternal grandfather, right?" This was Wes, looking interested. Lily stared at him. It seemed an odd point to bring up.

"Yes. Oddly enough, Lucy's father has the same last name." She knew Wes knew this, wondered why he mentioned it. At least it wasn't material they had covered ad nauseam previously. "He -"

"I don't see what this has to do with anything, Ms. Mossberg." Clement Fletcher was impatient. "Maternal, paternal, shmaternal, what difference does it make. What did he have to tell you?"

"It's interesting because Hmong culture is traditionally patrilineal and patriarchal but here it is the maternal grandfather who has the leadership of the family."

"Yes," Clement Fletcher looked bored. Lily was sure he wanted to say *so what?*

"And it is also interesting because Lucy and Mai's father, who has the same last name, Lee, is white."

Fletcher did a classic double-take and she saw a smile flicker just for an instant on Wes' face. Then it was gone. He had been waiting for this; had set Fletcher up for it. It was important, and Lily felt the faint prick of a correspondence, something she should remember. She filed away the information for further analysis.

"As for what Grandfather Lee told me," Lily continued before Fletcher could interject, "there is indeed some sort of predator who has been preying on children, Hmong children. Many imagine him as a shape shifting tiger.

Grandfather Lee believed he was in the area or had been recently.

He asked me to be careful but to keep an eye out for this person, to look for him."

"Let me understand this. Cooey, Chewie, ah George Lee asked you to look for this tiger man."

"Choua. Grandfather Lee. Yes." "And he said it was a shape shifter."

"He did. That's how they explain what has been happening to their children."

"Why does he think so?" "He's a txiv neeb. A shaman."

"Ah. A witch-doctor." He ignored Lily's wince. "And why ask you to look for him?"

"Because I am the teacher of his eldest grandchild, someone with a background in myth and legend and in different cultures. Someone, perhaps, who, even if she didn't believe him might at least help him." The implication hung in the air: the PDC Special Unit would not help much. Fletcher chose to overlook this but he gave Lily a considering glance.

"He said this man had been in the neighborhood very recently." Lily could have kicked herself as soon as the words were out of her mouth. There she went, volunteering information.

"And how would you find him? How would you know who he was?" Fletcher was leaning forward.

This was a problem and a big one. Lily didn't hesitate.

"A man, lurking about, probably trying to act like a tiger?" She raised her eyebrows. "Watching children?"

"I hope that isn't implied criticism of the police," said Wes. "A potential predator like that sounds rather difficult to miss." He didn't sound in the least insulted, only curious.

"No criticism meant. This is all rather new, and I suspect not just to me but to everyone. As far as I know, this is the first time something like this, something this, ah, weird, has happened around here. And I didn't come here to hunt child predators of whatever, er, stripe." She saw the answering gleam of humor in Wes' eye. "I came to check on a classmate of my daughter's and to return something of hers. Had I seen anything out of the usual I would have called 911."

She was only looking around because of Lucy's fear, Grandfather Lee's concern, she told herself.

"And you were only looking around because of the concern of the child and her grandfather," said Wes.

Lily blinked and stared at him. "Exactly. And as I have explained, my daughter is returning tomorrow." She glanced at her watch. It was two AM. Already. "Today. I really I have a lot to do. And if you haven't noticed, it's late."

"I"m sorry about that. Just one more thing, Ms. Mossberg," Clement Fletcher said.

There was always one more thing. Lily rubbed at her eyes and then hastily stopped. The eye doctor had told her not to do that.

"Yes, Dr. Fletcher," she said wearily. "What might that be?" "You are aware of the work your husband does?"

"I'm divorced."

"Your ex-husband. You are aware of his work."

"Only in the broadest sense, but of course. He runs a pharmaceutical research company." She paused but she knew what Fletcher wanted. "His primary focus is to find cures for the psi diseases."

"Have you been involved in this work?" "Not at all. It's not my field."

"But your husband, excuse me, your ex-husband, surely consulted you on various myths and legends concerning psi powers."

"I wouldn't say he 'consulted'. We had occasional conversations on the topic. As I dare say probably most people do these days, even those who don't read the tabloids." John hadn't consulted her on much of anything. It was one reason their marriage had failed.

"But you have more knowledge of the legends than most."

"I wouldn't even say that, Dr. Fletcher. My area of expertise is gender, not supernatural legends." It was best not show annoyance. Lily tried and failed. "Beth's father and I have very little do with each other since the divorce." In some ways it had been like that when they were married, but Lily didn't say it. She caught Wes looking at her with sympathy.

"Your daughter is with her father right now, is that correct?" Fletcher continued his questions.

"It is." Lily's voice was tight. "The visits are court ordered. It's a custody issue."

"And you accept tuition money from your ex-husband, Dr. Belkner, to send your daughter to her school. And you are considering accepting money from him to send her to a summer camp."

And just how the hell would he know that? It happened before she could control it. Her temper flared and she couldn't reign it back. "I don't see how any of this is your business, Dr. Fletcher! The arrangements between my ex-husband and me have nothing to do with you. My daughter is none of your concern!"

"If she is a normal human untainted by psi disease that's certainly true. I know she's been tested several times, but we may need to test her again. There are many more things of concern to me than you might credit, Ms. Mossberg."

"You leave my daughter alone!" She knew she was being baited but she couldn't help it. "She's been tested enough! The divorce was rough on her; this custody arrangement is rough on her. She doesn't need any more useless meddling and testing!" Her hands were under the conference table and to her horror she felt them begin to turn into claws. She had never been unable to control her change before; as far as she knew those other shape shifters, the werewolves, few though they were, changed, like it or not, at the full of the moon. She was not like that. Emotion had never caused her to lose control before, either.

Careful, said a voice in her thoughts. It sounded like Wes' but it couldn't be. She took a huge breath and felt the claws recede, retracting back into her fingers.

"My apologies," she said. "But this really is more than is called for." "I understand you are under a great deal of stress, Ms. Mossberg. I apologize for upsetting you." Fletcher did not sound as if he meant it, even remotely, but at least he went through the motions. "I am sorry we have kept you so late. I would not go so far as to ask you not to leave the state but please request permission of us - the PDC

Special Unit - before you do so. There are some standard forms and protocols."

"As you pointed out, it's quite late and I know you need to pick up your daughter tomorrow. Our interview is concluded for the present."

He stood up, leaned across the conference table and actually offered her his hand. Lily stared at it for a second or so before taking it and giving it a limp grasp. She was glad the claws were gone.

"I'll take you back to your car, Ms. Mossberg," said Wes. "The streets aren't as safe as we'd like this time of night."

They parted ways with Clement Fletcher outside the interview room.

Washington Street was really not all that busy at that hour of the morning. Lily expected Wes to take one of the Department's marked cars but instead he ushered her to a black VW Beetle, obviously his personal car, and beeped it open for her.

"Similar taste in automotive iron," he said with a faint smile. For a few moments they drove in silence, before Wes broke it.

"He really can be a son of a bitch, can't he? I was going to say that he's not all that bad to work with, and oddly enough, he's not, but Clem can be a real bastard at times."

Lily blinked at him in surprise. She had not expected one law enforcement official to criticize another to a civilian.

"I don't know how you stand him. I'm glad I don't have to work with him." She yawned. "I appreciate the ride."

They were back where she had parked her car. She couldn't help glancing around as she got out, but surely the shape shifter, whoever he was, would have more sense than to be here now. Wes got out, too, leaving the driver's door open so the light spilled out.

"Here," he said. "Take this with you and drink it." He handed her a styrofoam cup with a lid. "It's coffee. One cream, one sugar; I noticed you liked that during our, ah, meeting. It's from the Department. No sugar substitute, unfortunately; seems we ran out. I don't want you falling asleep at the wheel."

"Thanks." She would need the coffee; she was exhausted.

"Drive safely, Lily."

She wondered about Wes as she drove home, gratefully sipping the coffee. Fortunately, there was almost no traffic at three-thirty in the morning. The facts as she knew them tumbled around in her head, making no sense, but she could feel there were things that were missing, things that she knew or should know. It was a relief to pull into her little driveway in the predawn light. Stan's car, his old Saturn, was in the driveway; he was back. She hoped he was sleeping. She didn't feel up to any sort of debriefing, any sort of talk now.

She stumbled into the house, realizing how exhausted she was, and checked her voice mail: nothing. She frowned. John should have called to tell her when and where to pick up Beth. As she was replacing the receiver Monster crept out from behind the big arm chair.

"What were you doing back there, silly boy?" she said. "Did I interrupt your nap?"

The cat came to her and pressed himself against her. His eyes were huge.

After a moment she realized he was trembling.

"Monster!" Rather than attempting to scoop him up, Lily got down on the floor with him. "Are you sick?" She checked him over but could find nothing. Nothing stuck under his tongue, no sign of him having vomited, and he was hydrated; she did the skin pinch test. By the time she had finished her examination his eyes were normal again and the trembling had stopped. He rubbed against her and purred.

Not sick, then, but frightened. Something had frightened him. Lily frowned. There were coyotes in the area. Maybe Stan had left the inner door open and one had come up to the screen door. She had told him to never do that, but Stan was Stan and he tended to forget. She checked but the screen door was closed and the inner door closed and locked. She gave Monster a final cuddle and headed up to bed, dumping her clothes in a heap on the floor, something she never did, and climbing into bed beside Stan, wondering vaguely if he had discovered anything as she drifted into sleep.

It was the phone ringing at seven-thirty that hauled her out of sleep. She glanced at Stan but he had pulled the pillow over his head. Besides, it was best for him to not answer her phone. Lily fumbled around, almost knocking the phone from the night stand but managing to answer before the voice mail kicked in.

"Hello," she croaked.

"Good morning." John didn't sound as if he had been up all night, probably because he hadn't. "I'll be bringing Beth back today at three o'clock. Meet us at Quonset, the usual."

Lily avoided the impulse to say, *Roger, wilco.* "Fine," she said.

"Excellent, 'bye," said her ex-husband.

Lily sat up and rubbed her eyes. Stan rolled over. "John?" he said.

"Who else. I thought you would be out hunting the werewolves in Providence all night."

"No luck."

Of course he hadn't had any luck. Not if he had been tiger hunting in Providence or trying to talk to Hmong. But at least he hadn't denied it. She sighed. She had virtually no sleep but it didn't look as if she stood to get any now. She swung her feet over the side of the bed.

"Where are you going?"

"I've got some papers to grade," she said.

"They can wait." Stan reached over and pulled her back into the bed. "At least a few minutes."

It was an energetic few minutes. Even as Lily responded to Stan's passion she felt a certain unease. There was something she was missing, some important fact. She wasn't quite sure why she felt it had to do with Stan but it did. She soon forgot the issue. She and Stan were physically compatible but she was becoming convinced there was something wrong here. Perhaps it was time to call off this relationship.

Stan left shortly thereafter. Lily really did have papers to grade and Stan knew she didn't want him there or with her when she went to pick up Beth. This time he did pack up his laptop before leaving. On his way down the stairs he almost tripped over Monster. The cat backed up, his eyes getting huge again.

He hissed.

"Damn cat!" Stan was not an animal lover. He brushed by the cat with what was almost but not quite a kick.

"Hey!" Lily was outraged on behalf of her pet. She let Stan go by and knelt by the big Maine Coon who was both trembling and hissing. Not wanting to be on the receiving end of displaced feline aggression, she spoke softly to the cat. "Poor old Monster," she said. What the hell was wrong with Stan? She stood up. "Nobody's going to hurt my Monster! Stan, if you can't be good with my cat, you're out, and I mean permanently!" They had had this discussion before and Stan had always promised to do better. This time there was no response.

Eventually the cat settled down by that time Stan was gone. At least he hadn't called her "babe" but it really was time to end what had been a rebound relationship after her divorce.

Lily frowned and got to work. With the help of numerous cups of black coffee and absolute concentration she managed to make her way through almost all of the papers by two o'clock. There was just time to have a quick snack, lock the house (no Monster in sight), climb into her car and head to Quonset.

It was a cool afternoon with high clouds. A front was due to come through later. Beth would be home well before, not that it mattered. All of John's pilots were IFR rated and had, in fact, been hired away from commercial carriers after amassing a sufficiently impressive number of flying hours.

Although Lily had planned to be early, she walked into the little terminal just in time to see John's new Cessna Citation business jet turn off onto the taxiway. Lily pushed through the doors and ran out onto the tarmac, anxious to see her daughter.

First down the ramp was John, looking slightly less impatient than usual, and then her daughter, clutching her backpack despite the fact that one of her father's employees would have been glad to carry it for her. Lily trotted over, beaming.

"Sweetheart!" She opened her arms.

Beth came into her embrace and returned it but it seemed to Lily that there was something held back.

"You okay?" Lily held her daughter at arm's length and examined her. "Fine. Mom." Beth sounded lackluster.

"She's fine," said John simultaneously. "You want to get a sandwich or a soda before I head back?"

Lily turned from watching the fuel truck attach a static line to the small jet and stared at her ex-husband in surprise. Normally, he unloaded his daughter like a package and left again.

"I don't know if the cafe is open," she said. There was something behind this sudden friendliness.

"If it isn't, I'll get a car and we'll go into town somewhere." "I have a car," said Lily, drily.

As it turned out, the cafe was open. Beth got an ice cream and took it out into the small terminal to watch a tiny, ancient Ercoupe does touch and go while her parents got coffee and took it out of the cafe. There was no one near the internet weather facility so they both took chairs and watched the front silently approach on the computer screen. Lily kept her eyes on the screen. The video was looped so the front approached again and again but it was preferable than looking at John right now. Lily had a very bad feeling about this.

"There's something I wanted to talk to you about," said John. "I figured as much," said Lily. "What's wrong with Beth?" "Lily, you know the nature of my work."

Lily felt her heart squeeze and stop. "Only in general. But yes." "Beth may have come into contact with some of it."

"What do you mean 'come into contact'?" She swung around to look at him now. "I thought you took her to the Beechland place, the farm?"

"I did. That's where we always go, unless I tell you otherwise. But I also have a small, well, I guess you call it a research facility, at the farm."

Lily stared at him. "You what?" It was the first she'd heard of this.

"It's more like a summer camp, but year-round. I have a few cabins for some volunteers. Nothing much. We just keep track of them, draw some blood samples, stuff like that. Beth may have run into some of the kids."

"Kids? Kids 'volunteer'? Since when can kids volunteer for a pharmaceutical trial? How old are these kids? And what do you mean by 'run into'?"

"A few kids. A couple Beth's age. It's mostly just a few adults. But as I said, Beth may have run into some of the kids. I try to keep everything separate, of course. But something slipped up."

Slipped up. Lily stared at him. Kids.

"Just what are you trying to tell me? Spit it out, John. What did Beth see?

What happened to her!"

"Some of the side effects of some of the drugs we test, well, they can be disturbing for a child to see. You know, tremors, ah, seizures. Uncontrollable drooling. Diarrhea. Just side effects."

"John! And she was exposed to this - illness?"

"It's not an illness. Nothing to worry about there. But I wanted you to be aware in case Beth seemed disturbed by it in any way. But you know how it is. Kids get over these things pretty quickly. It won't happen again."

"Your damned right it won't happen again! She's not going up there again! She's not going to come into contact with any of your - experiments!"

"Lily, I promise this won't happen again but you know she will be coming to the farm again." It hung in the air unsaid: unless you are willing to go to court again and challenge the custody arrangements and risk losing child support. "I will make sure she's safe. I just wanted you to know about this."

"John, did she come in contact with any - any of the drugs?" "Of course not!"

"I think we should take a break from her visits to the farm. You can see her on schedule but get a motel room down here. You can see her here, take her out, do whatever. But here."

Would she really go back to court, risk all that? His lawyers were the best money could buy. But to protect her child? She would. When she stared at John, her green eyes held such intensity and threat that he drew back. At that moment, had she known it, she looked like a tigress protecting her cub.

"Okay," he said, surprising himself. It was unusual for him to give way to anyone, least of all his ex-wife. "Maybe just next time." Next time was three weeks away. "Flying much these days?"

It was a deliberate jab and Lily refused to give him the satisfaction of seeing her wince. She held a private pilot's license and when they had been married, she had had her own Cessna 172 Skyhawk. It had been in her name but she had been forced to sell it after the divorce. Hangar fees, annuals, insurance, it was all too much on her small salary. She occasionally rented a plane from a service up at Green International Airport in Warwick and she was considering joining a local flying club at Quonset when she could scrape up the initial cash, which looked like it might not be any time soon.

"Keeping current," was all she said.

He smiled slightly. He needed a victory, even one this minor, to salve his ego. He tossed his coffee cup in the trash and went to say goodbye to his daughter.

When Lily drove her daughter home Beth was silent the whole way.

CHAPTER FIVE

S HE TRIED. WHILE SHE AND Beth ate Beth's favorite dinner, salmon and asparagus (Beth was in some ways not a typical nine-year-old), Lily asked how the weekend went.

"Fine," said her daughter. And nothing more. At bedtime, Lily tried again.

"If there's anything at all you want to talk to me about, ever, you know I'll listen. I love you, Beth."

"I know, Mom. I love you, too." She was clutching Bunny-buns, her old stuffed animal, a sure sign of distress. But the tightness around her mouth was an indication that nothing more would be forthcoming, at least not now.

When Monster jumped up on the bed with her, Beth went to sleep holding the cat. When Lily checked on her later, child and cat were still curled up together.

In the morning, it was obvious that Monster was sick.

"He threw up, Mom! On the bed! And he just lies there; he won't move!"

Lily went to look. Monster lay not just in a pool of vomit but of diarrhea and he wasn't moving. She pinched up his skin and it stayed tented up. He was severely dehydrated. It didn't seem like he had a fever; if anything he was too cool.

"Get ready for the bus; make sure you have your books. Can you get yourself some cereal? I'll call the vet. I'll get Monster to the doctor right away." She had a ten o'clock class which fortunately gave her enough time to get Monster to the vet clinic first.

Beth nodded, obviously fighting back tears, and went to get herself some breakfast. As she left the room Lily tried to catch her with a hug.

"Monster will be okay. Dr. Flower will do everything possible, you know that." Sandra Flower was the vet.

"Whatever," said Beth, avoiding the hug, still fighting back the tears.

Lily stared after her daughter, shocked by the uncharacteristic response. It was obvious her daughter was upset. Why was she trying to pretend she wasn't? Then she went about phoning the vet clinic (yes, they could get Monster in right away but she would have to leave the cat for the day), stripping and changing Beth's bed and putting the soiled bedding in the washing machine, cleaning up the cat and loading him into the carrier. By then, it was time for Beth to leave and she did, without giving her mother the customary kiss. Lily frowned in concern after her only child.

But there was no time to brood. She grabbed her coat and her lecture notes and loaded Monster's carrier into the car. The cat had not moved and Lily had a sinking feeling. She stuck her fingers between the slats: he was still breathing. She was surprised to find herself gulping back her own tears.

"Poor old Monster; what happened to you?" she whispered.

At the vet's, she was told she could call any time after ten-thirty and that they would put Monster immediately on fluids, which should help. She got herself a cup of Dunkin Donuts coffee and a bagel on the way to class, and ignoring the signs posted everywhere that said "NO FOOD OR DRINK IN CLASSROOMS", sailed pass the janitorial staff known to students and faculty alike as "the food police". One of them moved forward, ready to admonish and to confiscate the food, took one look at her face, and stepped hastily back. Lily placed her breakfast on the desk that she preferred to the lectern, took a big swig of the coffee and then somehow managed to conduct the class.

It was noon before she had a chance to check her cell phone. There were four messages: one from the vet, one from Beth's school, one from John and one from Stan. The message from the school was delivered in person by the vice-principal when Lily returned the call.

"She what?" Lily couldn't believe what she heard.

"She hit Sarah Lattinger. She told Sarah to stay away from her."

"I can't believe it! Not Beth! And not Sarah!"

"I assure you, Dr. Mossberg -"

"No, no, that's not what I meant; I believe you. It's just that those two are best friends. Is Sarah okay? They're working on their science project together. What could have happened?"

"I know. Sarah's fine, physically." The vice principal's voice softened slightly.

Lily explained that her daughter was going through a bad time with her father. She even mentioned the sick cat. In the end, it was decided to leave Beth in school for the day and not to suspend her but to give her detention and a stern warning. This meant that Lily would have to pick up Beth after work, as Beth could not take the bus.

The next call was to the vet clinic. After a few minutes wait Lily was put through to Sandra Flower.

"Monster's going to be okay, I think, but he'll have to stay here for a couple of days, probably, until we're sure. He's responding to supportive therapy, which at this point is all we can do. Lily - "

"Did you take x-rays? What about some sort of intestinal obstruction? That big boy will eat anything, I mean, there could be something blocking him, a piece of string, who knows -"

"Lily." There was something in the vet's voice that stopped Lily immediately. She and Sandra Flower had a long history together and were on the verge of becoming personal friends.

"Lily, we did all that. I think it's panleukopenia." "What?"

"Distemper."

"Yes, I know," Lily knew the term, "but he's been vaccinated! I mean, he's up to date! He got his booster from you just a month ago! How is this possible?

Are you sure?"

"I can't be one hundred percent certain but it's a really good bet. I'm waiting for the ELISA results but his symptoms - Lily, I think it's a new strain of the virus."

"Oh my God." Too many thoughts were crowding her mind. Where could this virus have come from? She knew that typically the mortality for feline distemper was something like ninety percent.

"My poor Monster." She felt near tears again.

"I think he's going to make it, Lily. His previous vaccinations must have given him some resistance to this strain, new though it is. He's on an IV and getting really good supportive care and you got him here right away. He's perked up a little already. It would be okay, in fact a good thing, if you paid him a visit. It should help his recovery."

"I will. Oh my poor cat. He just can't - he just can't die!"

"Calm down, Lily; I really don't think he will. You know I'll do everything possible. I love your big boy, too. Lily, are you on a land line?"

"No, my cell."

"Okay. There's something I need to ask you. It would be better in person. When you get here. When can you come by?"

The clinic normally closed at six p.m. She could probably just make it. "Right before you close. But what's wrong with my cell -"

"Good. And try not to worry about Monster. He's going to make it." She hung up before Lily could ask anything more.

Next was John. To her surprise, she got right through.

"Lily, I want you to know that the court-ordered visitation stands. Beth's next visit will be here. Beth will come to the farm."

"I thought we had an agreement that you would come down here."

"We have no such agreement and I will not be dictated to. It's the farm. She will come to the farm."

Lily was silent for so long that John said, "Are you there?"

"Yes, I'm here. And Beth is not, I repeat not, going to the farm. If you don't like it, talk to my lawyer."

She hit the "end" button and resisted the impulse to throw the phone against the wall. The next call was to her lawyer who was also, amazingly, in. She agreed to get at least a temporary injunction against John taking Beth to the farm.

"I think we can get it." Claire Franks had been Lily's lawyer through the whole divorce. "Based on the perceived harm from her last visit and the fact that we are not attempting to deny visitation, just change the venue. But you know you could be opening a can of worms here, Lily."

"I know. Open away."

There was no time to return Stan's call. She had office hours with actual visits from students, astonishing in a day when most preferred email, and then she had another class. By the time afternoon classes were over it was four-thirty. She would just have time to get Beth and then go to the vet's. And to call Stan.

But apparently that would not be quite yet. Her last class had been her anthropology seminar, and there was Mai Lee, lingering in the classroom, wanting to talk to her. Lily repressed a frown.

"I just wanted to thank you," Mai said.

Now Lily did frown. "For what?" Returning the sweater, she thought. For talking to Lucy, to Choua. She realized she was being rude, felt embarrassed, and attempted to smile.

"For coming to see my grandfather. And for offering to help us."
"Offering to help -"

"Professor, I know how off the wall this sounds but it means a lot to my grandfather, to my whole family. To me. I am the first woman in my family to go to college. And I mean in my father's as well as my mother's family. I know I seem like a typical American and in many ways I am but you know how important my culture is to me. My family is not making me marry yet and I am getting my degree. But there are some things I still believe. I think my grandfather is right." Mai paused and looked intently at Lily.

"You mean about the tiger - the shape shifter." There was no point in pretending she didn't understand.

"Yes. It is not someone in my family who is preying on our - on Hmong - children but there is someone. I also believe that you are one who can help, just as my grandfather does." Mai's gaze was intent, full of both knowledge and expectation.

By changing into a tiger myself, Lily thought. She didn't say it. She closed her eyes, trying not to shake her head.

"Please, Professor. We need your help."

Lily opened her eyes. "I will do what I can," she said. Just what did that mean? She didn't want to think about it now.

"Thank you." Mai's whole face lit up with her smile. "Thank you, Professor.

And one more thing. For grad school I need references. Do you think you could write one for me? Please?"

That she could definitely do. By the time Mai left it was quarter to five. This was going to be tight. She had to get Beth and she had to get to the vet. She called Stan. He wanted to apologize for the odd and truncated weekend and make plans for the future. Maybe a dinner date, during the week. She cut him short. She explained about Beth and that she had to go to the vet's. A time constraint was something Stan could relate to.

"I can get Beth for you," he said.

Lily waffled. She didn't want her daughter to think her relationship with Stan was super-serious, especially since she had more than half decided that it had to end or at least become a friendship and nothing else. And today, especially, Beth needed a maternal lecture.

"I won't say anything about her fight with her friend," Stan promised. "Nada, zip, lips sealed. If she wants to talk, I'll just listen. You're the big guns here; I'm not even an opening salvo. Scout's honor."

"You were a Scout?" "Just say, 'thank you.'"

"Thank you." She still did not feel right about it but she couldn't be in two places at once and she had an odd feeling about whatever

Sandra Flower wanted to tell her. She called the school and explained that Stan was coming in her place.

She got to the vet clinic by five-thirty. Monster was in a big cage by himself, the feline equivalent of a hospital room all to himself. There was some sort of soft fuzzy thing in the cage with him; it had once been one of Lily's sweaters which Monster had taken over and loved, and she had brought it as a sort of feline security blanket.

"Private hospital room," said Sandra Flower, echoing Lily's thought.

As they approached the cage, the cat looked up. He had an IV line taped into one fore leg. He looked dreadful but nonetheless better than he had that morning.

"Oh Monster!" Lily dropped her purse and ran toward her cat. "Meep!" said Monster. He pushed his head out toward Lily in a rather wobbly fashion.

"Will you look at that," said the vet. "He is definitely going to make it."

She unlatched the big cage. Lily reached up to stroke her cat and then on a whim grabbed the sides of the cage and chinned herself up, holding herself, pull-up position, so she could gently butt heads with her cat.

"Damn, you're strong!" Sandra Flower was shaking her head. "I've never seen anybody do that and my partner is a bodybuilder." Sandra was in a long- term lesbian relationship. "Want a chair to stand on if you're going to do that?"

"Please." Lily kept herself in position until the promised chair was brought.

Then she stood. Monster began to purr. The vet produced a jar of baby food from somewhere and Lily put some on her finger. Monster licked it off, still purring. Lily did this several more times before the cat pulled away.

"He is definitely going to make it." Sandra took the baby food jar back, wrote "Monster" on it with an indelible marker and put it in a small refrigerator. "He may be able to go home in a couple of days. I thought it would be longer. Anyway. Lily. Come on back to my office and have a seat."

When they were both settled Lily waited. She had discovered, in both tiger and human forms, that waiting, saying nothing, just waiting, sometimes produced interesting results.

"It is definitely distemper," said Sandra finally. "A new variety. Highly contagious, highly lethal. I got the test results. Monster's gonna be okay not only because he has antibodies from the more usual strain but more because he's lucky. You caught it immediately and brought him in right away." She paused staring at Lily. "A couple more things. They don't think this strain is a natural mutation. And I was warned to not even consider publishing an article on this." Her mouth turned down; it was obvious she really wanted to publish.

"What? How could anyone know already that this isn't a natural mutation?

Who's 'they'? And who won't let you publish?" She had a sudden flash of insight. "The PDC? And why not? Someone is waging a terror war against our cats? With a new virus? That's ridiculous. I don't get any of this."

"It didn't make immediate sense to me, either. But you remember back when we met, years ago -"

Lily did. Details of that meeting suddenly came flooding back. They had been new in the area, she and John and a much younger Beth. She had brought Fluffball, Monster's predecessor, in as a kitten. The clinic was new, they were new, but John and Sandra Flower knew each other. That had become more than clear at dinner when Lily had mentioned the vet's name. John had forbidden her to use this clinic but Lily had stood her ground. She liked the vet and the clinic was close by. When she felt strongly about something it took a lot to change her mind. John had been unable to do so then.

"I worked for your husband, ex-husband, very briefly, at his big research facility back in New Jersey, as you know. I quit. For a lot of reasons. When I quit, I had to sign nondisclosure forms, not just for the company but for the PDC, the Department of Defense, and Homeland Security."

"What?" Lily whispered the word. She stared at the other woman.

Department of Defense. Homeland? Thoughts began to coalesce. She knew John. A word appeared magically in her mind and she spoke it.

"Weaponize," she said. "John isn't just looking for cures for psi diseases, he's trying to control them, alter them. Make them - transferable. Weaponize them for the government."

Sandra said nothing. She didn't move, didn't even incline her head, but there was confirmation in her eyes.

"But this makes no sense." Lily couldn't help attempting to work out her puzzle out loud. "I can see something like fire-starting. Maybe even telepathy. I don't believe in teleportation, no matter what the tabloids say. Lycanthropy.

Shape shifting," she paused. She had said too much. "But feline distemper? Something went wrong."

"Something always goes wrong," said Sandra. Her face was completely expressionless but her eyes spoke volumes.

"A vaccine for something mutated. You think Monster's illness has something to do with John's research." She had a sudden flash of Stan with his hypodermic. Maybe things weren't at all even that simple. Not that anything was clear yet. And Stan was picking up Beth. Lily rose suddenly to her feet.

She felt as if the world had shifted under her and she could trust no one. Nothing.

"Lily, you can't say anything about this."

"I don't know what I would say, what I could say. Or to whom." Wes' face filled her mind. She pushed it away and looked the vet in the eyes. "You told me nothing."

"Thank you, Lily. But Lily -"

She knew what was coming. She knew it and she couldn't stop it.

"You know John. You still see him. This has to stop somewhere. If you have any influence. If there is anything you can do, anything, without putting yourself in danger, of course -"

"I don't know what. I wish I knew what." As she spoke a vision of John's farm formed in her mind. The old Beechland farmhouse, the out buildings. Out buildings now used for what? And cabins. If she wanted to find out more, if she wanted to do - to do something - what? - about this she would have to go to the source. She would not be allowed access to the big facility in New Jersey, or if she were, it would be just the standard tour. What there was to find was at the farm, where John took her daughter.

Sandra Flower nodded, just as if Lily had spoken. For the first time Lily wondered if the vet did not have a touch of a psi disease herself, of telepathy.

"Lily, Monster will be okay. I'm sure of it. You can call me again tomorrow, any time." Sandra was showing her to the door. The clinic was closed now, the techs finishing up with the computer work.

"And Lily. Be careful." Everybody was saying that now.

"I will," she said. She had to say something.

CHAPTER SIX

B ETH WAS NOWHERE TO BE seen when Lily got home. Stan was there, laptop set up in the living room, frowning at something. He barely looked up when Lily came in.

"She's upstairs in her room," he said.

"Thanks for picking up Beth. Did she say anything?"

"Barely a word all the way home. She did look for that stupid cat when we got here. Couldn't find it."

Lily's eyes darkened. "Monster is at the vet. That's why I had to stop off there, to check on him. He's very sick and Beth is very upset. He'll probably live."

"Shit! I'm sorry. I had no idea. I don't like the cat much, I have to admit, but I'm sorry. You should have told me. I would have said something to the kid."

She had told him. She hesitated, then said it.

"I did tell you. And the kid's name is Beth. Stan, we need to talk about some things."

Stan had promise when they first started out and there was no denying he had his good points, but he was becoming less and less what she considered boyfriend material. It wasn't just his treatment of Monster. There was something odd about him now, something that wasn't there before. She paused, thinking. And then there was that syringe she had been meaning to ask him about. What was happening here, to Stan, to her, to all of them?

"It'll have to wait, babe. I gotta go. Got an appointment." He was packing up his laptop.

"Stan, this is important -"

"I'll call you about dinner later in the week. Who knows, I might just drop by." He grinned at her, the old charming grin that had been one of things which attracted her to him. "You know I love you, right?" He winked. Then his expression turned serious. "I'm not going to let you go. Your mine. You should know that."

With that he was out the door, leaving Lily standing with her mouth open.

That wasn't like him. Not the way he used to be, she thought. He had never said he loved her before. And that thing about never letting her go, that was just creepy. Drugs? That would explain a lot. But what kind of drugs? For now, her suspicions would have to wait.

Beth was lying across her bed, her face in her pillow. She didn't look up when her mother entered the room.

"I saw Monster just a little while ago." Lily sat down on the end of the bed. "Dr. Flower says he'll make it. He meeped at me. He even licked some baby food off my finger."

Beth rolled over. "Really? Oh Mom!" She threw her arms around her mother. "When can he come home?"

This was the daughter Lily knew. She smiled.

"A day or two, maybe. He has to get well enough for us to take care of him here."

"What is it? What caused it? Did Dr. Flower say?"

"It's a virus. A new one. But it's related to an old virus he had shots for so he'll be okay."

"A virus." Something shut down in Beth's face. She didn't lie back down on the bed but she stared at the floor, saying nothing else. Lily followed an instinctive connection.

"Beth, I don't know exactly what happened up at your father's farm this past weekend. I do want to know but you don't have to tell me until you are ready.

But there is something I want you to know. You will not be going to the farm again."

Now Beth did look up. "Really?" There was a sudden hope in her face, which just as quickly shut down. "But Dad said, he said the courts gave him the right to see me and to have visits no matter what."

"The court gave him the right to see you. And I'm not trying to take that away. You can see him, just not at the farm. Claire - you remember Claire. My, our, lawyer, - is going in front of a judge to get that stopped. I won't let you go up there, not if you don't want to. Do you want to?"

"No! No! It's weird up there now. Dad - he wanted to test me for something. And he said to vaccinate me against something! I told him I'd scream so he said okay he wouldn't, he'd do it next time. After he explained it to me some more. He said I was probably okay for now. He said he loved me and wouldn't hurt me, and this was to keep me safe. But Mom, I don't know if I believe him!" Beth burst into tears.

Losing trust in a parent, thinking maybe they didn't love you, even a parent like John, that was hard. Lily felt her heart tear. But beyond that, what the hell had John been trying to do? This went beyond Beth seeing a few "side effects" of some new drug.

"Oh sweetheart," she said. She put her arms around her daughter, who sobbed into her shoulder. "He loves you. You shouldn't doubt that." She hesitated but decided to say it. After all, Beth already knew. "It's just that his judgement isn't always the best. He tends to get ahead of himself."

"Like with the vaccines."

"Maybe. Beth, I won't let anything happen to you."

Beth sniffed and leaned against her mother. Lily sniffed back a tear herself.

She knew it was time for the lecture, the one she had promised to give. But somehow this didn't seem the right time.

"What happened today with Sarah?" she asked instead. "Can you tell me? I think you need to."

"I don't want to see her anymore." Beth's voice was full of tears and at the same time hard. "I - Mom - I don't want anything to happen to her."

"What could happen to her? Your science experiment isn't dangerous, honey."

"I know. I'm not an idiot, Mom. I'm sorry I hit her. It was a stupid argument. I know you're not supposed to hit people. I don't know why I did." Lily got the distinct impression that Beth knew exactly why and that somehow it wasn't related to any argument. She had the impression it was deliberate.

"I apologized. It won't happen again. The science thing is good enough as it is. It doesn't need more work." Beth turned away and flopped down on the bed again. "I'm gonna do some homework in a minute. I just want to rest, okay? And I miss Monster."

"Beth, if this has something to do with anything up at the farm, anything your dad is up to there, don't worry. It's not going to hurt Sarah."

There was silence in return and Lily knew she had overstepped the temporary bounds. She also knew she was on the right track.

She checked later, bringing her daughter a sandwich. Beth was indeed doing homework. Later still, after Beth was in bed asleep, Lily finished preparing her lecture notes while eating a bowl of soup. She was exhausted. She stretched out on the couch and turned on the tv. The local news was on; she hadn't realized it was that late.

There had been another attack in Providence. Another child, this time not Hmong, had been found comatose. The pugmarks, the paw prints of a large cat, had been found around him. Hysteria was mounting. There was talk of calling in several more Psi Disease Center Special Investigators.

Wes will love that, Lily thought, before going to bed.

In the morning she called the vet first thing. Monster was doing much better and had eaten a little on his own. Sandra Flower wanted to keep him another day but there was no doubt now that he would survive and recover completely. The news cheered Beth, who actually gave her mother a hug before heading to the bus.

Once Beth was gone, with strict instructions to make up with Sarah, Lily sat down at the kitchen table with another cup of coffee. She had only one class today, at noon. The semester was winding down in its usual frenzy of papers, meetings and student presentations. Lily was giving no final exams; it was all final presentations and papers. This left her both freer and more constrained than some of her colleagues. She sat down to finish another batch of papers when the phone rang.

It was Deb Lattinger. "I didn't want to bother you last night," she said. "I heard your poor cat was sick and Beth had some sort of awful time at her father's and was upset. I tried earlier and no one was home."

Word traveled faster than light, it seemed. Lily wondered how Deb could have known all this so fast unless Beth had told Sarah.

"Deb, I'm so sorry; I still can't believe what Beth did. I'm glad Sarah wasn't hurt."

"Not to worry. These things happen between girls. Especially with everything that's going on with Beth. They'll make it up. In fact, I wondered if you wanted me to pick up both girls from school and bring them over here.

Finish up the science project and have dinner. I'll bring Beth back by nine." "Is that a good idea? So soon? I mean, after yesterday -"

Deb laughed. "Sarah said it was a stupid argument. Trust me. I tell you what. Text your daughter. If she says okay - when she says okay - call me back."

The response part didn't take long. It took Lily the better part of several minutes to compose the text message but the result came back almost immediately. Beth must have been between classes.

"Luv 2 go. Thnx, mom, UR the best!"

That was an improvement in attitude, at least. Things might be looking up. On an impulse she checked the FAA site online: good weather. Just to be sure, she called the FAA weather service: it was more than good, it was perfect weather, the briefer told her. She called the service at Green Airport and rented a Cessna 172 for the afternoon. She needed both the practice and a break, she decided, and this was it.

By two-thirty that afternoon she was outside the hangar in Warwick looking at the Cessna. It was gassed up and ready to go. It would be nice to get up and away from everything, to be completely free, at least for a short time. Maybe she would fly to Block Island, not a long hop, or the Vineyard. Just away, somewhere -

"Lily? Hey, Lily! Is that your plane? I didn't know you were a pilot."

"Detect - uh, Wes? Wes, what are you doing here?" Then she noticed the flight bag in his hand.

"I got a 172 of my own. And I got the afternoon off. I was just going to the hangar to get her; the weather's so good. Nice plane you got there."

"It's not mine. I had one but I had to sell it when I -" why was she telling him this? "This is rented. I got it for the afternoon." She looked at Wes, really looked at him. Physically he was not exactly what most would think handsome. He was round but muscular, but she saw the genuine interest and empathy, saw his infectious smile.

"You going somewhere particular?" she asked.

"Nope. Just flying around. Thought I might get a sandwich on the Vineyard or something. I missed lunch and I'm starved."

"Me, too."

It was an impulse and she wasn't really sure why she did it. She just felt she could trust him and she genuinely liked him. Lily knew she was in need of friends but she also knew she had to be careful. This time the desire for friendship won out.

"Want to come with?" she said. "I'll fly left seat one way and you can fly the other."

"And we'll split the cost," said Wes. "I bet you've already paid for that.

Dutch treat." He grinned again and Lily felt herself responding with a grin of her own.

It was a perfect flight, if short, but Lily found she didn't miss the free and alone time in the air she thought she had been looking forward to. She flew flawlessly. They landed and parked, and ate at the airport restaurant.

"Fried clams," said Lily to the waitress. "A big order, not the dinner, and some curly fries on the side. And iced coffee with cream and sugar."

"Same here," said Wes, glancing at her. "I thought you might be the health food type. Guess I was wrong."

"Usually I am. But there's a time for health food," said Lily, "and this isn't it."

"Do you ever have that right!"

They grinned and sat for a moment in comfortable silence. Lily found herself wondering things: how could Wes afford a plane on a detective's salary? Was he married? She really knew very little about him. He undoubtedly knew more about her from his investigations. She looked up to find his bright blue eyes on her.

"I imagine you're wondering stuff about me," said Wes. "Let's start with this: I'm not married. I was." His eyes shifted away from her and looked into the distance. "It didn't work out. It very much didn't work out."

"I'm so sorry," said Lily, after a moment's silence.

"Yeah. Well. She was rich. Lots of family money, and I mean lots." He gave a lopsided smile that held no humor. "And since she was the one who wanted to break it off - she found this other guy, more at her level, she said - she gave me a stock portfolio. Nothing pharmaceutical," he glanced back at Lily, "as a, well, I suppose, some sort of bribe. I was angry enough that I took it. I get nice dividends every year, very nice. Extremely nice. Her family knew how to do stocks. I just leave it alone and collect the dividends. That pays for most of the stuff for my plane."

Lily found herself staring at him. He had answered most of her questions without her asking them. Although there was one more. "At least we didn't have any kids," he said.

Lily felt her mouth drop open and closed it, hoping he hadn't noticed. "I'm really sorry for what you are going through with your ex, and what that's got to be doing to Beth." He didn't say "your kid", she noticed. "She - Cynthia - took Buster. My cat. That's the closest we got to a kid. He died three years later; kidney failure. I think she hastened his death; she wasn't the nurturing type. She would have made a lousy mother. You know, I always wanted to have kids, just never with my wife, which I guess says something. "

"I'm so sorry." She seemed to keep saying that.

"It's one reason what's happening with these kids in Providence is getting to me so hard. But we didn't come here to talk about this stuff."

They were saved from further immediate discussion by the arrival of their food. They both dug in and Lily was amused to note that Wes used ketchup for his clams more often than tartar sauce, just as she did.

"At this rate," she said, "I'm glad you're flying back. I'm so full I can't think straight."

"Why don't we take a cab into town, walk around a bit before we head back. Do you have time?"

Lily glanced at her watch. 4 PM. "Plenty of time," she said, but she got out her cell phone and checked. No messages, voice or text, from anybody.

They took a cab to Vineyard Haven. On the way to town, she found herself telling Wes about Beth's fight with Sarah and about Monster. She even briefly mentioned Stan. She almost said she didn't think he was right for her and how could she have been so wrong and what could have happened to him before she shut herself down on that subject. She heard a little more about his own failed marriage, about how his ex-wife, Cynthia, had never been convinced that he measured up to her socially and her family had been certain of it.

They walked around the old streets commenting on the dress of the early tourists, as if they weren't tourists themselves. They looked for osprey nests near the harbor as it was about the time for the big raptors to return from their winters in South America. They discussed science fiction and briefly wondered why themes of supernatural fantasy seemed to be entering the realm of reality.

That struck too close to home, though. Then, even though the late afternoon had turned chilly, they stopped and got ice cream cones. Coffee ice cream for both of them.

"We should get back," said Lily, looking at her cell phone again. No messages.

The cab rides back to the airport transpired in a comfortable silence. Wes flew them back. He was an accomplished pilot and they were back in Warwick all too soon.

"Thanks," they said simultaneously.

"Let's do it again," said Wes. "Or something else. Soon."

Lily debated but then said it. "This has been the most fun I've had in a long time." Longer than I remember, she thought. They stared at each for a moment, grinning stupidly like kids on a first date. For the very briefest of moments, Lily thought he might kiss her but then they headed for their cars.

The relaxed glow lasted until she got home. Even the thought of the remaining papers to grade, of the call to the lawyer she would have to make did not bother her. But as she pulled into her driveway at 7:30 she saw Stan's car.

She frowned. He had no reason being there without her prior consent, and especially on a week night. He had no way of knowing whether Beth would be there and he knew she didn't want him there with Beth if she were absent, not without permission. She was out of her car almost before it stopped moving.

There was no sound in the house. She knew he was here; there were lights on but there was no sound. Then she heard a cat cry. It was Monster.

She was up the stairs and into the bedroom before she realized it. Her purse and her flight bag were still in her hands; her coat was still on. There was Stan, in the bedroom, with Monster on the bed. Stan was leaning over the cat and there was a needle in his hand. She dropped the flight bag and threw the purse. Her aim was accurate, hitting Stan on the back of the head. Stan staggered.

"What the hell do you think you're doing! Get away from him! Get away from my cat!"

She grabbed Stan from behind, yanking him away from the animal. The hypo full of - something - it looked like blood - dropped to the floor without breaking. She slammed Stan against the wall with a force that should have knocked him out. Instead the plaster of the wall cracked. Stan's eyes flashed briefly golden, the pupils slitting, reflecting back light. He reached out as if to grab her but then with an obvious effort let his hands fall. His eyes returned to normal and Lily, breathing hard, was not even sure she had seen them change.

"What are you doing with him? He's supposed to be at the vet's!"

"She released him early to me. She -"

"The hell she did!" Sandra Flower would not have released Monster to anyone but Lily, not without authorization.

"Get out! And don't come back!" She heard the snarl in her voice and hoped Stan didn't hear it. "Get your stuff and get out! And give me my key! If you ever come here again I'm calling the cops!" She moved between him and the dropped syringe; he wasn't getting it. It was evidence of some sort.

"Yeah, well, you got a special relationship there with cops, don't you?

Flitting around all day with your new boyfriend." He backed away from her.

How did he know that? she wondered. Not that Wes was anything close to a boyfriend. Stan had a sudden shift in attitude and made an attempt to be charming but Lily wasn't buying. He told her he loved her; he apologized and promised to explain all. But when Lily asked, no explanation was forthcoming so he was packed and gone soon enough. And she had her key back. She decided she might change the locks. Even as she thought this she felt tears prick and then angrily wiped them away,

She checked over Monster but found no damage. She picked up the syringe carefully, with a tissue, trying to remember what she had learned from the forensic dramas on tv. A call to the vet clinic brought disturbing news: it had been broken into, while still in business hours. Someone had gotten back into the hospital section and it had taken the staff a little while to discover the incursion, so clever had the intruder been. Her cat had been stolen.

When Lily got there, carrying Monster in his old disintegrating carrier since her regular one could not be found, the police were there, investigating and taking statements. They almost didn't let her through until Sandra Flower herself motioned to the cop at the door.

"This is one of the animals that was stolen," she told the cop. "Oh my God," said Lily, "there were more? How many?"

"Eight others, all cats, all from the feline section of the hospital. But they were found, all in carriers, right at the edge of the wood lot. Monster was the only one missing. We were trying to find him. I didn't know how I was going to tell you. Where was he?"

"At my house. Stan had him." Why had Stan brought him home? She saw the cop moving in, note pad at the ready. "I will tell you about Stan," she promised him, "but first I want my cat examined."

Such was the power of the combined stares of Lily and her vet that this was exactly the way it happened, with the bemused cop backing off.

It turned out that Monster was actually well enough to be released, to Lily's surprise. Whatever had happened since he had been stolen, it hadn't harmed him. Sandra took the syringe.

"I have a feeling we shouldn't tell the cops about this until I find out what it is," she said, glancing sideways at Lily.

"You want me to leave the whole syringe thing out of the interview?" Lily had the feeling she was getting even deeper into something than she could imagine.

"For now."

"There is no 'for now'. If I don't tell them now, I don't tell them."

The vet nodded her agreement. As a result, the police later heard that Stan had been leaning over Lily's pet when she came in and heard the cat scream.

Lily said nothing about the syringe nor did Sandra.

Time wore on and Lily could not break away. She ended up calling Deb Lattinger to ask if if Deb could keep Beth another hour or two even though it would be late. Alarmed at the cat-theft, the boyfriend problem and Lily's police interview, Deb offered to let Beth spend the night. The girls were getting along famously, she said, just like before their "spat", as she called it. Lily talked to her daughter who sounded thrilled to spend the night with her friend. One of her questions surprised Lily.

"Stan is gone for good?"

"Yes, I broke up with him. What made you guess?"

"I dunno; I just did. And I don't have to go back up to the farm." Assured that she didn't, Beth sounded much happier. The juxtaposition of the two issues was odd. Lily decided to ask her about it later.

Lily didn't get back home until almost eleven, carrying Monster in a carrier borrowed from Sandra. The cat ate some dry food and then went upstairs and settled comfortably on the bed. He seemed to know that Stan was gone, too.

After her interview with the cop, Lily had been offered "police presence" overnight, which she assumed meant a car in her driveway in case she needed help. She turned it down. She doubted Stan would have the nerve to come back even if he wanted to, and she felt more than capable of handling such a matter by herself, should it occur.

She changed the sheets on the bed. This temporarily dislodged Monster, but not for long. The cat went right back. Lily took a hot a shower and then settled back in bed with the cat and the tv remote. Oddly, she was not worried about Beth and it was rather nice to have the house to herself. It had been a very long day. She flipped on the tv. There had been five more "tiger" attacks in Providence, two of them Hmong, three African American.

African American? Lily frowned. It was getting worse. The police were making no progress. She wondered what Wes thought of this media coverage; she could guess. What had she said to Grandfather Lee? Had she made him a promise? Whether she had or not, it was beginning to look as if he were right. Someone or something needed to stop this shape shifter. It would have to be another shape shifter, one who knew the signs, knew what to look for. In short, she would have to do it. But not tonight. Definitely not tonight.

She got out of bed. She was way too tired to do anything now except make a check of the house. The best way, the way that would yield the most information, was to do it in tiger form.

Lily pulled off the t-shirt she slept in. She stretched, yawned and then shuddered. A tiger stood beside the bed, looking down at the pillow and the curled up house cat.

Monster looked back at the tiger. He was accustomed to her; she was his family. He blinked his gold eyes in a friendly hello. The big gold eyes of the tigress blinked back at him. Then the huge feline leaned across the bed and gave a very gentle head-butt to the small one. Monster purred. Lily took a four- footed step back from the bed and almost tripped. She glanced down and saw that she had forgotten to remove her underpants before changing shape. They were now ripped beyond repair. She puffed in annoyance and stepped out of them.

"It's always something," she tried to say, but what came out was a tiger's moan.

She didn't need light. She prowled the small house carefully, even pushing up on her hind legs to sniff toward the attic crawl space. There were mice there; it figured. But all was secure. At last, exhausted, she padded back to the bedroom, jumped up on the bed and curled up beside Monster.

CHAPTER SEVEN

THE RINGING OF THE PHONE woke her. Lily yawned hugely and glanced at the clock: 6 AM. Monster was no longer on the bed but she could see he had eaten more kibble from the bowl on the floor, a very good sign. Who could be calling this early? Was Beth okay? She remembered the night before. The police? Deb? Lily reached for the phone.

Just in time she saw the stripes along her arm, no, make that her foreleg.

And the extended claws where fingers should be. She had fallen asleep in tiger form. Horrified, she shuddered and started to change, while the phone continued to ring. This had never happened before. She glanced in the mirror opposite the bed. Her head was now human but most of the rest of her was still in tiger form. It was startling. She didn't want to miss the call. She managed to hook the receiver with a paw.

"Mrrello?"

"Lily? Is that you? It's Sandra Flower."

Lily coughed. In the mirror she could see her hand become human now.

She looked away. The mixture of tiger and human was too unsettling. "Yeah, it's me. Sorry, Sandra, it was a late night."

"You okay?"

"Yeah, I was just changing."

"I just thought you'd want to know the results of the lab analysis. Of what was in Monster's syringe."

"It's back already?"

"I've got connections at the lab. Anyway, it was nothing but a little blood.

That's all. And what appear to be antibodies against this new variety of panleukopenia. I don't think Stan was trying to inject poor Monster. He was trying to extract blood. He did extract blood. He just didn't get to do whatever else he wanted since you came home in time and caught him. He probably thought he was doing you a favor by bringing your cat home to do it. It looks like he took blood from some of the other cats he took, too."

"He wanted the syringe. He wanted my cat's blood. This doesn't make sense." Lily scratched her head and then winced. The claws were still out on her left hand. Paw. She hastily pulled it away from her scalp. There was a little blood on one claw.

"It doesn't. There is something very strange going on. Lily, I hope you don't mind me saying this but Stan's a creep. Except I know you wouldn't get involved with an outright creep. Lily, I think Stan was normal, more or less, and then something happened. Something changed him. I thought you should know about the lab results."

"Thanks." Both her hands were hands again, not big tiger paws. "Are you safe from Stan?"

"Absolutely." If Stan dared to come back she could meet him in tiger form. "Besides, the cops will pick him up soon. He won't dare bother me." She missed him, though, or maybe it was just the thought of a relationship that she missed. She could feel a lump that wanted to start in her throat. She was so alone. She had to be. She felt like crying; it was ridiculous. She couldn't afford this emotion.

As she was talking, Monster came in. The cat jumped up on the bed to give her a quick head-butt and then jumped down and went to his dry food. Lily swallowed, then smiled.

"Monster seems better this morning."

"Lily, I've been meaning to ask you; do you want to get together for coffee some time, just talk?"

Lily hesitated. One of the drawbacks of being a secret tiger was that she had few friends. In fact, right now, except for Deb Lattinger, she had none. She had colleagues at work and she seemed to be becoming friends with Wes, which was dangerous, but someone she liked, another professional woman -

"Sure," she said. "I'd love to. Just say when. My schedule is more flexible than yours and it's about to become even more flexible when the semester ends." A glance in the mirror showed her completely human now. Thank God.

No sooner was she off the phone than it rang again. "Mom?"

"Beth! How are you? Isn't this a little early for you to be up? School doesn't -"

"Mom, how is Monster?"

"I think he's going to be fine. He was eating just a minute ago."

"Can you come pick me up and bring me home so I can see him before I go to school? Please? Ms. Lattinger is awake and everything."

"I'll be right there."

She had plenty of time before class, so why not? On the way, she picked up a box of blueberry and cranberry muffins from the local bakery and some of the hazelnut coffee she knew her friend liked. Deb Lattinger met her at the door and was suitably appreciative. It said a lot that Beth didn't try to beg a muffin on her way out. She did stop to whisper something to Sarah so apparently the girls were in fact on good terms again.

Once home, Beth found Monster and gave him a gentle hug. The cat purred and licked her hand and then went to find his favorite catnip toy.

"Look, Mom! He's okay now!"

"It would seem so." Lily was smiling at both daughter and cat. "And Stan's really gone."

"Really." Lily felt her smile fade. What had happened with Stan? A look at her daughter's face told her that Beth wished she hadn't drawn attention to this question.

"I better get out the door, Mom. The bus will be here soon." "I have a better idea."

Beth looked at her warily. "We both play hooky." "What?"

"I'll call us both in sick and we can take the day off and just hang." "Mom? Mooom! You wouldn't! No way!"

"Yep. Way. It's not like we're gonna make this a habit or anything but I think we both need it pretty badly." She picked up the phone again. A bit too early for the university but she left a message that she was sick and her introductory classes, all she had today, were to get into groups and work on their final presentations. Then she emailed both classes to try to catch the students before they left for class. By that time the office at Beth's school was open. She explained that Beth was feeling "under the weather and exhausted".

"Not surprising," said the secretary, "considering everything she's been through. You tell her to take it easy."

"So," she said, turning to Beth. "What do you want to do? Go to the mall?

Take a bike ride? A movie? No, not not a movie. It's too nice a day."

They ended up riding down the bike path for a while. The path was almost deserted since it was a week day and early. They got off their bikes at a small stream and craned their necks toward the pond where there had been a beaver lodge. It was almost impossible to see it now, with all the new spring growth.

Lily smiled and turned to say something to her daughter about the beavers but the words froze in her throat.

Her daughter had one hand on the railing of the small bridge on which they stood and the other keeping her bike upright. She was not looking for the beaver lodge or the beavers. Her eyes were following a woodchuck that trundled along near the path. That the woodchucks were out already probably meant a warm summer. Lily had always thought that woodchucks were cute. It wouldn't be surprising for Beth to watch one but it was the way her daughter looked at the rodent. There was something predatory in Beth's gaze. Lily felt herself grow cold. Until now, there had been no signs, nothing at all to suggest that Beth might have inherited the strange shape shifting ability of her mother. In the next second, however, the look was gone, and Beth was smiling at her mother.

"Can we go to the mall next, Mom? You said I could get new sandals for summer. And maybe have lunch at the food court?"

Lily blinked. It was her imagination, it had to be. "Sure," she said.

The sandal shopping turned out to be a little more rigorous than Lily would have liked. But she found a new pair of comfortable clogs for herself, too, and then Beth insisted on going into the pet store to get some special catnip for Monster. Then it was time for the food court. It was over a lunch of Thai noodles that Lily heard what was bothering Beth about Stan.

"Mom." Beth's normally bouncy nine-year-old self had turned somber and slightly edgy. She had stopped eating and was pushing the noodles around, even though they were one of her favorite foods.

Lily looked up from her own food. When Beth said nothing more she

reached across the little table and tried to take her daughter's hand. "You can tell me, Beth. I promise I will try to understand."

"It's about Stan." Beth was still looking at her food. "He was up at Dad's." "What?"

"You don't believe me. I knew you wouldn't. I knew -"

"Whoa, hold up there. I do believe you. I'm just surprised. Very surprised.

You mean up at Beechland, right? At the farm." Beth nodded.

"When did you see him? And what was he doing there?"

"He spent a lot of time with Dad. And in the cabins. Where the, um, I don't know, the Experiments are." Lily heard the capital letter in her daughter's voice. "Those drug trial people Dad has there. And then, well, Stan was lurking around. It was creepy."

"How long have you known about the drug trials and the people in the cabins?"

Beth shrugged, looking away. "I dunno. A long time. Dad said not to tell you. That it didn't have anything to do with us and you'd freak and go ballistic. But I met some of the kids there and they, well, they didn't want to be there.

They were scared. When Dad found out I met them, he was wicked furious. And worried. He wanted to draw blood - from me. He said it was like a vaccination, only to make sure I wasn't sick instead of preventing it." She shuddered. "He wanted to test to be sure I hadn't caught some psi thing. He didn't say it but that's what it was; I'm not stupid. And I'm not sick, either. Stan was there, and he was lurking around. Mom, he was around the cabins; I saw him. And he was outside the house. I went out to, like, look at the stars. And Stan came out, it was like he had been under a bush or something, and his eyes glowed. I'm not making that up, I swear. I yelled or screamed or something and Dad came out. Dad went to talk to him and told me to go inside."

Lily leaned across the small table and put her hand on Beth's arm. "You don't need to worry about that anymore," she said. Beth might be exaggerating a bit about Stan lurking under bushes with glowing eyes but she didn't doubt the rest of the story. It explained some things. "You are not going back to the farm, your dad is not going to 'vaccinate' you or draw blood for anything I don't know about and don't approve of, and you won't be seeing Stan again."

Beth sighed. Then she jumped up and hugged her mom. "Good!" Her grin was blazingly bright. Then it dimmed slightly. "Um, Mom? Those kids there.

They don't want to be there. Can you do something about that?"

Lily took her daughter's hand. "I don't know, sweetie. But I will look into it and I'll see what I can do. I'll ask Claire." It was a job for a lawyer, certainly.

She said as much. "That's lawyer stuff." Not tiger woman to the rescue. She had to stop thinking that way. Wes' face flashed into her mind. And maybe it was a job for the cops.

By the time they got home, it was late afternoon. Lily called Claire.

Amazingly, the injunction to keep Beth away from the farm had come through. John would not be pleased but Beth definitely was. Lily mentioned there were other kids at the farm but Claire couldn't do anything about that, not unless their parents were her clients. Lily frowned over that but put the problem aside.

There was a message from Beth's school, with a list of homework.

"You didn't think you'd get off completely, did you?" Lily asked her. "Playing hooky only goes so far." She was thinking of her own work.

Beth grinned and with Monster rubbing around her ankles went up to her room with her new sandals to do the homework.

There was also a message from Sandra Flower asking if she could stop by later. There was no chance to answer that call. There was a knock on the door and there was the vet, with a bag of something steaming.

"Tea, Earl Grey, two cups, not in a pot, unfortunately, and butter cookies.

Do you like tea? If this isn't a good time we can do this another day."

"Come right in. I have more Earl Grey in the kitchen. This is obviously just what the doctor ordered. Wait, you are the doctor."

"So are you," said Sandra.

"Can I have some cookies? Did you come to check on Monster?" Beth seemed to have materialized from thin air.

"I thought you were doing homework." Lily tried to glare at her daughter. It didn't work, or at least Beth was unintimidated.

"How is Monster?" Sandra wanted to know.

"He seems fine," said Lily to Sandra. Then, to her daughter, "Yes, you can have some cookies if you take them upstairs with you. I said 'some', not half the box!"

She and Sandra ended up at the kitchen table. Lily waited for the subject of the visit to come up. She knew it would have something to do with her ex-husband, something to do with the vial of Monster's blood. But nothing like that came up, nothing at all. They talked about cats; Sandra and Leslie had five they had rescued, three of them with disabilities. Then they talked about books, then politics and found themselves in accord. Lily felt completely at ease. They finished the Earl Grey Sandra had brought and Lily made a pot of it.

Finally, Lily felt she had to bring it up herself.

"Don't you think we should tell the police about the blood Stan was trying to steal? I'm not sure I feel right about hiding this."

Sandra paused with the teacup halfway to her mouth. She put the cup down and then shook her head.

"We didn't tell them right away, Lily, and you know how they are about things like that. Besides there was nothing really unusual about the blood except -" she looked at Lily and then sighed. "Oh hell. That's not the problem. You know it and I know it. The truth is that I don't want the Specials nosing around me again. It was bad enough when I worked for John. With everything that's been going on in Providence, this supposed shape shifting, you know the Psi Disease guys would be all over me again, just because I worked for your ex-husband. There was absolutely nothing in Monster's blood that could have anything to do with what's happening in Providence. Even though Stan -" she paused. "Lily, please. I just don't want to deal with the PDC again."

For a moment Lily remained silent. Then she shrugged. Sandra had to be right. Stan was pursuing one of his strange theories, and there was nothing about Monster's blood that had anything to do with Beth or anything else that mattered.

"Completely understandable," she said. "I don't want the PDC around here anymore than you do. John's involved with them and that's his business, not mine."

After that it was more talk of books, the strange things clients and students had done, and more tea. At last, Sandra got up.

"I need to get home," she said. "I've got tomorrow off and I plan some serious vegging out tonight and I'm gonna sleep late tomorrow. We should do this again. Come over to our place for dinner, maybe next week?"

"Oh my God, look! We've eaten all your cookies. I think I owe you a dinner. Besides, I have a problem getting a sitter -"

"Bring Beth. I mean, if you don't mind. She always struck me as the kind of kid I would want." Sandra had no children, although Leslie did. Leslie's kids were older and lived with her ex-husband, and she had no desire for any more.

"Leslie is good with younger kids," said Sandra ruefully, "as long as they aren't hers."

Lily walked Sandra to the door, the two of them still talking. It felt great to have another friend, someone with whom she felt so relaxed. It was just a shame it had taken so long for them to get to this point. The fact that she had her odd ability did not have to mean that Lily needed to cut herself off from the rest of humanity.

While her mother and her friend were downstairs ,Beth ate her cookies on the bed, with Monster beside her. She admired her new sandals and posed in front of the mirror with them. Then she carefully removed them and put them back in their box. She took the scrunchie out of her brown hair and shook it loosely around her face. Then she shrugged it back and stared at herself again in the mirror.

There was no posing this time. She stared intensely at her reflection. Slowly her ears began to change. They rounded and grew furry. Her eyes changed, developing a slit pupil. From the bed Monster watched her, completely unalarmed. Still staring at herself, Beth watched her face change. The rest of her remained human but her face was the rounded, open face of a tiger cub just entering the juvenile phase. Beth puffed at herself, pleased. Then her face began to gradually change back to human again. After a few more minutes the face of a human child looked back her. The rest of her body had not changed at all.

"What do you think, Monster? Which looks better? Am I better as a tiger or a human?"

The cat looked back at her and then meeped.

"You're probably right. Cats are always better, right? But this has to be our secret, so it's a good thing you can't tell Mom about this. She'd freak. And it's an even better thing that Dad won't ever know now." She shuddered slightly. "He's my dad but he might want to make me into one of those experiments up at the farm. No way that's going to happen now. And no way he's getting my blood to test. Mom's gonna keep me safe, mom and that lawyer. And Sarah didn't get sick from anything I brought back from the farm. I think we're gonna be okay."

In completely human form, she sat down on the bed and took the cat into her arms.

"It's weird we call you 'Monster'," she said, "considering it's me and my mom who, well, do what we do. What do you think? Are we monsters?"

"Mmmrrp!" said the cat.

"Yeah," said Beth. "I know my mom would freak big time if she knew what I can do and if she knew I knew that she - is this making sense?" She sighed as the cat jumped off the bed and headed for the door. "I guess I'd better do my homework. I can get it done before dinner. Which Mom would never believe.

She knows I'm smart, she just doesn't know how smart. Someday, I'm gonna figure out this shape shifting thing without the help of Dad or the stupid creepy nosey Psi Special people or anything. I know there's more like Mom and me, and there's gotta be a reason. Like for the good of the world. Or something."

"Mrrr," said the cat.

"You said it. You and me, Monster."

"Damn it!" John Belkner was furious. Usually people shrank from him when he was this angry but the object of his fury stared right back at him, unintimidated.

"It wasn't my fault that Lily came back when she did."

"I don't know what you think were doing, trying to get blood from her cat! What is the point of that!"

Stan was trying to be patient. He was a far better scientist than the man in front of him, the man on whom he relied for funding. It obviously wouldn't do to point that out. "Her cat is now immune -"

"Shut up! I'm not finished yet. All the researchers have discounted that theory. They -"

"The other researchers are full of shit." Stan suddenly lost it. "If Lily's cat has the answer to this distemper strain that's been screwing up the research I figured I -"

"You work for me! You do nothing without my authorization! Nothing! I never wanted you to have anything to do with Lily from the beginning!" John stared at the man in front of him and saw the beginnings of a smirk, quickly wiped away. "No, it isn't jealousy. But I want you away from my wife and child. If there is any investigative research to be done there, I will do it. If you want to continue working for me, you do as I say! Understood?"

"Understood. Sir. But sir." "What?"

"Think about what I had to say about the child. In contact with the cat and with the cabin kids."

"Dr. Brentworth. Get yourself out of my sight now, before I kick you out. Just consider yourself lucky to still be employed."

"Yes, sir." That was all Stan felt was safe to say. He had his other contact but that meant nothing if he lost support from the head of Skyline Pharmaceuticals. This was where his research was.

CHAPTER EIGHT

FOR A COUPLE OF WEEKS, it seemed as if things might be normal again, or as normal as they could be. Lily's semester ended in its usual harried way. She turned down the opportunity to teach two summer courses, accepting only the one scheduled for the weeks Beth was supposed to be in camp. Things were financially tight but she could manage and she wanted to spend some time with her daughter. She had a feeling there were things going on that she needed to know about and besides, these days would never come again. She believed parents owed it to their children and themselves to enjoy as much together as they could. John didn't appear to be insisting that Beth visit Beechland so even that problem could be temporarily ignored.

They had dinner with Sandra and Leslie on several occasions at both their houses and both women semi-adopted Beth. For her part, Beth began to take an interest in the veterinary clinic. She wanted to hang around there and help out, especially with the cats, so Sandra let her help the techs clean the cages and do other chores. Beth was thrilled and expressed her desire to become a vet herself.

Beth's science project, her collaboration with Sarah, earned them both an "A" for the year.

The frosting on this cake of normalcy was that there were no more reports of shape shifting tigers or shape shifting anything else. Lily thought often of her conversation with Grandfather Lee but she had delayed looking into the problem until the end of the semester and now perhaps there was no more problem to look into. After all, the reports had stopped and Mai said nothing about to her before or after class. Lily was sure she would have if there had been any real concern.

Then out of nowhere came the report that the "child predator" had been caught and shot resisting arrest. The police and the PDC investigator had staked out a park where there had been reports of a big cat lurking. A young Asian man was apprehended where the cat had been reported but was shot when he drew a gun and fired at the PDC investigator. The detail the media loved was that the man supposedly had a tiger's tail while otherwise human. Lily tried to imagine Clement Fletcher on stake-out and decided she wouldn't blame the suspect for shooting at him. The danger was over, in any event, and it seemed the whole little state breathed a sigh of relief.

Things seemed to be looking up in other ways. Her forays into the woods in tiger form attracted zero attention. She allowed herself to shift without too much anxiety and she enjoyed her time in her other skin.

There were a few things that bothered her. She found herself desiring the tiger form more and more. She still maintained control over her change but the desire seemed to surface more often. Once in tiger form, the urge to hunt, or at least to chase, was strong. She kept an iron control over this aspect of what she refused to consider a psi disease, but it frightened her. The hunting part was easier. If she ate before she shifted form she had less desire to hunt without the stimulus of hunger, and only the desire to chase, which was much easier to control.

In tiger form the light sometimes hurt her eyes. When this persisted in human form she decided it was time for her yearly physical, or at least an eye exam. But she put it off. She was not only busy but sometimes flat-out exhausted, and in human form even a little nauseous.

She found herself in idle moments thinking of Wes. She thought of Stan, too, with a sort of regret and the realization that she missed what he might have been. It made her doubt, once again, her ability to choose men. She had thought she was pretty well recovered from her divorce and then this happened. She couldn't afford the closeness of a romantic relationship; she had to protect herself and her secret. So why was she thinking of Wes? He seemed to be the sort of friend she could confide in, the sort of man - she cut off that line of thought quickly.

She couldn't find the courage to call him but she thought about him daily. Something told her, some odd feeling, that he was also thinking of her. So it was with no real surprise that when her phone rang, on one of her last days of the semester in her office, it turned out to be not a student but Wes.

"Hi there," said Wes. He sounded a bit unsure of himself. "I wondered if you - well, I mean, well, I know this is last minute. But I'm going to be down in your area this afternoon and I wondered if a late lunch - I mean, if you have time, I don't know what your schedule is like -"

Lily grinned. "I'd love to," she said. "When are you going to be here?" She realized later that she hadn't asked him why he was going to be "in her area".

He met her at one-thirty at a small restaurant near the campus. To her surprise he wasn't in his VW but in a police car.

"Got some business down here," he said cryptically. "And this way I save a little wear and tear on my car and they don't question my mileage." Lily noticed that the car got looks from other restaurant patrons.

She found that she didn't care. She was grinning like an idiot and couldn't seem to stop. The only redeeming factor was that Wes was grinning in a similar fashion.

"It's good to see you. It's been too long," he said, wincing at his own platitudes. And then, "Are you okay since that Stan thing? Has he been bothering you?" He could have bitten his tongue as soon as the words were out of his mouth. He seemed to have deeper feelings for this woman than he thought he should, given their relatively short acquaintance. Ye,t here he was reminding her not just of an ex-boyfriend but of the circumstances surrounding their own relationship, whatever it was, and its odd beginnings. Despite the nature of his job, the first bothered him more than the second. Fortunately, the implications seemed to sail past her and didn't darken her mood.

"Stan hasn't been around," she said. "Haven't seen hide nor hair of him," she noticed something flicker on Wes' face, "and he wouldn't dare bother me." She almost added that she'd eat him alive if he tried anything but decided that the humor might be a bit misplaced.

"If he hasn't," Wes agreed, "he probably won't."

She detected the worry at the edge of his words but put it out of her mind.

It was a beautiful day. They ate lunch. Wes asked after Beth. He asked after Monster. They went down to Narragansett, with Lily following the police cruiser in her VW, to take a walk along the sea wall. They watched cormorants dive and a couple of surfers in wet suits over near the town beach. Lily wondered if he liked tea and debated asking him home for some. Then she glanced over to where their cars were parked. The cruiser stood out like the proverbial sore thumb.

"You didn't come down here just to eat lunch and walk on the sea wall," she said. She had the impression that his "business" involved her, but she didn't say it. "What's going on, Wes?"

"I wanted to see you," he said, "but yeah, you're right." He turned and looked out to sea where a sailboat was hauling close to the wind.

Please don't hate me for this. But it's a police matter, too. He didn't say it but Lily heard it clearly. It echoed in her mind as if etched in bold letters.

Startled, she stared at him. She remembered the interview that night in the police station, remembered a couple of times on the Vineyard. She had heard his thoughts then. Hadn't she?

"Wes," she said, unsure of how to continue. He shook his head at her.

"Just listen," he said. "I did want to see you again. Really. I mean see you, not see you on business. I could have asked you to come up to Providence for this, but -" he paused, realizing how that sounded. "Oh hell. Lily, I need your help. There have been more attacks in Providence. And well," he sighed, looked around. "This isn't the place to talk about it."

"Want to come to my place? We could have tea." The invitation was out of her mouth before she thought about it. Tea, she thought. She had really asked him over for tea, not just thought about it. Did American men even drink tea?

Did cops? And more attacks? She thought it was over, the shape shifter killed. "I'd love it, if you have any Earl Grey. But I don't want to disrupt anything with your daughter. When is Beth due home?"

"Not for a while. I'm picking her up later at the vet's." She grinned at his double-take. "The bus lets her off sometimes at Sandra Flower's clinic. She volunteers there and says she wants to keep it up during summer vacation when she's not in camp. Now she says she wants to be a vet when she grows up.

Before this it was a vulcanologist and before that a tv meteorologist. This time, though, it might be for real. Sandra says she's got a feel for the animals. And Beth loves it."

"Jeez." Wes sounded impressed. "Smart kid."

They went back to her house. The house was cool and quiet. Lily didn't bother about what the neighbors might think if they happened to see a police car parked in her driveway. Some of them knew she had had "trouble" with an ex-boyfriend and might assume it was related. Monster met them as soon as she opened the door, friendly and completely unfazed by Wes, whom he apparently remembered. Lily put the tea on to boil without comment and then started rummaging for her tea biscuits. She was sure she had some left.

"Just the tea will be fine; no cookies, thanks," said Wes. "I really don't need anything more now, not after that lunch." Lily turned to look at him. She opened her mouth, shut it, then said it anyway.

"Can you read my thoughts, too, or just project yours?"

For a moment Wes didn't answer. Then he leaned back in the kitchen chair and sighed. "I don't know why it is that I trust you so much, but I do. I can't read your thoughts. I can project. Sometimes it takes a lot of effort and it's always hard masking the fact that I'm doing it. I've never been able to do it so easily before, and I've never had anyone pick up anything I didn't intentionally project. At least not before this. I think you can read my thoughts sometimes without my trying."

The kettle began to whistle and Lily busied herself with making the tea. "Honey? Sugar?"

"Just black. Thanks,"

"How did you get into the police force? I know they check for these things."

"I can control it. I discovered when I was young that I can control it really well. When they started testing me for real I had learned about statistical patterns. I could create a perfectly normal statistical response to any test. This was before they had gene testing. Which your ex-husband developed."

Lily said nothing. For a few moments they both sipped tea.

"By the time they got to gene testing I was already a cop. Not a detective but a cop. They tested me and found I was, as they put it, a carrier, since the disease obviously hadn't manifested in me, they thought. And I didn't have kids with Cynthia since she didn't want them. So I hadn't passed anything on." He paused and closed his eyes for a moment. "They wanted me to get a vasectomy. So I did. No chance of any kids of mine getting the disease."

"I'm so sorry."

"There's no use being bitter about it. In the general scope of things, I'm lucky, I suppose."

"You don't really think it's a disease, do you?" "Do you?"

"No," said Lily, "I don't. It's a mutation, or several mutations. As with all mutations, they can be benign and do nothing, or they could be advantageous or harmful. I think the mutations we're talking about here can be all of the above, in different degrees."

"But they can be hard to live with."

"Yes," said Lily, "they can. Especially given our social climate." He had been so open with her. He could lose his job, any chance for a normal life because of what he had told her. Of course his boss knew, the hierarchy knew at least some of it, but his life on the job could be over if they knew what he could really do. Why couldn't she open up to him? She wanted to, but the habits of a lifetime got in the way. She had to protect herself.

"Why do you need my help?" she said at last.

"There have been more tiger attacks. We've been keeping it out of the press, which isn't easy, believe me. We don't want a panic. It's not just children now and not just Hmong."

"I thought they got the guy. Mai said nothing, and Lucy -"

"We asked them not to talk to you or to anyone while we got this under control." Wes sighed and grimaced ironically. "We are far from getting it under control. The guy who was shot was just a gang banger. Fletcher had some suspicions about you. He thought you might at least be connected to the attacks. I tried to convince him you aren't but I'm not sure he's a hundred percent convinced. Mostly convinced but not all the way there."

Lily felt cold. "Why?"

"Lily. I don't think he believes you are the shape shifter. It's not that it hasn't crossed his mind." Wes leaned forward and his eyes were intense. "But I think he believes you know something about your ex-husband's business, something you aren't telling us."

"And you don't think that."

"No. I don't. I think you know a tremendous amount about shape shifting legends." He was silent for a long time. Lily knew what he wanted to ask her, knew he was giving her a chance. She said nothing. At last he sighed and broke the silence. "And I think you are a shape shifter yourself."

Lily pushed back her chair, trying to get up from the table. She had no idea what she was going to do, where she was going to go. Wes reached across and caught her hand.

"I don't for a second believe that you are the shifter responsible for these attacks, the illness and the deaths."

"Deaths?"

Wes nodded somberly. "It's a homicide investigation now. A number of the children have died."

Lily drew in a breath and sat down again, slowly. What happened to someone if their soul was "eaten" by a shape shifter tiger?

"I think you are a shape shifter. I think you are a tiger. But I think you are like me - you can control what you do. The other shifters we know of, all of them wolves except this one tiger out there, can't control their behavior and they can't control how they present themselves to the world, or when. You can do all of that. And whoever is killing people can do at least some of it." Through all of this, Wes had not let go of her hand. "I also don't believe you ever killed or attacked anyone in your life, not in any form you might take." His eyes were warm and gentle with something soft and intense in their depths.

It was hard to see. Her own eyes were blurry and she could feel the tears slipping down her cheeks. She sniffled a little, pulling her hand out from under his.

"Wes, if anyone knew. If they guessed - I could lose, I could -"
"You think I don't know?"

Then somehow she wasn't sitting at the table and he wasn't any more, either. Lily found herself in his arms. Her sniffles became sobs and she buried her face against his chest. Somewhere deep inside she realized that he smelled good. His arms tightened and Lily clung to him.

"Sshhh," said Wes. "It will be okay. Everything will be okay." He didn't know what he meant by that, but at least for the moment he believed it, too. Everything had to be okay. He had never felt about a woman the way he felt about Lily. The feelings he had had for his ex-wife did not even begin to compare to this. He pulled back slightly, lifted her chin and kissed her, tears and all.

She kissed him back. She knew her mouth tasted of salt tears and tasted sweet at the same time. She could see it in his mind, read it there, feel it. She could feel desire run through her like an open flame at the same time that it ran through him.

God help me, I love her. I don't just think I do, I know I do.

She heard it as clearly as if he had spoken. For a moment she thought he had. She pulled back to answer him and then saw the truth in his eyes.

"Wes," she whispered. "It's too soon and - did you mean me to hear that?" He shook his head. Neither of them knew what he meant by the gesture.

As if by mutual consent they both sat down again at the table. They kept glancing at each other and then away again. Lily reached for teapot but it was cold.

"This is awkward," said Wes, at last.

"It doesn't have to be." Lilly sighed. "I don't know, Wes. I might love you, it's possible, but - well -"

"It's too soon," said Wes. "You're right. You need time. You're still getting over Stan -"

She laughed. She couldn't help it. She knew she had never been in love with Stan. Initially, it had seemed like the relationship would be a good thing, back before Stan had changed. But even then she had never felt about Stan this way. Had she ever felt about John this way? She didn't think so. She saw the puzzlement in Wes' eyes.

"Stan," she said with a grin, "is not what I'd call a serious contender here." Then her smile faded. "But Wes, I have to tell you something." She hesitated. How to do this?

"I'm a shifter. A tiger. That's true. And yes, I control it and no, I have never hurt anyone. Well, that's not quite true. I've eaten a few rabbits and there was a deer once," she stopped. This wasn't what she wanted to tell him.

"A deer?" Wes was intrigued. "Where? And when?"

"Over in the Great Swamp. About a year ago." She looked at him, puzzled.

Why did it matter?

"No shit! They didn't publicize it but the DEM people went nuts! It was spring, right?"

Lily nodded.

"They thought it was a cougar. They were debating whether or not someone had released an illegal pet or if we had a native population moving back into the state. I heard about it because a buddy of mine works for Environmental Management. But it was the only deer kill like that. There was never another. That was you?"

"It was. But. I, well, I didn't like killing the deer. I mean I did, it was good, delicious," she paused, remembering the stalk, the pounce, the kill, the taste, then shook her head. It seemed more desirable now than it had at the time, which was odd. She put the thought away. "It was good but it wasn't. I didn't like the look in its eyes. When I killed it. I mean, I did, but it also repulsed me at the same time." She looked over at him. "It helped turn me into a semi- vegetarian. In human form, anyway. Not as a tiger. I guess I'm a bit, uh, conflicted there." He was smiling at her and she could feel herself grinning back. Somehow he understood. How could anyone understand this? She couldn't believe she had found someone she could tell about all this.

"They finally decided the cougar had been an escaped pet, recaptured by its owner. Or that it died," said Wes. "Or that they had imagined it." He grinned ironically. "You should have heard the arguments Ed said that started."

Lily laughed. "Sorry about that. I guess anything but a cougar didn't occur to them."

"Ed said the pug marks were pretty big. They were thinking very large cougar. Very large."

Lily chuckled, then sobered. "There's more." She told him about Stan and the syringe of Monster's blood. She told him of Beth's report of seeing Stan up at the farm. Wes listened carefully, then shook his head.

"I don't get that," he said. "That's the sort of thing Clem would want to ask you about. You need to tell him, Lily, whatever you think of the Specials. It's obviously got something to do with the research your ex is doing. Clem is going to be very frustrated that you don't know the answer."

"If this all going into some sort of official record, why not just call Stan in and ask him? Ask him what connection he has with John?"

"We would if we could find him."

Lily frowned. "I don't like this. I don't like it all. His research means everything to him. I assumed he was still at the university. I haven't seen him there because I didn't want to."

Wes shook his head. "Then did you ask John?"

"We did. He claims he hasn't seen Stan in a long time. That yes, Stan was doing some contract research for him but there has been no contact in months."

"That's not true."

"I know that and you know that but proving it is another matter. It's hardly illegal, anyway. In any event, I want to ask you to officially become part of the team that's working on these attacks in Providence."

Lily gaped at him. "What could I do?"

"Official consultant. Expert in shape shifting legends. Cross cultural expert.

And someone formerly connected with Skyline Pharmaceuticals. I know, I know," Wes waved a hand dismissively, "but you may have insights. You could help us stop this."

"What does Dr. Fletcher think of all this?"

"One thing he thinks is that it's a good way to keep tabs on you, see if you are in cahoots with your ex or with anyone." John smiled sourly. "But I think he would actually appreciate the help, much as he would hate to admit it. He's coming around. He's not all that bad when you get to know him."

Lily stared out the window. "My ex is supposedly trying to find cures for psi diseases."

"Of course."

They looked at each other.

"What would be involved here? In being a consultant?" Lily asked, at last.

She was thinking of the time she wanted to spend Beth, and thinking of her summer course.

"Some meetings with us. Let us - let Clem - pick your brain. Maybe talk to the Hmong some more. Clem is not having the greatest success there." Wes grinned briefly. "Maybe talk to some of the families of other minority groups that have been attacked, some Hispanics and immigrants from some African nations who thought they saw striped lions, if you can believe it. It wouldn't take that much time. A few hours a week. We can meet anywhere. Here sometimes, if you want. Oh, I almost forgot. We pay you."

"You pay me?"

"Well, the Psi Disease Center Specials do. They have the deep pockets; we, the police, I mean, don't."

Lily just stared at him. She didn't ask but after a moment he answered. "A thousand a week."

"For a few hours' consult?" She was incredulous.

"For a few hours, yes. Maybe you can help solve these homicides and stop a killer."

And that way we can see each other every week for certain. He didn't say it but he thought it so hard that she heard it.

"We can," she said, "but I can think of other more pleasant ways we can see each other, too."

She had the privilege of seeing him blush.

CHAPTER NINE

S HE WAS AT HOME WHEN the call came. It was Claire, the lawyer. "Bad news," said Claire.

Lily was silent long enough for Claire to modify her statement.

"Well, not super bad news but Beth won't like it. John is refusing to pay for sending her to that camp."

"Jeez, Claire, don't do that to me! I almost had a heart attack! As it turns out, I may be able to send her to camp after all, even without John." Her consultation fees should more than cover it, if she took the job.

"No kidding? Cool! Yeah, well, there's more." "Spit it out, Claire."

"Reg says John wants things back on an amicable basis between the two of you." Reginald Finan was John's lawyer. "John says if you are willing to go up to Beechland and check things out, look around - without Beth, of course - you might see there isn't anything to be concerned about. Then things can get back to where they were."

"Yeah, right. Not gonna happen. Beth is really upset about that place." "Lily, I recommend that you do go up there and meet with John. It will calm him down at the least. Reg says he's really upset about all this and he might want to reopen the custody arrangement completely. He's threatening to go for sole custody of Beth. Whatever you're making now, Lily, I don't think you can afford that battle. John could possibly even win it, much as I hate to say that. We both know the resources he has. If you just go up there and meet with him you may be able to calm him down, head this off at that pass."

Lily felt cold. She knew she needed to go. Answers of some sort might be there. There was more to this than the obvious, though; she knew it. What could John want from her? "I'll think about it," she said.

"You do that, but think fast. Reg said John will have him file papers in two weeks if he doesn't hear from you."

"Great." She almost growled the word. "An ultimatum. John should know I don't do well with those." She could feel the rage beginning to rise; someone was threatening her cub. She blinked, startled at her own thought. Not her cub, her child.

"Lily -"

"Okay, okay. I said I'll think about it."

She put it off for a while, though. That afternoon was her first meeting with the "task force" created to deal with the shifter homicides and attacks. Clement Fletcher had insisted that the first meeting be in Providence, although not in police headquarters. He had a suite in the Westin Hotel and wanted to meet there "for privacy and discretion", as he put it. Lily had agreed, rolling her eyes since it was a phone conversation and he couldn't see her. The PDC was very big on secrecy these days, as much or more so than Homeland Security. She wasn't entirely sure she wanted anything to do with this and she was going as much to simply show good faith as to check out the consulting offer.

She found she could barely remember the old days, before the "psi plague".

She did remember that people had complained about the intrusion of government into their lives back then. In retrospect it seemed strange, almost silly.

Beth had gotten permission to take Sarah with her to the vet clinic after school today. Then Deb was supposed to pick up both girls and take them for fast food. This was something neither Deb nor Lily did often but they had decided that once a month they would alternate and treat the girls. This arrangement gave Lily plenty of time for her afternoon meeting and time afterwards for a quick sandwich with Wes. She couldn't imagine the meeting taking long.

It was a nice suite at the hotel, a really nice suite. It gave a whole new meaning to the term "government benefits". Lily stared at the living room, at the couch and the chairs, at the small buffet laid out. Clement Fletcher ushered her in and Wes looked up from where he sprawled in one of the comfortable chairs. He was munching on a sandwich. He grinned at her around the sandwich.

So much for going out later, Lily thought. There's enough food here for a small army.

"Thank you for coming," said Fletcher, "and for agreeing to work with us." "I haven't entirely decided if I am. I had the impression that my help was one of the last things you wanted and that, in fact, you considered me more of a suspect." She wanted the cards on the table, face up. It was only after the words were out of her mouth that she realized it sounded rude.

"Lily!" Wes coughed, choking around his sandwich. Then he tried to pound himself on the back.

"I'm sorry if I implied that." Fletcher sounded sincere. "We are trying to stop a killer here and I would like your help. I understand that you are quite the cross-cultural expert on shape shifting. I checked out your background." He smiled thinly. "And I hope there is a possibility that you might know something, some little thing you don't even realize you know, about your husband's, excuse me, ex-husband's business. That might help us quite a bit. "

"You should know more about that than I do. After all, he has a government contract. He gets money from the Psi Dsease Center for his research. From your organization."

Wes started to say something but cut himself of and rolled his eyes instead, behind Fletcher's back. He shook his head at Lily but it was obvious he knew it was a useless gesture.

"That he does. Would you like a sandwich? I understand you are a vegetarian, of a sort. We have tuna fish, if you eat that, and this really good tofu spread. In any event. Dr. Belkner is not telling us everything. Not that he needs to, you understand. We don't have to be in on every step of the research. But we think there is something very odd going on up at that farm of his." "Beechland."

"Yes. Where your daughter was recently. We understand you have refused visitation for your daughter at the farm because of some of your concerns."

"I have." Lily selected a tuna fish sandwich. It looked good, made with mustard and no celery, and on what looked like herb bread. She took a chair beside Wes.

It was then she noticed the fourth person in the room. He had been there all along, but in a corner, out of the way. There was no doubt as to what he was. He had his little bag with him and he already wore surgical gloves. In case there was any doubt, he even wore the stereotypical white coat. Lily frowned at him.

"Dr. Respin. He works for us, for the PDC. Anything we have said is quite safe with him but he won't be here for the rest of the meeting." Fletcher tried to smile reassuringly. It made Lily want to tell him not to.

"Why is he here?" Lily turned to the man in question. "Why are you here, Dr. Respin?"

Respin glanced at Fletcher before he replied. Apparently, he got the signal he wanted.

"We need to draw a little blood from you," he said. "We need to run a test."

"Another? You've already tested me for every psi disease known plus whatever else from Lyme to breast cancer."

"They're doing it again, Lily, because they are afraid some virus has escaped John's lab." Wes had said nothing up until now. "You need to let them."

"Fine." Lily rolled up her sleeve. "What virus?"

Fletcher hesitated so long that Lily doubted she would get an answer.

Finally, Respin had his sample, smiled at her and left the room. Through the whole procedure he had said absolutely nothing. Lily wondered if they were hiring mutes now at the PDC.

"A virus that induces shape shifting. He was hoping to control it, is hoping to control it -" Fletcher stopped, either afraid he had said too much or not sure how to continue. "In fact, we aren't even sure he has actually developed it."

Lily sighed. "Don't you want me to sign some security documents or pledges or something? Before we go any further? John has always been messing around with viruses and God knows what, ever since I've known him."

Fletcher flushed. It was obvious he had somehow and impossibly forgotten the security pledges. As Lily signed without even reading them, she wondered. Was it possible that new tests could detect her ability? She had to hope not.

From the way Wes was looking at her reassuringly, she assumed not. "There you go, Dr. Fletcher," she said, at last, massaging her hand.

"Call me Clem, please. If this virus is out of control," Fletcher passed her the platter of sandwiches; she decided to try the tofu this time, "there is no telling how much harm it could do, especially since there is no antidote, no cure. Of course we don't even know if such a virus exists. And there is no way we can find out. There is certainly nothing going on in the New Jersey lab, as best we can determine, but at that place in New York state - we can't get near anything there. Oh, we've been up there but there's no sign of anything secret going on. I don't know how we can find out. If anything has gone wrong, they won't want us to know. We ask; he doesn't tell. Skyline gets a lot of money from us. A lot." He was filing Lily's papers into a briefcase. "But there's no way we can get behind the front up at that New York place. Anything you can do to help us we would be grateful for."

"I may just be able to help you there," said Lily. She was afraid for herself and her secret but if John had done what Fletcher said, he had to be stopped. She told them of her conversation with Claire

Franks that morning. She saw no reason not to be candid. Clement Fletcher had obviously done his research and knew whatever was on record about her. And Wes knew more than that.

"So I can go up there legitimately," she said. "And I can snoop around a bit behind John's back. Talk to the people in those cabins Beth told me about or at least have a look, see what I can find out."

"Lily, no, I don't think it's a good idea." Wes had begun his third sandwich but now he put it back on his plate. "From everything you've told me about John, he's dangerous. I don't think you should go up there at all, let alone by yourself, and I don't think you should do any snooping."

"Hold on a sec." Fletcher was interested. "She may have something there.

How likely are you to be able to get around there safely, without Dr. Belkner catching on?"

"Clem, I really don't think," Wes began.

"A pretty good one." Lily put her sandwich down. "I know the layout of the place well; I've been there often enough. We used to go up for getaway weekends way back when." She could feel Wes' eyes on her and feel herself flushing. "I know the place. I don't think I'd get caught. Even if he has me watched it can't be for every second. I know how to slip out and slip back again from almost anywhere on the property." She didn't say it was because she had scoped the place out in tiger form. "Dr. Fletcher -"

"Clem."

"Clem, why can't you go in there? Even get a court order if you have to?

Go in unannounced and surprise him?" "A much better idea," said Wes.

"Do you really think that would work, Lily? May I call you Lily?" "Please." She tried to sound gracious about it.

"Do you really think we could surprise him?"

Lily stared at him for a moment. She didn't say the obvious "why not", and after a moment she nodded. "Someone in your agency would tip him off."

Fletcher looked both uncomfortable and as if he had just eaten something nasty. Lily knew she was in now, whether or not she wanted to be.

"I'm afraid it looks that way," he agreed. "There is the slight possibility of a leak. More than slight."

Lily looked at Wes. "Do you have any better ideas?" she said.

Finally, he shook his head. "If you have to go up, you go up with backup." "How would I do that? I'm serious, Wes. Can you suggest anything that wouldn't tip John off?"

Wes finally shook his head. "I don't like this, Lily."

"Neither do I but that doesn't change anything. How sure are we that John is behind whatever is going on here?"

"Not sure at all," said Fletcher. "And I don't think he's deliberately behind anything. But he may be covering up for something. Something gone bad, like this virus, maybe."

"The man is dangerous." Wes shifted in his chair.

"He can be." Lily smiled slightly. "But so can I." The menace in her tone was completely unmistakable.

Wes stared at her in barely disguised horror and Fletcher looked confused and a bit frightened, which gratified Lily.

"I held my own pretty well in the divorce," she told the PDC operative. "John knows I'm not a pushover. And he should realize I intend to check that place out and make sure it's safe before I allow my daughter to set foot up there ever again." She could hear the menace intensify in her own voice and it surprised her. *Dial it back,* she told herself.

"Well." Clement Fletcher drew back, eyes wide. Then he grinned. "I sure wouldn't want to tangle with you. I'm glad you're on our side. Now if we could figure out just why this problem is showing up in Providence - this whatever it is."

"You have the answer to that." Lily sat back in her chair. Both men looked at her. "Come on, you can't imagine I haven't figured it out. I know you have.

Stan." When neither responded, she clarified. "Stanley Brentworth. My ex, uh, significant other. He's got a connection to

John and Skyline Pharm. You know all that. You know he's contracted with John. If anything escaped any secret lab at Beechland, Stan probably brought it with him. Okay, it's a stretch but can you think of anything better? So what about him? Where is he? There's your connection."

Clement Fletcher just shook his head.

"That's what I thought," said Lily. "If you can find him you might get some questions answered."

The meeting took the rest of the morning and all afternoon. Clement Fletcher had, as promised, picked her brain fairly thoroughly on the subject of shape shifter legends. He also asked questions about the Hmong community, many of which Lily couldn't answer, and then about the native Narragansett community. Lily frowned at that one.

"You asking me that because one of my friends is a Narragansett Native?" she said.

"No, no, I just wondered."

"Wondered what? Clem, you've already proved that on this issue there isn't any 'just wondering'."

Clement shrugged.

So much for open communications, Lily thought. "I haven't heard of any attacks on the reservation or in Charlestown or anywhere nearby," she said. She was prickly and she knew it.

"You haven't heard of all the attacks there were," said Fletcher. "You don't need to know."

"Maybe I didn't then but I do now. Does that mean there were attacks in my area?" Lily demanded. "I need to know what's happening in my own community!"

"There weren't," Wes interjected. "Clem, you have to trust her. She can't work with us unless you trust her."

"I can go only as far as I am permitted," said Fletcher rather primly. Then he softened slightly. "No, there have been no attacks in your area, Lily. There have been attacks in minority communities here, including some Narragansetts in the city, and Hispanics - and you know the rest. But nothing outside of Providence, not even in the suburbs, at least not yet."

"The minority community thing disturbs me. Whoever is behind this thinks they make a better prey base, possibly because of culture. But in any case, the city makes a better hunting ground," said Lily.

"It would appear so," said Fletcher, "although I'm not sure why. You would think it would be harder for a large animal to hide here. Less cover. And people would notice an attack."

"On the contrary," said Lily. "There is plenty of cover. Lots of buildings, alleyways, shrubs, parking lots. And you are dealing with an animal that can become human again, blending right in with everyone else, although we don't know the rules for that transformation. And besides, think of this: how many attacks happen all the time in the city? Attacks of all kinds? Attacks that no one seems to notice?"

"Point taken," said Clement Fletcher, less grudgingly than he might have.

Fletcher took no offense but Wes was frowning now. Lily realized he might have construed her remark as a slap against the Providence police. There was something else in his attitude, something she couldn't read. She shook it off, ignoring it.

It was late afternoon going on evening before the meeting ended. She told Fletcher about the vial of her cat's blood but the incident apparently made no sense to him. It was obvious he knew about it, however. Lily did not glance at Wes. Of course he would have told his PDC partner. It was hard to think of them all as a team now but she was trying. The sandwiches were long gone, coffee sent for and finished. Lily yawned.

"When are going up to your ex-husband's farm?" Fletcher wanted to know. "We'll make sure you have someone nearby, not at the farm, of course, but nearby, that you can call on if you need to. We need to plan this."

Don't do it, Lily! said a voice in her head. She refrained from looking at Wes.

"I'll set it up through the lawyers," she said. "As soon as I can. John thinks I need the money for camp for Beth so sooner is better, not to mention more believable. I'll let you know; we can solidify plans then. I need to get going," she said, picking up her purse.

Before she could leave there was a knock on the door and Respin entered. He handed a sheet of paper to Fletcher, who looked it over and then glanced at Lily.

"No sign of any psi disease," he said to her.

"I could have told you that," said Lily. And then it struck her. "Damn, that was fast! You have accelerated testing now?"

"We do." Clement looked smug, as Respin left. Then the smugness faded. "In large part due to your ex-husband," he said.

"And doesn't that figure." Lily scooped up her purse.

"Let me walk you out," said Wes. "You parked here?" he asked, when they were out in the corridor.

"Nope."

"Why not? We could get you a parking voucher."

"Is that wise, since you want everything kept so hush-hush?" He stared at her.

"I'm sorry, Wes. I'm a little on edge. There were some weird undercurrents in that meeting." She also didn't like being told what to do.

"There are likely to be weirder things."

"You want to grab something to eat? I know it's early and I know I have to get home soon but we should have time. For something tasty." She suddenly realized how her remark could be construed.

"Lily." Wes stopped her near the elevator. His hands were on her shoulders and she would have sworn she felt warmth flowing from them. Suddenly she wanted nothing more than to bury her face in his shirt. Maybe even get one of the rooms right there in the hotel - she couldn't believe she had thought that.

She could not allow herself to fall for a man this way. Look at how far she had gone already; he knew her secret! And all she wanted to do now was climb into bed with him. She was furious with herself.

"Lily, you can't go up to Beechland by yourself. You can't." "Wes, we just went through this -"

"Lily, no. You don't understand. You are putting your life in danger and I can't let you do that. Something very odd, very dangerous -

geez, Lily. I love you. And I can't let you do this. I forbid it." He pulled her to him and kissed her.

Fire ran through her. She kissed him back with all the pent-up passion she had. She ran her hands up under his shirt, pulling it out of his pants. One slid down to squeeze his buttocks. She pressed herself against him, feeling him grow hard as she did. She wanted very little more right now than to throw him to the floor and take him right there. But there was one thing she wanted more. When he was breathing hard and barely in control she pulled away from him.

She was breathing hard, too, and for a moment she didn't know if she could go through with it. But she did.

"I want you, Wes, and I think I love you. But you need to understand something. No one, and I mean no one, tells me what to do. You can suggest, you can argue, you can make your case. But you can't tell me and you can never forbid me. Ever. One thing you don't understand, Wes, is that my daughter's well-being is at stake here, too, and I will protect that. I will protect her."

"LIly, I didn't mean - I just don't want you taking those chances. I can handle this another way; I'll come up with something. I can't have you go up there like that."

"Listen to yourself, Wes."

He ran his hand through his hair. It was short, but it was already disheveled. "Lily, you don't understand how dangerous this is!"

"You don't understand how dangerous I am." With that she stepped back again from him. Deliberately she began to change. It was only her ears and her eyes and the lengthening and broadening of her nose into the nose of a big cat, a tiger. Stripes began to flow through her reddish hair. The rest of her remained human. But it was enough.

Wes' intake of breath was audible and he took a step back from her and then another. With a third step he backed into the cart one of the housekeeping staff had left in the hallway.

Lily let the stripes fade from her hair, her nose thin and shorten, her ears return to human. She wondered if she had frightened Wes so badly that he would want nothing more to do with her. The thought stabbed through her with a sudden pain. Knowing she could transform herself into a tiger and actually seeing her start to do just that were two entirely different things. The elevator dinged, the door opened, and two men in business suits came out. They were engaged in conversation and walked around both Wes and Lily, barely noticing them.

That was a damn fool thing to do, said Wes' voice in her head. You need to be more careful.

"So do you," she said.

"If that's the way you want it," he said stiffly. He held the elevator door for her but did not follow her in.

All the way to the ground floor she thought about the incident. She didn't want to lose him. She couldn't lose him. Just the thought of it made her feel as if her heart was being ripped out. But she couldn't have him dictate her, either. Her life was her own and in the years since her divorce from John, she had become accustomed to making decisions, all decisions, for herself and her daughter. She also couldn't believe she had opened herself so much to this man. Telepath or not, he was still a cop. A cop who was working with the PDC Specials.

Well, she thought, so am I working with them. Can I protect my secret and do this?

It was not a comfortable thought.

CHAPTER TEN

I T WAS AFTER DUSK WHEN she left the hotel; she hadn't realized it was so late. She would get herself some fast food before she got home, treat herself the way Deb was treating their girls. She frowned at the pedestrians she saw, realizing there was someone out here who considered them fast food.

She was parked all the way over in the Convention Center garage. It had been a ridiculous and meaningless gesture of independence to park over there and now she wished she didn't have the long walk. People avoided her, involved in their own thoughts, except for a group of young men hanging out near one of the bus stops, and she made a point of avoiding them. They catcalled and made a few loud remarks in her direction, making her briefly regret that she couldn't shape shift right then. The thought made her grin briefly; it might do them some good.

She had parked on the second level of the parking garage. She was always extra careful and alert in such places even though she had never had any trouble there. She braced herself out of habit. This time there was trouble but the trouble came before she even reached the garage. There was a covered section of roadway, a lane between the north and south garages. It was off to the side of this lane that Lily came upon a struggle taking place.

At first she couldn't believe her eyes, for two reasons. Firstly, it wasn't yet dark. The attack she was witnessing was occurring at a time when it could very easily be interrupted. It was dusk, deep dusk, and the shadows in the covered lane were deeper still, but even so it was hard to believe that anyone would choose this time for an attack. Secondly, the attacker was a surprise, and a bad one.

The victim was a woman, not especially young or beautiful, just someone who had probably parked in the garage and was on her way to her car to go home for the evening: a working mother, a student from the university's urban campus, a shopper. The attacker was a tiger.

The woman was trying to scream but she couldn't. The tiger had a big paw across her throat, half-suffocating her. *Not exactly a killing mode, thought Lily,* analytically. A bite to the throat would do the job better and more quickly.

What the heck was he up to? There was no doubt in her mind that the tiger was a male.

The woman's belongings were scattered around her: her purse, a backpack, a plastic shopping bag, a set of car keys, a cell phone. She was struggling and squirming but there was no chance she could escape. And then Lily saw something very peculiar. The attacking tiger had ripped the woman's pants off with one giant paw and now he was attempting to turn her over while still controlling her with a paw on her throat to keep her from screaming. She couldn't scream now; she had almost passed out from lack of air from the paw across her throat. The tiger flipped her over onto her stomach and pulled her to him.

Tigers mate with the male covering the female from behind. Lily's jaw dropped. She was watching what was about to be a rape, and a very unusual one. The tiger grunted with satisfaction as he moved in.

"Hey!" Lily shouted and ran forward. "Get off of her! Get away from her!

Get off of her, you pervert!"

The tiger paused. He did not release his intended victim. One paw held her torso down, the other lifted her naked buttocks upward and toward him in an oddly human fashion. But he turned his glowing eyes on Lily. And he snarled.

It was like a physical shock. She could feel the mental force behind the gaze and the snarl. Both were meant to paralyze her, to hold her in place. The shape-shifted tiger intended to keep Lily frozen while he completed his rape and then devoured his victim's consciousness and perhaps a piece of her physical body. Lily could feel his intentions and knew the tiger was projecting them at her. His victim, if she survived, would never regain consciousness, would never be able to testify as to what had happened to her. Lily could feel the pleasure behind the thought, the lust and the hunger.

Despite the peril of the situation, Lily's analytical side kicked in. This shifter had abilities she did not have. As well as being able to devour a person's conscious mind (how did one do that?), he could project his thoughts, or at least some of them. Could he do it in human form? And he was accustomed to paralyzing his prey, at least partially, by his snarl and his gaze. There was also the strange sense that she knew this shifter and that he knew her. Lily wanted time to puzzle this out but she didn't have it.

The shifter turned his attention back to the woman beneath him. She had started to regain more consciousness and had begun to squirm again.

Apparently, the shifter liked it that way because he made no attempt to stun her by snarling at her. He was also satisfied that Lily would remain where she was until he could deal with her. He seemed fearless and unintimidated, a tiger in an urban jungle.

Lily dropped her purse and kicked off her shoes, simultaneously pulling off her sweater. It was all she had time for. Her shirt ripped and her pants split and shredded with the force of her rapid change. Her bra strap snapped and the undergarment sling-shotted across the road. Then another tiger stood there in the shadows.

Lily snarled. In the snarl was all the fury, frustration and pent-up worry she had felt for the past weeks. In a blur of speed, she was on the male tiger, claws extended and ripping. As if he were a cub, she grabbed him by the scruff of his huge neck and hauled him off his intended victim. The woman had regained complete consciousness now, and she scrambled out of the way on all fours, her eyes wide with shock, horror, and disbelief.

The male tiger rolled onto his back. Lily jumped back. A cat in that position was not vulnerable but dangerous, and indeed, all the other tiger's claws were extended and reaching for her. Her snarl of defiance split the air and echoed off the sides of the buildings. The male tiger lunged to his feet again.

Lily glanced to one side. The woman had scrunched herself into a small ball and was clutching her torn clothing to her. Her eyes were wide and glassy and she was shivering. Lily turned briefly from her opponent and made a motion with one big paw in the woman's direction. "Go, go!" said the motion.

The woman understood. She grabbed her belongings and scuttled backwards. Lily turned back to the fight. Her moment of distraction, brief though it was, cost her. The other tiger leaned forward and with one lightning- swift swipe, tried to rake his claws across the side of her face. She pulled back in time to avoid the worst of it but two of his claws caught slightly. The cuts stung.

Lily yowled and flung herself forward. Her own claws raked deep into the other tiger's nose. She followed up by clamping her huge teeth into his ear and then twisting her head sideways. She heard the cartilage tear and tasted blood as well as fur. A sudden nausea made her step back and the male tiger took that opportunity to run. He vanished into the shadows as she spat out a torn piece of ear.

Lily's stomach heaved. She wanted to follow him but the shadows were deep and she doubted she'd find him. And she had more immediate worries.

The intended victim had run but not that far. Lily could see her with her cell phone to her ear.

Lily stepped backwards and with a shudder changed back rapidly from tiger to woman. She looked down at herself. Naked, of course.

Damn. She saw her purse not that far away and reached out and grabbed it. The next moment she was on her knees, retching. She looked at the result.

"Great," she muttered. "A hairball. I threw up a hairball, just like Monster." But she knew it wasn't her own fur and that took any humor from the situation.

She found her clothing but most of it was torn from her rapid shifting. Her shoes were fine and she slipped into them. Her sweater, fortunately, was long and covered most of her body. She gathered up pants, underpants and shirt, all torn beyond use. At the last second she fished some tissues from her purse and scooped up the hairball she had just vomited up. Then she saw the torn piece of the other tiger's ear which she had spit out. Willing herself not to throw up again, she scooped that up as well. Then she ran for her car.

She saw no one else on the way to her car. She ran up the two levels rather than using the elevator; it was faster that way, even in human form, and she had the stamina of a tiger. By the time she was in her car and driving for the exit she found she was shaking. A quick glance at herself in the rearview mirror revealed two long bleeding gashes across her cheek.

"Damn!" she muttered.

Fortunately, the parking attendant in his little booth took her money without noticing her wounds. His attention was directed toward the flashing lights and sirens on the street outside. He couldn't see what was happening but he dearly wanted to know and he passed Lily through without a glance. She wondered if her had heard the snarls and roars and what he made of them.

She did not have to pass the cop cars and the ambulance but she saw them in her rearview mirror as she made the turn that would take her toward Route 95 South. She assumed the woman would be all right. After all, Lily had stopped both a rape and an attempted murder, and she knew the woman would be believed by the police. Not to mention the special psi task force. Lily intended to watch the news tonight but she was pretty sure there would be no coverage of the incident, no mention. More to the point, she had to figure out what action, if any, she would take.

By the time she was home some of the shock had worn off. Monster greeted her with huge eyes and then ran and hid under the couch. Lily locked the door, went to the kitchen for a zip-lock bag, into which she placed the vomited hair ball and then another one for the piece of ear. She dumped them on the counter. Then she shuddered again and then headed right for the shower.

The hot water felt good and she stood under the stream for a long time, ignoring the fact that she was a conservationist wasting both water and electricity. Sometimes you just had to. Blood washed down the drain with the water and she felt her cheek. The scratches had opened in the warmth of the humid shower and were bleeding again. Just as well; any infection would be washed out.

When she stepped from the tub, the room was so steamy that she had to wipe the mirror to see herself. The scratches didn't look good but at least they were clean. She patted them dry until the bleeding stopped and then spread some antibiotic ointment over them. She was not as bothered by the scratches as she should have been. What disturbed her most of all, the thing she did want to think about, was how much she had enjoyed the battle, how much she had enjoyed the feel of her teeth snapping shut on her opponent's flesh. The sight of him fleeing had filled her with a raging joy and made her want to pursue him.

Lily sighed and pushed the thoughts away. This was not like her. If she allowed herself to feel these things she was no longer truly herself. She went into the bedroom and pulled on a pair of sweatpants with her bathrobe over that. Then she went back down to the kitchen.

Monster came out from under the couch and meeped at her. She fed the cat and then stood staring at the plastic baggies on her counter top. Her stomach rolled again. Evidence. She couldn't let this go and she had to handle it before Beth got home. She would call Wes. She drew in a deep breath and picked up the cordless phone.

The knock on the door was loud and insistent. Still holding the phone, Lily went to the door and peered through the small glass window. It was Wes. She opened the door.

"I was just about to call you," she said.

"Lose something?" he said, simultaneously. He was holding out her bra, the one with the broken strap, the one that had sling-shotted across the covered roadway when she shapes shifted. Then he took a better look at her.

"Holy shit! Lily, your face! Are you all right?"

"Come in." She took his arm, pulling him in. "I'm all right. I need to talk to you."

"You need a doctor."

"I need to talk to you. Now, Wes." She fended off his attempt to put his arm around her shoulders. Not that she didn't want the support but she wanted his full attention more.

"I know, you ran into our shifter outside the Convention Center garage.

We've got the victim's report. She told us about the tiger who attacked her and tried to rape her, and about the tiger who saved her. Tigress. She was certain her savior was a female. That's what she told us."

"Who's 'us'? Does that include Clem?"

"It does. And some of my superiors on the force." "Damn."

"Clem doesn't know it was you, not yet -" "He's not stupid, Wes."

"No, he's not." Wes sighed and ran his hand through his short hair. "Lily, you need a doctor -"

"And I've got evidence." "You what?"

She told him about the hairball and about the ear, feeling sick again as she did so. She felt nauseous and dizzy and her cheek throbbed.

"Sit down," said Wes, "before you pass out."

He put his arm around her and guided her to a chair. This time she let him. "I really think you need that cheek looked at. It doesn't look good." He smoothed the hair away from her face.

"Wes." Her eyes had been closed while he smoothed her hair

but now she looked at him and caught his hand to make him look at her. "I must disgust you."

"What? Lily, why would you think that?"

"I - I'm one of the shifters. Look what I did this afternoon. I attacked a man - a tiger - a well, whatever he was, and I ripped his ear -" she put her hand over her face and then pulled it away as her cheek flamed with pain.

"Lily." Wes pulled the hassock over and sat on it, taking both her hands in his. "I think you are one of the bravest people I know. You saved a woman's life today. You defended someone." He sighed. "Battle isn't easy. War does something to you; I know. I was in Afghanistan. It's hard to keep your moral compass. But Lily, you've done that and under circumstances as strange - well, stranger - than war. I'm sorry about earlier today. I really have no right to tell you what to do. I don't want to tell you what to do and I know I'm being overprotective -"

There was a knock on the door. Wes stopped. He and Lily stared at each other, then at the door.

"Shit." Lily ran her hand through her wet hair. "I bet that's Deb bringing Beth home." She stood up. "Wes -"

The knocking came again.

"Do you want me to get it?" Wes stood up.

Lily shook her head. Even that motion made her cheek throb.

"Go in the kitchen," she said. "The evidence I told you about - two plastic baggies. Get them off the counter. Before Beth comes in."

She opened the door. It was Beth but not Deb Lattinger. Her daughter was with Sandra Flower.

"Hey, Lily, Deb asked me if I'd mind bringing Beth home since she forgot she had this spa day thing tomorrow morning and she wanted to get her clothes - oh my God, Lily! Holy crap!"

"Mom!" Beth pushed her way around the vet. "Mom, what happened to you! To your face! Oh Mom!" She stopped short as she saw Wes. "You're that cop! What happened to my mom?"

"Beth, I'm fine." Lily put her hands on her daughter's shoulders. "I scratched my face on some vines today. I went down toward the edge of the property and I thought I saw a jack-in-the-pulpit. They're endangered, you know. Anyway," she waved her hands around, "I didn't look where I was going. I walked into some briars. They got stuck in my face; it was awful. As for Wes, you know I'm working with him now as a police consultant. They need my knowledge of legends. Sandra, have you met Wes? Beth, take your stuff upstairs and take a bath. I'll see you in a few minutes."

"Mom -"

"I mean now."

To Lily's surprise, Beth went. Lily turned back to her friends and found them eyeing each other. Lily felt dizzy and swayed slightly. Wes put an arm around her.

"Get her on the couch," said Sandra, shortly. "I have my bag in the car. I'll get it."

"What?" whispered Lily.

"Sit down," said Wes, "before you fall down." She did.

Then Sandra was back with her veterinary bag. She opened it on the coffee table and sat down on the couch beside Lily.

"Vines, right," she said. "I know cat claw marks when I see them. You really should have stitches."

"No hospital," said Lily.

"I didn't say 'hospital'. I said you should have stitches. But first I need to make sure these cuts are clean. Cats carry some pretty nasty stuff on their claws."

"Monster isn't always as sweet as he looks," Wes interjected. "Good thing he's up to date on his rabies shots. That cat can be a demon."

Sandra looked up from rummaging in her bag and stared at Wes for all of a heartbeat. "Oh please," she said.

Wes' lips tightened but he didn't reply.

Sandra set about cleaning the cuts and Lily gripped the arm of the couch to keep from crying out.

"Sorry," said Sandra. "I really should have some topical anesthetic in here but I don't. The cuts are clean now but I'd like to put a tiny stitch in each of them. Just a little one."

"Just tape them," said Lily. "They'll scar."

"They'll scar anyway, won't they?" "Probably."

"And if anyone asked questions, I'd have to say you stitched them because there won't be any hospital records," she glanced at Wes and held up a hand, "and there won't be, because you know we can't afford the scrutiny."

"I think we could hush that up," said Wes.

"You want to tell me what happened?" Sandra sat back slightly. "The cuts won't get infected now, Lily, but you'd better keep them clean. Change the dressing twice a day. Don't get it wet. I've got some samples here of ointment," she rummaged again, then looked up, holding out a couple of small tubes. "Use this stuff when you change the dressings. You can be liberal with it. You gonna tell me what happened? I used to be the vet at a zoo, you know. I know what a big cat wound looks like." She watched as Lily and Wes exchanged glances.

Then she sighed.

"The PDC is involved, isn't it," Sandra said. It was a statement not a question.

"Yeah," said Lily. "It is."

"I knew it! Damn it." Sandra crumpled a gauze package in her hand. "It's got to do with that shifter outbreak in Providence."

"Yes," Lily admitted.

"Lily," said Wes, warningly.

"You can trust her, Wes. She used to work for John but she quit."

Sandra and Wes looked at each other. Lily had the sensation of the air crackling around them, of unspoken communication. She frowned.

"So what's going on?" said Sandra again. "Somebody going to actually tell me? Before Beth gets out of the shower, comes downstairs and wants to know the same thing?" She looked from Wes to Lily. "Lily, I want you to come see me tomorrow; I want to check on those claw wounds. Scratch that; I'll come and see you." She stopped when Lily and Wes both broke into laughter.

"'Scratch that'?" said Lily. All three of them broke up.

"Ibuprofen for fever and inflammation," said Sandra when they finally caught their breath.

"Clem isn't going to like this but I can see we have to fill her in," said Wes. "But I'm not sure where to start."

"Let me see if I can help." Sandra packed up her bag and then sat beside Lily on the couch. "Lily is a shape shifter. A big cat. I would guess a tiger; that suits you, somehow. I would say you got into it pretty badly with another shifter tiger today. That's judging from the claw marks on your face."

"Shit." Lily leaned back on the couch. Despite whatever Sandra had done, her cheek was still throbbing. "Did someone take out an ad? Have I got a sign on my back? Is it on YouTube?"

"Lily," said Sandra, "I guessed before this. Don't ask me how, I just did.

And Wes here is on the PDC task force -"

"Yes, I am," said Wes, "but I'm actually just a Providence cop."

"Lily?" said Sandra.

"I'm consulting. That's all. It's Clem, Dr. Clement Fletcher, who's from the PDC Specials. He's in charge, I guess."

Sandra was silent for a moment. They all were. Sandra finally broke the silence.

"Lily, Wes, I would just as soon that the PDC doesn't know that I am in even on the fringes of this. I'll treat you, Lily, since I've already started to and you're right. You don't want to have to explain hospital records. Just keep the PDC away from me."

"Not a problem," said Lily. "There's no reason for them to know a thing about you."

"Agreed," said Wes.

There was a knock on the door. They all looked at each other. "Now what?" said Lily. She was feeling definitely light-headed.

Wes got up and peered through the little window. Finally, he switched on the outside light over the door.

"It's Clem," he said.

CHAPTER ELEVEN

"SANDRA, YOU CAN GO OUT the back. Through the kitchen."
Lily felt as if she were in a bad tv drama.

"My car's in your driveway," said Sandra. She looked pale. "He knows I'm here. He's probably blocking me."

The knocking continued.

"I'd better let him in," said Wes.

Lily looked at Sandra, who shrugged. "Go ahead," said Lily.

Wes opened the door and let Fletcher in.

"Wes." Fletcher nodded at his colleague, unsurprised to find him with Lily, then turned to Lily. "I'm sorry to have to disturb you tonight, Lily, but I felt coming down here was better than calling, from a number of standpoints."

Hazily, Lily remembered that there was probably a leak somewhere in the PDC. But tapping the phones?

"Hi, Clem. Do you think my phone is tapped? I mean other than by you guys?"

"If you mean by other than the PDC, I doubt it. It's a question of who has access to that." He looked at Lily more closely. Then he turned to Wes. "How bad is she?" He paused for a second, then shook his head and turned to Sandra. "My apologies. You must be Dr. Sandra Flower, and I'm assuming you are the one who is treating Lily. I'm Dr. Clement Fletcher, PDC." He held out his hand.

Sandra stared at the extended hand as if it might detach itself from Fletcher's arm and bite her but finally she shook it.

"Glad to meet you," said Fletcher. He realized the feeling obviously wasn't mutual and hesitated for a moment. Then he waved his hand, as if pushing aside anything negative she might have thought. "I understand how our organization has rather lost its good reputation." He waited another moment as if hoping for a response and then looked slightly put out.

Lily, watching the exchange, grinned. Sandra wouldn't have done anything to make nice with the PDC doctor, whatever he expected.

"So how is she? Are the cuts infected? What did you give her?" Fletcher peered at Lily.

There followed a discussion of antibiotics which Lily did not even attempt to follow. The point that impressed itself rather strongly on her somewhat hazy consciousness was that Fletcher obviously knew what she was and did not seem even remotely surprised. The room seemed to fade in and out although she herself didn't move. What was wrong with her? She thought she heard Wes saying something about "delayed shock". Then there was more discussion between Sandra and Clem but she couldn't follow it.

"Here." It was Fletcher sitting beside her on the couch now. "Take these." He handed her four pills.

Lily recognized ibuprofen but she fumbled with the blue pills. "What?" "Incyclovir. In case your wounds are virus-laden. There may be a connection between shape shifting and immune disorders; we're not sure. But these should help with anything viral and nasty."

Lily came out of her fog and looked at Fletcher sharply. He shook his head at her.

"I don't think your wounds are going to turn you into a shape shifter." He grinned wryly. "Since you are one already. But there are all sorts of more mundane things you could catch. Come on, Lily, just take them. And then drink this." He held out a mug.

"What is that?"

"Chicken soup. Well, broth, actually. That stuff you had in the back of your kitchen cabinet."

"You were in my cabinet?"

"No, Sandra was. Come on, Lily. Just drink it. You'll feel better." "Go ahead, Lily; Clem is right." Sandra put a hand on her shoulder.

So now out of nowhere it was "Clem"? Sandra was friendly with a PDC agent? How long had she been out?

"Clem was prepared for something like this," said Sandra. "Go ahead and take his pills and drink the soup. It will help, really. Part of the problem is that you're hypoglycemic now on top of everything else."

She drank some of the soup with the pills and she did feel better. Suddenly she sat bolt upright.

"Where's Beth?"

"She came downstairs a while ago and you sent her to bed. You told her we were all having a business consulting meeting." Wes came over and edged Clement off the couch to sit beside Lily. "You were very convincing."

"Really?" Lily looked from one to the other of them and saw confirmation all around. "Why can't I remember? And did she really go to bed?"

"Shock and hypoglycemia," said Clement. "That's why you don't remember. It will come back to you. I hope you remember more about what happened earlier this evening, too. We need information."

There was the Clem she knew, thought Lily. She was still concerned about her daughter. Sandra picked up on that.

"Yes, Beth really did go to bed," said Sandra. "I went and checked on her.

She's in bed with Monster beside her." Lily sighed with relief.

"And we are, in fact, about to have a business meeting," said Clement. Lily glanced at Sandra.

"I am now part of the team," said Sandra, "although I am hoping to remain a relatively minor part. The secrecy oaths I took back when I worked for John are still binding."

"The ones you took for any government agency most certainly are," said Clement Fletcher.

The broth really was helping to clear her head, Lily found. In fact she was still hungry. She finished the broth and then grabbed her purse, on the floor near the couch, and rummaged through it, coming up with a granola bar of rather dubious age, which she ate nonetheless.

"So," she said to Clem. "Here we are. How long have you known about me? That I'm a shifter?"

"Known? As in for certain?" He shook his head. "Not until you admitted it right now." He smirked slightly. "But it didn't take much guess work.

Especially after I heard about the shifter attack outside the garage. And that another shifter saved our almost-victim. Interesting that nothing ever showed up in your blood work. No tracers in your DNA. Does your ex-husband have any of your blood, Lily?"

Lily closed her eyes. It was nightmare time. They knew. Now it would be time for her to disappear, for her to lose her life to the researchers in the labs, to be kept locked up as a medical curiosity. She wouldn't see Beth again, ever. Or even Monster. She could feel the prick of tears beginning. This above all was what she had wanted to avoid. But she would not cry.

"I'd like to run another test," said Fletcher.

"Keep your hands and your needles, and whatever else off her. She's not a lab specimen, Clem!" Wes' voice was low and intense.

Lily's eyes snapped open.

"And she won't become one," added Sandra, "not if you want my cooperation."

"May I remind you both," Fletcher began, rising to his feet, "that you are under my authority as a representative of the government -" he glanced at Lily and broke off.

Lily had been determined not to cry but when Wes and Sandra

sprang to her defense one fat tear slipped down her cheek despite herself.

"Damn it." Fletcher sat down heavily. "Nobody is a lab specimen. Lily.

I'm - my apologies. I'm sorry. You're a colleague. I will eventually have to report all this, one way or another. When that time comes I will make sure that you don't get locked away in some facility, that you have your life. Maybe we can even find a cure; your ex-husband is working on cures for psi diseases, after all."

"I think we all know he's not," said Lily, bitterly. She wondered just how good Clem's promises were. How much pull did he have in the PDC?

Clement looked nonplussed, then sighed. "For now I'm going to keep your ability completely under wraps. I promise, Lily. It's just between us in this room; no one else will know. Except perhaps that other shifter you attacked tonight. I wish we had some way of figuring out who he is."

"We might at that," said Lily. "I have some things that could help you out." She hesitated. She was feeling a lot better but she didn't know if she was quite up to facing what she had left on her kitchen counter. "Sandra, would you mind getting the couple of plastic baggies I left in the kitchen, on the counter?"

"I saw those," said Sandra. "I saw Wes put them back on the counter after Beth went to bed. I wondered what they were." In a few moments she was back with them, holding them with a mixture of curiosity and revulsion. She obviously knew what they were now.

"Give them to Clem," said Lily.

She watched as Sandra handed the baggies to Fletcher, expecting a wave of nausea. Surprisingly, they did not upset her. Clem took them. He stared at them for a few moments, then held up the one. The rounded, furry tip of the ear of a big cat could clearly be seen through the plastic.

"Is this what I think it is?" said Clem.

"Yup," said Lily, "evidence. And wait, there's more, for your $19.95. The other baggie? The one with - well, it's a hairball. The attacker's fur. I, er, threw it up. If you rule out my DNA you've got his. Not to mention the ear."

"Good work, Lily! Great thinking!" Clem was virtually ecstatic.

"Assuming," said Wes, "that our offender's DNA is already in a database." If it wasn't they were back to square one. He didn't have to say it.

"You might want to check with hospitals and clinics," Lily suggested. "Even when he shifts back he will still be missing part of an ear. And I ripped up his nose pretty badly while I was at it. He may need a little surgical reconstruction eventually."

There was silence in the room. Everyone stared at her. "Wow," said Sandra, finally. "You go, girl!"

"I'll get right on that," said Wes. "Can I use your phone - oh wait, never mind. I'll use my cell." He flipped it open, stepping outside the front door for a better signal.

"Lily needs to get to bed," said Sandra.

"I know that," said Clem, "but I came down here for a reason. Sandra, I was hoping to meet you, maybe bring you on board, just not tonight. But that wasn't why I came. I came hoping for help from Lily." He glanced at the front door. The outside light was on and Wes' head, just his head and his hand, could be seen, as he talked into his cell phone.

"I don't think Wes is going to have much luck with the clinics and hospitals.

At least not yet." Clem stood up and wandered around the room, glancing at things: the Maxfield Parrish print of "Daybreak" that hung over a chair, an African violet in bloom on the windowsill. Abruptly he turned back to the women.

"There were more attacks after the woman in the garage," he said. "Three Hmong children. Two are dead. One is comatose and in intensive care. Two adult Narragansett women, one raped and one killed; the rape victim survived but is comatose. One white woman who apparently billed herself as an 'urban shaman'. Sexually assaulted but she somehow fought off her attacker, she says through spells, but she's in the hospital. We suspect someone interrupted the attacker before he could finish her off. She gave us a description of her attacker: a tiger with a torn and bloody ear and a ripped nose."

"My God," said Sandra.

For a moment, Lily said nothing. Then she met Clem's eyes.

"So you should have plenty of DNA to match - or not - with the samples I gave you. It might not give you an ID but it's a start."

Clem nodded. "I am afraid, I think, I don't know but I think that this shifter is drawing power from his victims. Becoming more and more powerful."

There was silence after he spoke. Lily and Sandra avoided each other's eyes. Lily knew they were both thinking the same thing: how was it possible to stop someone like that?

"But you have no idea where this guy might be, or if he's still on a rampage." Sandra broke the silence.

"We don't," Clem admitted.

"I might," said Lily, "because I see a pattern, except for one thing." She sighed. She did not want to talk about this now, even though it was obviously of huge importance. She wanted to check on her daughter and she wanted to check on her cat and she wanted these people, friends and colleagues and whatever else they were or might become, out of her house so she could go to bed.

"What's the pattern?" said Clem. "Then we can get to the exception."

"The pattern." Lily had remembered what she had seen on Stan's computer and now some things were beginning to make sense. "'Initial attempts on a culturally primed population'," she quoted.

"What?" Sandra was confused.

Clem wasn't. "Oh my God," he said. "The Hmong, the Narragansetts,"

Sandra caught on. "No tigers native on this continent for millennia," she said. "They wouldn't be in Narragansett legends."

"No," said Lily, "but cougars would. It's close enough. The populations

attacked have been those with not just shifter legends but big cat legends. The exception, though, what I don't get - the woman in the garage earlier this evening -" How could it have been just this evening? It seemed like another age.

"Not an exception," said Clem. "She's Wiccan. Fascinated with shifter stories, actually looking for some material since she writes an occasional column for a local Pagan newsletter. Big cats, apex predators like wolves, are attractive to the human imagination."

"I guess she's got her column now. How did he know? How did he know she was Wiccan, that she was, well, primed for belief?" Lily sat up, felt dizzy and leaned back again. "How did our shifter know who she was?" It felt strange to be saying "our shifter", as if she weren't one herself.

Wes opened the door and came in, looking slightly sour. "No one has checked into a hospital or clinic with any wounds like that yet. I've got people still calling and all the hospitals will be on the lookout. The good news is that there haven't been any more attacks tonight. Yet."

Clem nodded; it was what he had expected. He picked up the plastic baggies with their gruesome contents.

"I'd better get these to the lab," he said. "Come on, Wes. We should let Lily get some rest. And we have a newspaper column to kill. Don't you just love to mess with the free press." He came over and handed Lily a small envelope. A handful of the big blue pills were in it. "Every six hours," he said, "until they're gone. And check with Sandra tomorrow."

"I need to go, too," said Sandra, with a yawn. "Clem, is your car blocking me?" He wasn't, as it happened. "Lily, call me during the night if you need to. Don't hesitate. Leslie is used to me getting emergency calls." She grinned wryly.

Then Sandra was gone, little vet bag and all. Lily blinked. Had she faded out again?

"I don't think I can stay awake much longer," she told the men. "I know you both want a full report, or whatever else I can remember but trust me, right now it's not much. I really need some sleep." She reached up to touch her throbbing cheek but drew her hand away at the feel of the dressing. It didn't hurt as much as it had before, which was surprising.

"So, boys, uh gentlemen, if you would excuse me, please, and show yourselves out -"

"Come on, Wes," said Clem again.

"I'm not leaving," said Wes. "Lily needs protection and I'm it. I'm cleared to stay with her tonight. Police protection." He opened his jacket and Lily saw the shoulder holster.

"Really, Wes," said Lily, "you don't have to do that."

"The attacker may be able to identify you. He may know who you are. I think it's a good idea for you and Beth to have a police presence here. We don't want to take any chances."

Nice touch, thought Lily, *to remind me that Beth could be in danger.* "I think I can take care of myself, Wes," she said, but she didn't sound convincing, even to herself.

"Not tonight," said Wes with authority. "I'll stay awake and spend the night in the car, or walking around the property. Let me say it again, we don't want to take any chances."

"He's got a point," said Clem. "I'll talk to you both tomorrow. And Wes, I've got your cell number if anything urgent comes up. With the help of these," he held up the baggies, "we may be a lot closer to getting our guy." With his free hand he tipped an imaginary hat to Lily. Then he, too, was gone.

Lily yawned. She found that she was grateful that Wes had offered to stay. She stood up, intending to head for the stairs, and wobbled slightly. Wes caught her.

"I'll come up with you," he said, "so you don't fall on the stairs."

Upstairs she peeked into Beth's room. Her daughter was asleep, with Monster in a large soft ball beside her head. Lily backed quietly away.

"They're cute together like that," whispered Wes, who had come up behind her.

"I told her not to let Monster sleep on her pillow," Lily whispered back. "Not much she can do to stop him," whispered Wes, "once she's asleep." They both tried to back down the hall together. Inevitably, they bumped into each other. Wes steadied her again, with his hands on her shoulders. The next thing Lily knew he was kissing her very gently, careful of the dressing on her cheek. She reached up and pulled him closer, kissing him back. She started to pull him toward her bedroom and for a moment he followed her. Then he stopped.

"Lily," he said softly, "I can't."

She stared back at him. She could feel the fire in him as well as in herself.

She knew she could.

"If you don't want to," she began. Then she couldn't think of how to finish.

All the reasons he might not want to were running through her head. "Oh, I want to," he said.

And she felt it again, a blast of desire. There was no mistaking it this time; she could tell exactly how he felt. She tried to pull him closer but he drew back.

"I can't," he said. "I'm on duty. I really do have orders to protect you. I can't do that very well if we -" Now he paused.

"You're blushing," she said, and he blushed harder. "I think it's cute.

There's coffee and tea in the kitchen, and help yourself to anything you want." She yawned; she couldn't help it. "And you really don't have to sit in your car. There's always the couch. Unless you change your mind." She grinned at him.

"Go to bed," he said.

She did, and fell asleep almost immediately. One of her last conscious thoughts was that it was nice, tiger or not, to have Wes protecting her.

Downstairs again, Wes took her up on her offer of coffee. He made instant in her microwave, found a travel mug and poured it into that. Then he checked his gun, took the coffee and quietly left the house.

He did not sit in his car but eased back into the bushes. He found a relatively comfortable stump to sit on and pulled his jacket around him. Tonight was chilly and the concept of global warming seemed remote.

For a long time, nothing happened and he began to believe that Lily was right and nothing would. Wes quietly finished the coffee and listened to the sounds of the night around him. Insects were out already, and soon would own the hours of darkness. He sat very still, feeling privileged, as an owl swept low overhead. After a while he yawned. He might have to go back to the house and make more coffee. After all, what were the odds that the shifter, their attacker, knew exactly who Lily was or where she lived or would even want to come here if he did?

It was then he saw the yellow eyes glowing, not all that far from him, back deeper still in the bushes. The tapetum lucidum of a cat reflects light, he remembered, even light that humans can't register. Wes' own night vision was pretty good, especially after sitting in darkness for so long, but there was no doubt that this animal was better. There was also no doubt, at least in Wes' mind, that it was a tiger, their tiger, and that it was watching him.

Drowsiness was gone in an instant. Wes was on his feet, his weapon, his own Glock 9 mm, drawn. He didn't remember doing it. He hesitated for a second. A gunshot would echo through the woods and wake the neighborhood. More than that, was he really sure that what he saw was a tiger, their own shifter tiger?

The hesitation cost him his chance. The eyes winked out and were gone.

With a whispered curse, Wes pulled his flashlight from his pocket and the powerful beam illuminated the woods.

There was nothing to be seen, nothing out of the ordinary. Only newly leafing trees, a couple of rotting logs, some old tangled dry grasses being pushed aside by this year' new growth. And there, in a patch of dirt, two big pug marks.

CHAPTER TWELVE

When Lily awoke in the morning she felt much better. Beth was going to the end of the year "field day" at school this morning and seemed quite willing to accept her mother's explanation of the scratches on her face. When Lily took the dressing off and looked at the scratches she could tell they were healing quickly, much more quickly than she would have thought possible.

On the other hand, her sensitivity to light seemed increased, and she felt slightly nauseous. She decided this was not surprising in the light of past events. She took more of Clem's pills and resolved to call Sandra as soon as Beth was off to school. Sandra should be pleased that there were no medical complications and nothing that would bring her any more official attention than she already had.

Being friends with me is dangerous, Lily thought. She paused to consider this idea. What about Wes? He was able to take of himself, wasn't he? Should she end things with him before they got serious - any more serious? It would be for his own protection. Just the thought made the morning darker, so she pushed it aside.

She looked out the door for Wes' car but it wasn't in the driveway.

The travel mug was washed and in the drainer so she knew he had availed himself of her offer of coffee but it seemed he had left. The front door was locked. It wasn't until she walked Beth out to the bus that she realized that Wes hadn't left after all. She recognized his car at the end of the street, and what she thought was Clem's, too. She frowned but then smiled again as soon as Beth looked at her; she didn't want to upset her daughter. She would go over and see what was going on after Beth got on the bus.

From the bushes he watched them, in human form now. Every so often he touched his torn ear and winced, even though the wince hurt his wounded nose. He wanted to growl and tried once, except that in human form what came out was a moan. He silenced himself. He wasn't out of the woods yet, literally or in any other way. He would need some medical attention and he would need it soon, and he knew of only one place he could get it without questions that would end up on some official record, although that place was unfortunately far from here. He couldn't understand how things had gotten so out of control.

Much of the time he wished he could have his old, normal life back. He had been on a fast track in his career with an opportunity for wealth and fame available to very few. He had what passed for a normal social life, at least, with a smart, attractive woman. He missed her. There she was, right there, yet out of reach.

The rest of the time, though, he knew he could never give up the power he felt in tiger form. He loved the terror he saw in his victims' faces; he fed on it. It was incredulity first and then terror, and in most of the victims, from a culturally primed population, he reminded himself, the knowledge of what was about to happen to them. Soon his prey base would be everyone, thanks to the media.

He wished the cops were not quite so successful at keeping his attacks out of the news. He couldn't really eat souls, not the way the Hmong thought, but he could certainly set them adrift, steal consciousness and feed himself on some of the mental and yes, psychic energy of his victims.

Their terror nourished him. The thought made him smile, despite his wounds. The idea of rape had been the frosting on the cake. It added to the terror and degradation of his female victims, so much so that it stimulated both his hunger and his lust just to think of it, even in his present circumstances.

There was so much power to be had that way. He had been stalking that Wiccan reporter for some time. He had read her columns and he knew she was perfect for him. He had imagined himself inside her, both physically and psychically, with her powerless but conscious, at least at first, and he had almost had his desire. He had been so close! No one should have seen the attack. The woman's body would have been found but her unconscious state attributed to a head wound (and he would have made sure she had one) from a more mundane sexual assault. He had even picked the perfect time, the dead spot before the start of the evening rush hour.

And then she had interrupted him, had spoiled his plans and his pleasure. From his hiding place he glared at Lily. That hadn't stopped him, of course, and he had made up for it later in the evening. But now he needed help. First he need to get out of the bushes and get away, and he couldn't do that very easily with the cars at the end of the street and the neighborhood awake now.

Looking at Lily, he regretted the normal life again. Not that Lily was normal.

Far from it; he knew that now. He didn't know how he could have missed it before. She might, in fact, be the perfect mate for him, more perfect than either of them could have imagined in the past. He wanted her back. He wanted to get her alone and convince her. He grinned, then winced again. His ear, what was left of it, felt as if it were on fire. He knew he shouldn't have stayed to see how she would react in daylight when that cop told her what he'd seen. He just hadn't been able to resist. Since this thing had happened to him he seemed to have less control over his impulses, and that was putting it mildly. He could see that the cars clustered at the end of the street showed no sign of moving and he knew he had made a big mistake. Even with the arrangements he had made, they might not be enough. And then he saw Lily turn to come toward him.

After Beth was on the bus Lily walked toward Wes' car. She could see now that it was indeed Clem with him. Her frown came back. More things had happened during the night; there was more information, obviously. Part way down the street she paused and looked back toward the woods. Then she turned and headed back, straight for the trees. Behind her she heard Wes call out to her. She ignored him and pushed back into the brush.

She didn't shift. She didn't want to shift here but she needed her senses heightened the way they were when she shifted. She wondered if it were possible to do that. Her run-in with the other shifter the previous night had alerted her to the possibility that there might be things she could do that she had not previously considered. She sneezed and then winced. Her stomach hurt.

As she stood there wondering, her glance fell on pug marks in the dirt. Big pug marks, tiger pug marks. It was all she needed. He had been here. She would do whatever she could, now more than before, to track him down.

She concentrated on shifting her senses without shifting her body. She found that her hearing heightened suddenly and also her sense of smell. it wasn't just that he had been here, he was still here. He was nearby and she could track him. She could find him.

"Lily! What are you doing back in here?" It was Wes, pushing into the trees, with Clem right behind him.

Lily held up a hand, trying to stop them, trying to hold them back and also to silence them. Clem got the point and stopped immediately but Wes continued in until he stood beside her.

"Damn it," whispered Lily. She could feel the presence fading, pulling back through the woods, heading - heading where? She started back along his trail, intending to follow him before it was too late. Clem's hand pulled her back. "Lily," said Clem, "he was here last night; there's evidence back here that we don't want to contaminate -" he broke off when he saw her expression. "He was here a lot more recently than last night," she snapped. "Look at that pug mark. It's pushed into the dew; the dew was not deposited on it. It was made after dew fall."

Clem dropped to examine the paw print. "You're right," he said. "He was here nearer dawn."

"And more than that," said Lily. "He was here just a minute ago."

"What!" Clem stood up suddenly. He reached toward the small of his back and Lily nodded to herself. She had known the good doctor was armed.

"Where is he?" said Wes. Wes had already drawn his Glock and was looking around him as if expecting the shifter to leap from the bushes.

"I don't know," said Lily. "He was here and then he knew I was here and then you guys came and he, I don't know, just faded."

"Right." Clem holstered his gun. "He just vanished." Lily shrugged.

"Look, Lily, I've seen some pretty interesting and strange things since I've been on this job." Clem brushed his hair back. It had been a long night and he was exhausted. "But I don't think this guy has been here since last night very late, or maybe around dawn. He was checking you out but Wes scared him away. Last night, early this morning, whatever. He wouldn't have stuck around."

"He did, though." Lily noticed that Wes had not reholstered his weapon. "He was just here. Checking us out. Me and you. He was watching you guys parked at the end of the street. And who knows, he was watching the neighbors, too, I suppose." She thought of Beth on the bus. Now she felt like she might vomit. She pushed it down.

"Lily," Clem began.

Suddenly she lost patience. "You want to know how I know?" She glared from one to the other. "You want to know? I could smell him. Hear him. Feel him! Right nearby! I don't have to be in tiger form to do that, so it seems! Not anymore."

"I believe you." Wes obviously did.

Lily looked at Clem, who did not hide his skepticism. How could he work for the PDC and have such a closed mind?

"Clem," said Lily, "have you ever seen anyone shift? Those werewolves you guys were studying, ever seen them do their thing?"

"No," admitted Clem, "I haven't."

"Seems to me you should have, before they put you on a case like this.

Seems to me you should know what it looks like to see someone shift." She was feeling sicker by the minute and less in control of herself. Obviously.

"Lily," said Wes, warningly.

"I think he needs it, Wes. And it doesn't matter now. We all know he's going to turn me in just as soon as this is all over. Take me away from Beth. There's no way he can't." She glared at Clem, daring him to contradict her. He didn't.

He was staring at her with his mouth open like a fish. He deserved this. Did Wes? She didn't stop to think. She knew this was potentially self-destructive, but then that was all water over the dam, wasn't it? She wasn't thinking straight and she didn't care. She was nauseous again.

She deliberately began to change, starting with just her ears. They enlarged, rounded and grew furry. She had the satisfaction of seeing Clem step backwards, of hearing him gasp. Then she changed her eyes. It was always slightly disorienting to have the color shift that came with feline vision and she felt slightly wobbly. And there was that nausea.

"Damn," whispered Clem. His own eyes were huge.

"You ain't seen nuthin' yet," said Lily with vicious satisfaction. She kicked off her shoes, dropped her thick sweater and pulled her shirt off over her head, wincing slightly as the shirt caught on the dressing. Then she unzipped and stepped out of her jeans. She stood there in the woods in underwear and socks.

"Lily!" said Wes, caught in a mesh of horror, admiration and desire.

Lily grinned. She debated removing her underwear but modesty oddly won out. Instead she threw herself into full change. She heard her bra snap and her panties rip. *I really need to go underwear shopping,* she thought.

Now she was looking up, but not far, at the men. Both of them wore stunned expressions. Lily knew she had made whatever point it was she had wanted to make, although she was no longer entirely sure what that was. She had probably made a few other points as well. She moved forward and then, with a tiger's lightning speed, before either man could react, she rubbed her huge feline head against Wes' waist and chuffed. She looked up at him and gave a long, slow feline blink.

Wes understood both enough of feline language and enough about Lily. A surprised grin flickered across his face, partially erasing the shock. Then he blinked back.

Lily turned to Clem. She did not make a move toward him. Instead, she gave him a big feline grin. Then, before he could react, she did move. She was beside him so fast he barely had time to gasp. Then she rammed her head against his legs. Clem staggered backwards.

"She's being friendly," said Wes, hastily.

"I know that," said Clem, sounding shaken. "I have a cat."

Surprise brought Lily up short. Clem had a cat? Then she realized she had a problem. She wanted to change back to human form. And there were her clothes, all except the underwear, in a nice little pile on the ground. If she shifted back now, she would be stark naked. Well, damn, she thought. Now what? The nausea was gone and she was thinking more clearly again. Just why had she done this?

She turned away from Clem and went to her clothes. She tried to get pants, shirt and sweater in her mouth simultaneously. Of course it didn't work. She had to settle for picking up pants first and carrying them in her mouth behind a tree. Then she came back for her shirt, nosing at it and then picking it up as if it were a cub. One of her clogs was caught in the shirt and got dragged along.

Clem started to follow her but Wes pulled him back. Lily stepped behind the tree and emerged a few moments later in human form in pants and shirt with one shoe on. She picked up her sweater and slipped on her other clog, looking mournfully at her socks and underwear. Her bra was missing.

"Here," said Wes helpfully, holding it out. "Second one in two days." "Clem," said Lily, intercepting his look, "get your mind out of the gutter.

Now you know what I can do." She looked at Wes. "And so do you." Lily's head suddenly snapped around. "Hear that?" she said.

Both men looked at her.

"A car! Do you hear it? About a street over! Just starting up!" "I hear it!" said Clem, surprising her again.

"He must have gone back through the swampy patch, pretty nasty stuff, to get to his car!"

"Damn it!" said Wes. "If only we knew what he was driving! We could put out an APB!"

"I have a pretty good idea what he's driving," said Lily. "It's a purple 1999 Saturn." She gave them the plate number.

"Purple?" said Clem.

"It's Stan. Unless he's changed it, that would be his car. I knew there was something familiar about this shifter from when I first went after him in the Lee's neighborhood, under that house -" she stopped but Clem nodded at her, unsurprised. How much did he know or had he guessed? "And I recognized him for certain this morning. I should have last night. But it's Stan, there's no question." She frowned. "He wasn't a shifter when I was involved with him or I didn't guess he was. I would have known." "Are you sure about that?" Clem asked. "Yes." Was she?

Wes had his gun put away and cell phone out. Now he put it back in his pocket. "We'll get him," he said. "He won't get far. He's got no head start, and a purple Saturn, for Chrissake." He shook his head. "Gone rogue on your ex, on everyone, but in a standout car like that, the idiot."

Lily wasn't so sure. There was something bothering her and she couldn't quite think what it was.

"You'd better let me have a look at those cuts," said Clem. "I don't suppose you've seen Sandra yet."

"Not yet," said Lily, pulling back. "I'll go there next." "Suit yourself."

Did Clem look hurt? Lily blinked. That was surprising. Even PDC Special Agents had feelings, it would appear. Or at least Clem did.

"Stan won't be going to a hospital or a clinic." Wes sounded definitive. "He knows we've got them watched, or he should; he's not stupid. If there's any way he can make it to one of your husband's facilities, either in New Jersey or upstate New York, he'll try for that. Your ex won't be too pleased with a rogue consultant who's just killed people but I'll bet he'll help him, maybe before he locks him up as another lab rat, uh lab tiger, himself. He certainly won't want it known that he helped create this mess. But Stan won't get there. We've got every exit watched near the state line, all of them. He can't get through. We've got the truck stops on alert. He won't get past us. Personally, I'm surprised if he's able to drive far at all, hurting the way he must. And then there's the probable blood loss -"

"Tigers are pretty tough," said Lily.

"Yeah, well, I doubt he's traveling in tiger form. Although maybe we should alert Environmental Management. Clem, what do you think?"

Clem shook his head. "In how many states? No. Not even in one, not even in this one."

"We just tell them somebody's illegal pet tiger escaped. We need to cover that base, Clem, just in case."

"I dunno, maybe. It's still the PDC doing the asking and we don't want the media alerted."

Lily was tired of the whole discussion. Her face was starting to itch. The dressing was gone now, fallen off when she shifted. Healing already. Amazing. She wanted to see Sandra and she wanted some time to puzzle out a couple of things that were nagging away at the back of her mind. And she needed a bathroom, badly. It felt like an episode of diarrhea might be in store. Again, not surprising, considering. She couldn't do any of that standing here.

"Guys," she said, "I got stuff to do. I'm going to see Sandra. My cell will be on. You can reach me."

"Okay," they said simultaneously.

Lily shook her head. They sounded like a comedy act. She had the sense not to say it. It was all surreal.

It was indeed an episode of simultaneous nausea and diarrhea, but fortunately it didn't last long. She felt much better when it was over, and she headed out for the vet clinic.

Sandra wasn't in surgery and saw her immediately.

"I'm sorry I didn't call ahead," said Lily, contritely. "I know I should have." "It's okay," said Sandra, "I've been expecting you to call all night." She looked as though she hadn't slept and Lily said so. "You look awful," she said. "Did you sleep at all?"

"Not much. Fortunately, I have no surgeries scheduled today, just exams and vaccinations. I hope no emergencies come in. Let me see your face."

"It's itching. I think it's healing." Sandra confirmed it.

"This is going to be more fun for Clem," said Lily wryly. "Another interesting ability."

"Lily, I don't think Clem is the only thing you need to worry about here. Yes, the PDC's Special Unit is going to try to get its hooks into you, no matter what Clem promises to the contrary. But that's not your first concern. I don't think he's the one you need to worry about right now."

Lily frowned. She was leaning back in a chair in one of the exam rooms while Sandra worked on her face. Now that the vet was finished, she sat up.

"I don't follow. If you mean Stan, he's gone. Or will be. The cops will have him soon, or Fish and Wildlife or somebody, and then the PDC Specials. He hasn't got long. He's gone rogue on John and he's wounded, and he's got everybody after him and well, he's driving a purple car." "He may have longer than you think."

"What?" The nagging at the back of Lilly's mind grew stronger. "I don't think he's rogue."

"What!"

"Well, in a sense he is. I'm sure John didn't mean for him to kill people.

But I suspect John's been testing out variants of this virus on human test subjects and one of them was probably Stan. If that's so, you're in danger. Stan knows what you are now, and if he gets word back to John and tells him, your ex will be coming after you. It's just a matter of whether or not Stan can make it back to upstate New York and I'm betting that he can, that he can make it past the road blocks -"

"Oh my God!" "Lily, what is it?"

"You're right. John might know about this. And Stan doesn't have to make it over any state line. He doesn't have to make it very far at all. All he has to do is make to Quonset or Westerly, any airport with a runway long enough for the Citation. John will send the plane to pick him up. Oh my God!" She was fumbling for her cell phone and got it open. No signal.

"Use my phone," said Sandra. "You'll have to use the land line and we'll just have to hope it isn't tapped, except maybe by Clem." She made a face and then something occurred to her. "And Lily, call Wes, not Clem. Just a hunch. In case they - someone - can monitor Clem's calls from his end. I don't know if any of us really know what's going on here." "I know we have to stop Stan," said Lily.

CHAPTER THIRTEEN

HE KNEW AS SOON AS heard from Lily that they were going to be too late. It just wasn't that far to Quonset and Stan had enough of a head start for that, not to mention that the cops weren't looking at the smaller airports. Wes called ahead to the Quonset tower and found that the Citation had already landed some time ago and then recently taken off again, no flight plan filed. He had pretty good idea where they were going, of course, but that didn't help.

"Damn it!" Wes smacked his hand against the side of the car. "Think we can get anyone to meet them up there in New York, arrest them?

"At Belkner's private airstrip at his farm?" said Clem. "With no warrant? On what grounds? We don't have 'em."

Wes stared at him. "Can't you arrange it? I can try to get a warrant through the state police up there, but it won't be fast enough. There must be something you can do!" He couldn't believe he said it. He was encouraging the detention of citizens without due process.

Clem smiled faintly, as if he guessed his partner's thoughts. "You're forgetting my - our - little problem, Wes. If I call ahead for a team to do that, on whatever grounds, Belkner could know we're coming even before we do."

Wes sighed. "True, we don't know for sure Belkner's working against us but we can't just let Stan get away like this! Buy a throwaway cell phone, for crap's sake!"

"There's no time for someone to see a judge, do all that. And Stan's not getting away. We know exactly where he's going. We know where to find him. Well, we know where in general. We need a little help with that, somebody who can get in there without arousing suspicion, find out what we need to know, and guide us in. Once we're in, I have no doubt we'll find all the evidence we need."

Wes stared at the PDC man. Clem wanted Stan to get back to Belkner. "You think Lily won't arouse any suspicion after last night?" he said, finally.

"You got a better idea?"

"No. But using Lily is a flat-out bad one." "I suggest we leave that up to her." "Damn it!"

"Wes, listen to me. It doesn't take the third sight or any other paranormal talent to see that you and Lily have a thing."

"You have the third sight? What thing?"

"No, Wes, I don't have the third sight. All I meant was that anyone who's made it through adolescence can see that you and Lily - well, have a thing isn't right. Are in love." He glanced at Wes. They were both sitting in Wes' Beetle, Clem with the seat pushed all the way back to accommodate his long frame.

"Hey, do you guys even realize you're in love?"

Wes stuttered but nothing comprehensible came out.

"Never mind. Whatever is going on between the two of you, Wes, you don't stand a chance unless you stop crowding her. She's gotta make her own decisions, you know."

He wanted to ask just what Clem knew about this. He wanted to say sure, Lily had a right to make her own decisions, just not if it involved putting herself in danger. But he said none of it. He remembered his discussion with Lily. No, their argument. She was right. Clem was right, not that he liked it. Finally, he sighed.

"You're right," he said at last. "But I don't have to like it." "No one said you do."

Stan had never been so sick in his life. The flight from Quonset to the farm hadn't taken all that long but it had seemed like forever. The doctor on board, one of John Belkner's staff but someone he had never seen before, had run an IV to hydrate him and had given him something for fever. It didn't seem to be helping. By the time they got to the farm, he was delirious. He barely noticed when John Belkner came to his bedside in the small clinic on the farm property.

"Is he going to pull through this?" Belkner asked.

"I don't know. I've never seen anything like it." It was the chief doctor at the farm; Stan couldn't remember his name. Sanity and comprehension seemed to come and go in waves.

"It's not infection from his ear wound or the wounds on his nose. I thought so at first but those infections are responding to treatment. This is something else entirely."

Stan moaned. He had abdominal cramps that were so intense that he writhed. "Pain," he whispered. "Please..." They ignored him.

"He's dehydrated. Severely, despite the IV. We're running blood tests but so far there's nothing definitive." It was the doctor again.

"Please," whispered Stan.

"We're not sure just what to give him for pain," the doctor continued. "Considering his shape shifting capacity, it's possible that even something as simple as an NSAID could be dangerous. Even fatal; it can be in cat species, you know. We can't risk it until we know more. The anti-retroviral won't work on him."

"I don't want him dead," John said, "but I don't care if the son of a bitch is in pain. Give him nothing for pain. He's responsible for the deaths of I don't remember how many now. And in the area where my ex-wife lives. And my daughter!"

Stan heard the steely coldness in John's voice. Suddenly he was furious, and with the fury came a little clarity.

"And whose fault is that!" he said. He had wanted to shout it but it came out as a whisper. "It's all because of your damned experiments! You know what you did!"

"I know what we did." John turned to address Stan directly. "But we didn't do this. You did this thing on your own. A lot of things on your own. The only reason I want you alive is because the gene virus worked on you. It worked too well. After we figure it out, you can die and die in pain, as far as I'm concerned." Belkner turned back to the doctor. "Keep him alive. Get him through this. But that's all."

"John, if we can figure out something to ease his pain, it will help him stay alive."

Belkner looked sour. "If you have to," he said.

Stan moaned again. The pain in his stomach was becoming even more unbearable. "Please," he whispered again, "please help me."

No one paid him any attention. He wanted their attention. He wanted Belkner's attention in any way possible.

"Lily," Stan said. Now Belkner turned back to him. "Lily is the same. As me. The same as me. A shifter. A tiger. And she's going to be mine! We were meant to be together. She's my mate! I'm going to have her. Often." He grinned weakly. "And your daughter, John, your little brat." He paused, gasping for breath. The light in the clinic hurt his eyes. "I bet she's the same as me. A shifter, a little bratty shifter. She is. You know it, she is. And when I find her, I'll kill her. Because she's your cub. And then Lily will bear my cubs, my children, whether or not she wishes to.

And I'll kill you." He knew he shouldn't be saying these things, even if on some level he meant them, but he couldn't stop. "My children will have everything, John, and yours will die-"

He said no more. Belkner leaned over the bed and took him by the throat.

"Your stupid son of a bitch! Shut up!"

Stan snarled. It was a very weak snarl but he put everything that he could into it: the power to paralyze prey, the power to hold them immobile while he had his will. Belkner's hand went slack and he froze. The doctor gasped and gave a slight scream, an odd, high-pitched sound coming from a man. Stan grinned. He still had it. He had the talent. Right now he wished he had the power to follow through. To kill and eat these ridiculous humans. Immediately he regretted the thought. Just the idea of food made him suddenly nauseous and his control over his victims slipped and fell away.

"You're dead when this over," said Belkner. His fury was gone, apparently, and he was as calm and as controlled as ever.

The doctor was less calm. "You try that again with me," he said, his voice shaking, "and there won't be anyone here to treat you."

Stan laughed. Or he tried to, but the effort backfired. The pain in his stomach was suddenly so intense that he couldn't bear it. Now he was the one who screamed. Then he threw up. He was so weak, so sick that he couldn't even lean over. The vomit ran down across his chin and onto his chest. At the same time the pain expanded into his intestines and his bowels released with explosive diarrhea.

"Sometimes," said John Belkner to the horrified doctor, "I don't think I pay you enough."

As soon as he was out of the clinic, Belkner motioned to Rick, his right hand man for the sort of business he had in mind.

"I want my daughter brought here immediately," he said. "It shouldn't be hard. She's got some field day end of the year thing at her school so she won't be with my ex. It lets out early so you have to get there ASAP." He thought for a second about Stan's ravings. Could Lily in fact be a shape shifting tiger?

Possible, but doubtful. She had been tested extensively when they were married, but if Stan had deliberately infected her he supposed it was possible. He frowned in thought. She'd never do what Stan had, no matter what shape she took. But to protect her child, a tigress with her cub, a mother with her child, any mother, he thought - "Stay the hell away from my ex, under any and all circumstances. Don't let anyone see you but get my daughter. Get Beth.

Get her and bring her back here safely. Take the plane. The Citation. It should be refueled and ready to go by now." John insisted that one plane always be in readiness.

"Fred said he was glad to get on the ground after picking up -

well, he was glad to get back. There's some sort of spring weather front coming through later, thunderstorms." Rick was a pilot who sometimes flew the Citation and often co- captained with Fred. Belkner believed in hiring people with multiple talents whenever possible.

"I don't give a crap. You're both IFR rated. Get in the air, get my daughter and get back here." He hesitated. "If you're fast enough you'll beat the damn front." He wanted Lily as well as Beth but getting Beth meant he would almost certainly get Lily, too. Beth came first; it would be easier to get her without Lily, but Lily would follow her. Oddly, he still cared about his ex-wife. They were divorced but that in reality meant very little. She and Beth were his. They both belonged to him. He had not become what he was by letting anyone else control his property.

"Yes, sir," said Rick. He knew when not to argue.

Lily knew she had to do it. She would have to go up to the farm and check the place out. She would try very hard not to be confrontational and she hoped beyond all hope that she would not run into Stan. It wasn't likely, she decided. John probably had him in the clinic under lock and key, and he probably had all the cabins under lock and key, too. She didn't know how long she'd be there but it would be at least overnight. She'd get her regular pet-sitter to take care of Monster, if Sandra was too busy. She would set up whatever precautions Clem and Wes wanted, whatever backup they wanted her to have, although she knew that should she need help, it was highly unlikely anyone could reach her in time. She would be truly on her own. There was one thing she needed to do, though and the sooner the better.

She knew her ex-husband and she had a pretty good idea what Stan would be telling John. She also had a pretty good idea what John's response would be. Both she and Beth would be in danger. She would get Beth as quickly as possible, before John could. She would take Beth some place safe, some place John would never think to look, if she could manage it. John might think he was going to keep their daughter safe but he couldn't, not up at the farm. And he wouldn't, not if he thought there was a profit to made through her. Lily needed a really good place to hide her.

It wouldn't be the cops. She couldn't ask Wes and she couldn't ask the local police. Wes might claim to understand but she doubts he would truly comprehend the danger involved here. He didn't know John. The danger to herself, she could handle but Beth must be protected.

She could ask Clem to protect her child and she was sure he would. Clem was a good guy as far as it went, which was totally surprising, but she had no doubt he would whisk Beth away into the protective custody of the Special Unit of the PDC. She did not want to trust her daughter to the government. She knew a place that was safe, or she thought she did, a place they'd never think to look. The problem was that she needed to set it up first; she needed a little time.

She checked her student data base first. She had Mai's number and she called it. It was Mai's cell phone and Mai wasn't answering. Lily left a message. There was no other number listed for Mai. She looked up Choua Lee in the phone book. No listing. There were eight listings under George Lee and she tried them all but with no luck. She reached five voice mails, obviously not the Lees she wanted, was hung up on twice, and the last time reached a woman who claimed to know nothing of any George or Choua Lee. Next was the school, Lucy and Beth's. Lily could have kicked herself for not thinking of this first. They had the number and amazingly they gave it to her. When she finally got through she got someone who spoke very little English. It was a child.

"Choua?" she asked desperately, "is he there? Grandfather? Choua?" There was silence for a moment on the line. Lily could hear people talking in the background, the child who had answered the phone, a woman, Jen maybe, and someone else. A man? Was Choua there? Finally, the child came back.

"You want Choua, you come here," the child said. Lily want to throw the phone against the wall. "Please let me talk to him," she said.

"You want Choua, you come up here, Tiger Lady," said the child, and hung up.

Lily stared at the phone in her hand and finally hung it up. Tiger Lady. She was that easy to identify. Did all the Hmong know, or just Lucy and Mai's family? Well. Fine. She would go. She looked at her watch. It was still before noon. She could get up to Providence, talk to Grandfather, arrange things, she hoped, and then get back in time for Beth. Maybe not in time to pick Beth up from school but at least to meet the bus. At least that. She didn't have a choice. She would see how fast her Beetle could go, and thank all the gods, spirits and ancestors for radar detectors.

It was almost one o'clock when she finally parked on the narrow Providence street. She was prepared to beg, as time was of the essence, but Choua was waiting for her.

"Things are very bad now," Choua said, as Lucy accepted Jen's offer of tea.

She didn't want the tea but she couldn't refuse the hospitality.

"That other shifter has killed many people now." Choua shook his head. "Too bad you did not kill him last night when you stopped him." He smiled at Lily's shock. "Your face hurt?"

Lily blinked. "No. Well, yes, but not nearly as much as it did." Choua nodded. "I send you healing. During the night."

He sent her healing? "Uh, thank you," said Lily. "You don't believe me."

Did she? She wasn't sure. Perhaps she did.

"It does not matter. What matter is that bad shifter got away."

"He did," said Lily. "But I know who he is and I know where he is. I even have an idea why he is."

"Good." Choua nodded. "And you will go and kill him."

Lily stared at him. Kill Stan. She had planned on stopping him but could she kill him? And what about John, John's whole program? She couldn't kill John! And the CDC Special Unit involvement? The government? How could she stop them all?

"I'm not sure you know what you're asking," she said.

"I have pretty good idea. And I know it is hard to kill. I know this from personal experience. But you must do this."

"Kill Stan. Kill - the other tiger. Choua, Grandfather, do you know how many other people are involved in this?"

"No. But if the government is in it, a lot. Enough. You do not have to kill them all. Just the killer tiger. Other things will follow from that. Some things will turn to right after that. Some things will heal. That part will not be so hard and you do not even have to do that; it will do itself."

"Mr. Lee -" She needed formality here.

"Oh come now, you know I am Grandfather."

"Grandfather. I promise you this. I will go after the other tiger. He must be stopped. I will do everything I can to stop him."

"Even kill him."

She had a flash of the woman near the parking garage. Of the pug marks near her house. She swallowed.

"Yes," she said. "Even kill him."

"Good. But that is not why you came to see me, what you want from me." "I don't know how to ask this, Mr. Lee -"

"Grandfather, please. Choua, if you must."

"I'm not sure how to ask this, Grandfather. But if - since - I am going after Stan and he's with my ex-husband -" she paused and tried again. "My ex-husband is a very dangerous man. Or can be. In his own way more dangerous than Stan, the other tiger. I am very worried about Beth, my daughter."

"She is welcome to stay with us," Choua said. "She and Lucy are friends and Lucy has been asking about having friends for sleep-over." He smiled but the smile did not reach his eyes. "She will be safe here, Tiger Lily. No one will guess she is here. But first you must get her and bring her here. You must do it very quickly. Very, very quickly. You are right that your husband is a dangerous man. Go and get your child, and bring her here. Do not go home to get her anything; we have everything here she could need. Go now, and hurry."

Lily stared at him. Then he had her gently by the elbow and was leading her to the door.

"Thank you," she said softly.

"It is we who should thank you," he said. "And I will help you any way I can, and I know many ways. Now go."

Lily went. It was one-thirty. She ran two red lights getting back on Route 95 and broke the speed limit recklessly, weaving in and out of traffic. It was two-fifteen when she reached Beth's school. The field day was just wrapping up; she had beaten the busses, which were lined up waiting for their passengers.

Lily pulled into a parking place and left the car at a run, not bothering to lock it. The feeling of urgency was mounting.

The halls were full of kids. Where would Beth be? In her home room or in the gym? Frustrated, she looked around.

"Ms. Mossberg!"

Lily turned. It was the assistant principal, a cheerful man named Hendriks, whose first name she could never remember.

"Mr. Hendriks! Do you know where Beth is?"

"Why yes. She left. Someone sent by her father picked her up. About an hour ago."

"What?"

"He had paperwork. A note from Dr. Belkner's lawyer, a note from Dr Belkner - I recognized his handwriting - and a note from you."

"I never signed anything!"

"I recognized your signature, Ms. Mossberg."

"Forgery!" Lily had already turned away and was striding down the hall toward the exit, trying not to mow down students. Hendriks hurried to keep up with her.

"Do you want me to call the police?" Hendriks asked. "Who picked her up? What was his name?"

"Rick something. He's been here before. That was another reason I didn't think anything of it -"

"The pilot," she bit off the words. "One of them."

"Do you want me call the police?" he asked again but she had already left him behind.

She was out the door and in her car. It wouldn't do any good to drive to Quonset. There was no way she could stop them now; they were undoubtedly in the air already. There was only one thing she could do and she intended to do it.

CHAPTER FOURTEEN

S HE DID GO HOME. SHE had to. She was on the phone the whole way. Wes and Clem met her at her house, and they were there before her.

"Quonset tower said the Citation made two trips today but they don't know why, of course. Nobody got on or off but the pilot and copilot."

"Right," said Lily. "Idiots."

"Lily, I'm calling for a PDC plane," Clem began. He was pulling out his cell phone. "I just wanted to check with you - "

"No!" said Wes and Lily simultaneously.

"Oh, right." Clem looked abashed. "I can only hope they are still in the dark about what we're up to."

"We're in the dark about what we're up to," said Lily.

"We'll take my Cessna," said Wes. "Civilian plane, we'll land at the nearest small airport and find, rent a car somehow. No flight plan; let me check the chart, see where we can land -"

"John has a private field," said Lily. "Yes, but we can't use that -"

"I'm not talking about the one he regularly uses. There's a grass strip back in the woods. It's long enough. I'll show you the layout. It has runway lights and I know the frequency for them. We'll be landing after dark, but it's better if we don't use them. Can you do that, Wes? Land in the dark?"

"I hope so."

"After that it's a bit of a trek through the woods but we don't need a car." Clem was looking distinctly uneasy, she noticed. That didn't help things. "Clem," she said, "is there anyone you are absolutely certain you can trust?

Anyone in your unit? We may need outside support." "There is."

"Then get on your cell with them now, get them headed to Wegland. That's a town close enough to the Beechland farm to get there quickly if they have to. There's a Motel 6 there on the main highway."

"Right." Clem looked relieved to have something to do and pulled out his phone.

Lily wanted to shake her head. She had expected more from the Specials, but she supposed nobody had experience dealing with anything like this. She went upstairs and looked into Beth's room. Some of Beth's stuff was gone. They had been back here first. Monster was under the bed, but Bunny-buns was gone, and some other things, including one of Beth's new sandals. Just one.

Lily frowned. That was deliberate; her daughter was leaving her a message. They had been here and out again, and not left any sign except for this.

"Damn!" She reached under the bed to give her cat a reassuring scratch and then took the stairs down two at a time. Clem was on his cell phone still but Wes was waiting for her.

"Speaking of outside help," she said, "where's that number for my pet sitter?"

There was a knock at the door.

"Damn!" Lily had been pulling her old back pack out from behind the coats in the closet. She needed the pack and there was so little time.

"It's Sandra." Wes was looking out the door. "Damn!" She couldn't stop saying that. "Ignore her."

The knocking turned into a pounding. "Lily! I know you're in there! It's your car in the driveway! I know you're all in there! Wes, Clem, somebody open the door!"

Wes glanced at Lily, shrugged, and did. Sandra pushed her way in, looking furious.

"So, what did you think, you were leaving without me?"

"What?" Lily turned and stared at her friend. "How did you - what makes you think - how did you know I - we - were - are going anywhere today, er -" You didn't want to be involved, she thought. She didn't say it.

"I'm not an idiot, Lily. When that little Lattinger girl got sick, Beth's friend, I knew something was up. A Mr. Lee, your Mr. Lee, called me and told me that his Lucy, his granddaughter, told him - I guess this is getting complicated -"

"Told him what!" Lily, Wes and Clem spoke in unison. Sandra looked taken aback.

"That little Sarah was sick with the 'tiger disease', was how he put it, and I should come here and make sure you were okay and get Beth to him if you didn't have time. So," She stared at the three shocked faces staring back at her. "That's why I'm here. To get Beth. And take her to the Lees. If that's what you want. Leslie will look after her if you prefer, at our place. And come feed Monster, or I'll take him home with me, too, if you want, Leslie can take care of him there, and if Beth is with him - what?"

"Beth is gone." Even saying it now, Lily found it hard to believe.

"What do you mean 'gone'?" Sandra blinked. "Oh shit! Oh Lily! John took her!"

"Yes. He did. He kidnapped her. They were here. Beth left one sandal behind. It's a message," she said to their confused looks. "But supposedly, I don't know John has her yet."

"I'm going with you." Sandra crossed her arms, as if daring them to contradict her.

Lily stared. What had happened to the woman who wanted to

stay as far away from John as possible, as far away from the PDC Specials as she could get?

"I'm part of this team and I'm coming," said Sandra, as if answering her unasked questions. "And Beth is like - well, like I always imagined a daughter of mine would be. I'm coming. These sick kids -"

"Okay," said Wes. "Enough, you can come."

"I'll call Leslie and tell her to come get Monster. He'll be safer at our place." She flipped open her phone but before she could place the call, Clem was off his phone and turning to her.

"The tiger disease," he said. "I should get one of our doctors down here for Sarah -"

"Not just any doctor," said Sandra. "I'm afraid what you need is a vet. I'm afraid it might be the new distemper, not just your shifter virus. Don't look at me like that; what am I, stupid? I used to work for Belkner, remember? Have them send a good vet, and make sure no one knows? If there's a vet who's had any med school training for humans, that would be best. Don't know if you guys have that but you have everything, right?"

Clem's mouth opened and then closed again. "Right," he finally managed, getting back on his cell phone.

"You can do that in the car," said Wes. "It's the better part of an hour to get to Green and then more to get pre-flighted and in the air. Let's move. Sandra, you can call Leslie from the car. We'll take mine. Let's go!"

Knowing that her cooperation would make it so much easier for them, Beth had made a scene. She hoped someone at the school would do something.

Call her mom. Even call the cops. She knew the pilots. Well, she knew Rick, anyway, and was sure they wouldn't hurt her, so she yelled.

"I need my stuff!" she yelled loudly, unfortunately they were in the car already. The two men had bundled her off before she could do this more

publicly. "You take me home now! Now, or I'll stick my head out the window and yell!"

"C'mon, Beth, please. You know your dad will have anything you need up there at the farm -" It was Rick. He was the younger of the two pilots she usually had, Fred and Rick. He was nice enough but Beth liked him slightly less than she liked Fred.

"He doesn't have Bunny-buns! I've got to have Bunny-buns!" She considered saying that she wanted to say goodbye to Monster but she was afraid mention of the cat would make the men snatch him up, too. Her father would have no qualms about using Monster in the stuff he did, she thought. The experiments. If she didn't mention Monster, he'd probably hide when he heard strange men in the house. So instead she started to cry.

"Beth don't cry!" Rick turned sideways and tried to look at her.

She was in the back seat and some guy she didn't know, the copilot she hadn't met, was in the passenger seat in the front. Beth cried harder, great gasping shrieks.

"Jesus!" said the copilot. "Just do what she wants, Rick! How long can it take? What, fifteen minutes?"

"And then another fifteen to get back on track, never mind the time at the house. I want to beat that front," said Rick.

"At this rate we won't beat anything. The cops'll pick us up and it's over and we're fired and -"

"Point taken. Beth! Stop crying, Beth. We'll go to your house. You can

grab a little stuff. Do you have a key?"

She hadn't meant to cry, not really cry. She meant to only cry as a, what was it called, a ploy. But now that she had started, it was hard to stop. She took some deep breaths, swallowed and nodded. Then, because maybe they hadn't seen her do that she said, "Yes, I have a key."

"We have to make it fast," said Rick. "There's very bad weather coming in and your dad wants you home - his place - safe. We'll go in, you grab your stuffed bunny, whatever else, and we're out, fast. Okay?"

"Okay," she sniffled.

And then Rick turned around and they were going to her house and she felt a great burning sense of something. She wasn't sure if it was hope or triumph or fear or a mixture of all of them. She knew it wasn't over. It was really just beginning. And she had to help Sarah somehow. She just knew it was her fault Sarah got sick, she just knew it. And her dad - or that creep Stan, or maybe both, had the answer. But she was going to get it. And then look out.

Rick was nervous. He had good right to be. He was very much afraid what they were doing was kidnapping, never mind that Dr. Belkner was Beth's father. Custody cases were the worst, and although his boss had plenty of money and power it hadn't seemed to buy him his own kid. His boss' ex, Lily, was a woman to be reckoned with. If he got indicted in a kidnapping, custody, whatever it was, conspiracy, there went his pilot's certificate, and here came a prison term. But now that they had let Beth pick up some stuff, her stuffed rabbit and a few clothes and stuff, she was quiet and seemed cooperative. Rick had stayed with her every step in the house, to make sure she didn't leave a note for her mom, and she didn't. Of course, it wouldn't take Lily long to put together who had her kid but by then they would be safely back at Beechland. He just hoped they could beat the storm. After that, it would no longer be his problem.

When they finally got to Quonset, after what seemed like an age, the Citation was fueled and ready. Beth let them smuggle her aboard quietly, wrapped in a tarp, like baggage. Not a peep. Amazing. Rick decided not to question his luck, especially when the weather briefing proved wrong. There was turbulence, all right, but not bad, not a SIGMET, not yet. And only spatters of rain ahead of the front. It was going to be okay.

Her dad met her right there on the tarmac at the strip near the big house.

He usually didn't do that. He must have been really worried, Beth thought. He hurried up and gave her a hug.

"You okay?" he asked.

She had given some thought to the answer to this inevitable question. "I'm okay," she said, "but my best friend Sarah is really, really sick." She swallowed back tears, and they were real. "They think, well, they didn't say, but you know all that shape shifter scare stuff at home? They think he got her.

Infected her somehow. Dad, you have to find a cure! She's my best friend!" All he did was give her another hug, which told her nothing.

"And I didn't get to say goodbye to Mom."

Now he did have an answer. "There wasn't time, honey. I wanted you here safe and sound, and there just wasn't time. I'll let her know."

Which told her he knew what was going on back home and that he maybe had something to do with it. And that he wouldn't call her mom. He was lying about that. But she would bet that Stan was here and her dad had him stashed away safely. She hoped. She was going to find out.

Her dad was leading her toward the house now, away from the airstrip. As they walked, the skies suddenly opened up and a torrent of rain poured down. A huge blast of wind nearly ripped her backpack from her hand. She hoped her mom had gotten the message from the one sandal. Thunder boomed.

"A real spring storm," said her dad. "We'll get you warm and dry inside.

I'll have Jenna make you up some cocoa, if you want."

"I'd rather have tea," said Beth. It wasn't even that she liked tea that much or that her mom let her have it that often but she smirked at her father's look of surprise. That was worth it.

The front was already coming through when they left the Providence airport. The rain was pouring down and the winds in the runway environment were bad and aloft they were worse. Lily was up front in the right seat, copilot, and Clem and Sandra were in the back. Clem was green and was clutching some plastic bags since they didn't have standard airline "air sickness bags", and looking as if he might need them any second. Sandra's face was white. A gust caught the little Skyhawk and pitched it sideways. Wes compensated with a cross-control of rudder and yoke. Lightning flashed.

"Oh God," said Clem, and then he threw up, into bag, fortunately.

"What is - can you - should we be flying in this?" Sandra tried to keep her voice calm but she couldn't hide the edge of panic. "Maybe we should have driven."

"No," said Wes, "we most definitely should not be flying in this. It's a SIGMET - a significant meteorological event. The commercial heavies stay grounded in this stuff. But we want to get up to Beechland. This is the fastest way to do that." Another gust almost flipped the plane over in the other direction and again Wes compensated.

"Assuming we get there," whispered Clem. Then he grabbed for another plastic bag.

"You better tie those things up tightly," said Sandra. "I don't want your puke all over me if we go upside down in this crate."

"Cessnas are good planes," Lily tried to reassure them. "They're like trucks.

And Wes is a good pilot." She kept her voice steady. "He's got a lot of hours. At least I don't think we have much to worry about in the way of traffic tonight." It wasn't much of a joke but it silenced the passengers, and Wes rewarded her with his glance and a faint smile.

She believed what she said but she knew how dangerous it was and after a seeming eternity of turbulence and rain, it was with a sense of both vast relief and surprise when the GPS told them they were nearing the Beechland coordinates.

"What's the frequency for those runway lights," said Wes. He was exhausted from trying to keep the plane in the air and level, and he knew they hadn't even begun with the evening's activities yet. "I can't see a damn thing in this storm. I need the lights. Nobody will see us, Lily. I can't land this without lights."

Lily told him the frequency.

"At least we're less likely to be noticed, even with the lights," she said, "on a night like this."

Wes keyed the radio.

Like magic lights came on, almost directly below them. Through the driving rain and the gusts of wind, they could see a long grass strip with a hangar at the edge of it, surrounded by woods,

"Oh thank God," said Clem. He was still green but he hadn't vomited in some time, probably because there was nothing left in his stomach.

"We're not on the ground yet," said Sandra. Lily glared at her.

Wes said nothing. Sandra was right. Landing was in many ways the most difficult part of the endeavor so far. The wind was against them and they went straight in. The grass was slick and when Wes applied the brakes, they hydroplaned slightly, causing Lily's heart to turn over but then they were stopped and safe on the ground. Clem moaned with relief and Sandra sighed audibly.

Wes passed a shaking hand over his face and then began flipping switches off. "Get out," said Lily. "Get out now, let's get the plane turned around and ready for takeoff again but back at the edge of the runway, near those trees. There's a tie-down there; we need it. Wes, do we need fuel? There's a pump over there; if the code isn't changed I can unlock it. Clem, you okay? Drink some water when we get out, I mean it. Sandra, you all right?"

There were heartfelt affirmatives from both of them. The rain did not let up as Wes topped off the tanks and they got the Cessna turned around. Despite the rain gear they had brought, they were all soaked. Just as they finished turning the plane and chocking it and tying it down, the runway lights went out.

"Thank God," said Wes. "That was beginning to worry me, in case they register at the main house, somehow."

"Not at the house," said Lily, "but at the main strip. If anybody's monitoring, they'll assume it's the wind. And they won't want to check in weather like this."

"You hope," said Clem. He was sipping water from a canteen, as ordered, and he looked quite a bit better.

"We all hope," said Sandra.

"Okay," said Wes. "We have our plan. Clem, you need to make contact with your team, see if they're where they should be. I hope they're here."

Clem already had his cell phone out. "No damn coverage here," he said. "Shit, I forgot about that." Lily wiped her wet hair away from her face. The rain wasn't really bothering her, not the way it was with the others but her stomach was upset again, and not from the ghastly flight. "Reception is better down there." She pointed. "Call your team. Hike out to the road; you've got your GPS. Meet them there, go with them and stand by. Take Sandra with you. Wes and I will wait to hear that you're in progress before we move out to the house and the compound. We've got our cells. There's coverage near the house."

"This may take a little while," said Clem.

"I know. But make it as quick as you can. Wes." She looked at him. "Let's wait in the hangar. It'll be cold but at least it's dry." Wes was shivering and that wasn't good.

They watched as Sandra and Clem disappeared into the dark and the rain.

For a while Lily could hear them crunching through the woods and winced. She had told them to be quiet. Then she realized it might be her tiger hearing, preternaturally sharp. She hoped so.

She and Wes headed toward the hangar. The side door was not locked. It never was, but Lily held out her hand to halt Wes. With a slight effort she shifted her sight to that of a tiger. Had she known it, her pupils slitted and gleamed in the darkness, taking advantage of every trace of light. The hangar was empty except for clutter in the back and some coils of rope, an old office chair, and other miscellaneous stuff. No sign of motion, no one there. Lily opened her mouth wide to check for scents with her Jacobsen's organ. Nothing.

Just engine oil, aviation fuel, and mustiness. She shifted her senses back and looked at Wes.

"It's safe," she said. "Let's get you out of the rain."

Wes knew what she was doing. He saw it when her eyes changed and gleamed, and then changed back again. It did not frighten him. She did not frighten him and he was surprised to find that her abilities did not disturb him at all, not on any level. He knew, too, that there was no way he could keep her from doing what she felt she had to. They were in this together, to catch a killer, to rescue a child, to perhaps stop a dangerous virus. Whatever it was they were doing, they were partners and colleagues and far more than that. He had never felt this close to anyone before.

"Lily," he said. He wasn't sure how to say what he felt. He had never been good with that. Besides, his teeth were chattering. "Lily, I l-love you." He wanted to say, marry me.

Lily looked at him. She could read the expression in his eyes, feel the pressure of his emotions. But more than that. He was shivering, dangerously so.

"Wes, come here. You're freezing. You're going to go hypothermic."

He came to her and she sat him in the broken down chair. She looked around. There wasn't much available for warmth, and they certainly couldn't start a fire. There was an old tarp but it smelled nasty. She took off her rain poncho and then her jacket and sweater. Wes' eyes widened.

"What are you doing?"

"Get your wet clothes off," she ordered. "We're going to use body heat, share body heat, to try to warm you up a bit. Come on, Wes, you know about that stuff. Get your wet clothes off."

Wes peeled off his rain gear. Then his jacket. "My sweater's only damp," he said.

"Get it off. Shirt and undershirt. And pants. Wes, this is no time for modesty. We can't have you going comatose." Lily had removed her shirt and her bra and now she was working on her own pants. "My God," said Wes.

Lily went to him and helped with his pants. She did not feel remotely cold.

I must be a Siberian tiger, she thought. And then she grinned. That most certainly wasn't all there was to it. She pulled Wes' arms around her and sat on his lap, completely naked, wiggling to make herself more comfortable.

She was tired of waiting. There was a chance, one she tried not to let herself think about, that they wouldn't survive this night. She knew how Wes felt about her. She couldn't admit to herself exactly what it was she felt about him. Or could she? She knew she wanted him.

"I think you're getting warmer," she said. She tried to pull her jacket, which was dry, around them both. The chair wobbled and almost spilled them to the floor. She laughed and ran her hands down Wes' body. "I don't know how long we can stay in this chair," she said. "It's gonna dump us on the floor. She kissed him, running her tongue along his lips and then she slipped her hand down his chest and then lower still.

"Oh my," she said, "you are warming up nicely."

"So are you," said Wes. He considered asking if she really wanted to do this but decided he needed to stop making stupid remarks.

"There are other ways of doing this," he said. He pulled them both up and then backed her against the wall. He was really hoping that nobody came to check out the airstrip, the hangar, not now. And he really, really hoped that Clem and Sandra would call on their cells, as they were supposed to, and not come looking for them. And he hoped it wouldn't be too soon. And then he stopped thinking at all.

CHAPTER FIFTEEN

S HE GOT HER TEA. It was orange pekoe, with lots of honey in it and it really wasn't too bad, as these things went. She was warm and she was comfortable, and she was worried. Her father had made sure she wasn't left alone, not for a minute. Even when she went to the bathroom there was somebody waiting for her outside the door. It was ridiculous. She finally decided that she had to take the bull by the horns.

"I want to talk to my dad," Beth said. "And I want to talk to him now."

Her guardian of the moment, Jenna, the housekeeper, blinked. She had heard that tone of command before, from Lily, when Lily had been living here, but also and frequently from her employer, Dr. Belkner. Beth was her parents' child, no question.

"I'm sure he'll see you when it's time, dear. You know he's a busy man -" "I need to see him and I need to see him right now," Beth said. "Now. I'm not going anywhere. I'll stay right here in the kitchen. You don't have to watch me. Just go and find him."

As it was, Jenna did not have to leave the kitchen. She just picked up her cell phone. Not too long afterwards, her dad came into the kitchen.

"What's this about, Beth? You know you don't have anything to be afraid of here with me. Why don't you come out into the great room and sit with me?" The great room was an enormous living room. There was even a deer head on the wall, which Beth hated.

"In a little while we can have one of the doctors come and draw a little blood, and run a couple of tests to make sure that you're okay. Come on, sweetheart, let's go." He stood there impatiently and Beth felt a flash of annoyance.

"Dad," Beth did not move from the kitchen table. It wasn't the big one, it was the little old one that she and Jenna liked to eat at sometimes. "Sit down, Dad. Jenna, thanks, I can take it from here. I need to talk to my dad alone."

The housekeeper gave her a surprised look and left. Her dad frowned. "Dad," said Beth, "you and I have to talk. Right now. It's about this sickness back home," she did not consider the farm to be home, "and about that creep Stan - well, he used to be an okay guy, I guess, but now he's a creep. And maybe a murderer. You know something about all this, Dad. And I want to know what it is."

"Beth, sweetie, you're right. Stan is a creep. But you're safe from him now.

You're safe here."

"Dad, I deserve to know." She noticed that her father had sidestepped the main issue and she didn't like it. "Don't think that just because I'm a kid, I can't understand. Stan did stuff to people. And I think you know what. I think he made people sick. Maybe even some kids I know. And that's because he was working on some virus stuff, stuff that you're interested in. Stuff like you work on."

"He did make people sick." John frowned. Kids his daughter knew? It had come that close to her? She had said something about her best friend, hadn't she? "He's a carrier, Beth, at least we think so, of a bad disease. That's why I want to have one of my doctors draw a little blood from you, to make sure you haven't been infected."

John wasn't really all that concerned. He had caught this just in time, just before it went out of control. It had been close. He had Stan locked up safely now. He wouldn't admit it, not yet, even though it was obvious his daughter guessed.

He had heard nothing from his contact at the PDC, the man he paid handsomely to keep him informed of any inside workings that might affect him or his operation. There was no indication that the team in Providence, which now included his ex-wife Lily, was doing anything other than a headless chicken act. It made him smile to think of Lily consulting for the PDC Specials. It was just too silly. If it weren't for people like him - well, there were no other people like him, only a few very far behind him in second place - the Specials would have no good research, let alone good pharmaceuticals to work with. And to hire someone like Lily - he could only assume it was because of the influence of her new boyfriend, the Providence detective, Wesley Martling. What a mistake.

Beth could see she wasn't going to get much of a direct answer so she tried again.

"Dad. Dad, listen to me. This is important. If Stan is a carrier of some el sicko creep disease, do you have the cure? I mean, do your scientists, your research doctors? People like that? Do you have the cure here? A vaccine or something? I need it! My friend Sarah -" she broke off, feeling suddenly and to her horror as if she might cry. She hadn't meant to mention Sarah's name; how did that happen?

John considered various responses and finally decided for the truth, or close to it. "Not yet, honey. Not yet. But we will soon. Is your friend in the hospital?"

Beth nodded.

"That's good. That's best. I think she has a good chance, a very good one, with supportive care."

That was all there was to it. Beth found herself next having blood drawn and then being shown to her room. It was her usual room but she noticed immediately that there were bars on the window.

"To help keep you safe," her father told her, which was creepy, as he gave her a kiss.

He left and she sat down on the bed. The bars would make things harder but not impossible. She had seen the way her dad shifted his eyes when he told her there was no cure. There was one, and it was here. She knew it. There had to be, there just had to be. She knew where the hospital section was and she knew where the labs were, and she had made friends with a couple of the doctors. She would have to find a doctor and make him show her where this drug was, and make him show her how to use it. A tiger could convince a doctor, she thought, if necessary. She would have to, even if it meant her dad finding out what she was. She didn't want to think about that.

So she waited, even though waiting was hard. The room had its own bathroom so there was no reason for her to want to leave on that account. She could shift into tiger form and take out whoever was guarding her door. But if she did that she might do the guard some real harm and she didn't want to hurt anyone, not really, not seriously, and she certainly didn't want to kill them. She shuddered; that would be awful. But she had an advantage, aside from being the boss' kid. She had always been a pretty good girl - well, with a few exceptions - when she was here. She could trade on that now.

She looked around the room to see what was available. Could she use the little stool in the corner? Then she could have smacked herself. She had the ability to change her form partially. Surely with the strength of an almost-grown tiger cub in her hands and only her hands she could accomplish what she wanted. She hoped. She wished she knew something like that Vulcan grip she had seen on an episode of that ancient tv show, "Star Trek".

She opened the door to her room. Outside, as expected, was one of her father's thugs. At least, that's how she was trying to think of them, although in this case it was really a nice guy named Chad, just out of college. Chad treated her like an adult and a human being, which almost gave her second thoughts about what she was going to do. Almost. "Hey, Chad," she said.

"Hey, there, Beth. What can I do you for?"

"I'm sorry to bother you but I was really hoping for some milk and cookies." "Yeah?" said Chad. "I heard you had turned into the tea type."

She had forgotten that her father kept his people briefed on everything he thought it was necessary for them to know.

"Not really," she said. "I was just trying to impress to impress my dad. So he'd treat me more like a grownup."

Chad grinned. "I hear ya. I'll get that milk and the cookies. What kind of cookies?"

"Chocolate," she said.

"Now you're talkin'. Yum." Chad pulled out his cell phone and started to punch in the number for Jenna, or whoever was on duty now in the kitchen. He did not turn away. So Beth resorted to one of the oldest tricks she had read about.

"Oh my God!" she said. "Is that a spider?!" She let out a little shriek.

Chad couldn't know that she found spiders of any size fascinating. "It's huge!"

She pointed. Chad, his call uncompleted, turned to look. Beth concentrated. For a moment she was afraid it wasn't going to work but then her hands turned into big paws. She made sure her claws were retracted and reached for Chad.

She hadn't taken into account that he was so much taller than she. He heard her behind him and half turned, still holding the cell phone. His eyes widened. He hit two buttons on his cell. One, she knew, aborted the call he had placing, the one for her cookies and milk. The other was an alert, transmitted immediately throughout her father's telecommunications system. Then he reached for the taser on his belt.

Beth had no choice. She shifted completely into tiger form and launched herself at Chad. Her big paws, claws sheathed, went around his throat. Surprise and her weight tipped him over backwards, sending the phone skidding from his hand. His head hit the floor with a smack.

Beth jumped back. Chad lay still on the floor. Horrified, she leaned over him. Had she killed him? No, he was breathing. And she could hear his heartbeat. She hoped he wasn't badly hurt. At least help was coming for him, and coming soon. The alarm he had sent out would have people here any second now. She glanced her clothing on the floor, ripped from her sudden change.

She took a brief moment to grab it with her teeth, take it into her room and shove it under the bed. With any luck it would buy her a few more minutes as people wondered what had happened to her.

She had already left the room when something occurred to her. She went back in and gently took Bunny-buns from the bed. With the stuffed toy in her mouth she glanced around the room. Finally, she trotted over to the big old horrid ancient chest that sat in the corner. She had always hated the thing and never used it, although her parents said it was antique. She pushed the toy behind it, leaving only the tip of one cloth ear sticking out. She had to hope that her father's people wouldn't find it.

As she left the room, still in tiger form, she could hear footsteps coming quickly. No other sound, no shouting. Her father's guards were too well trained. She slipped into the shadows and headed for the stairs, then realized that she would certainly be found that way. The bathroom for the "help", as father called them, was open. Its window was, too. It was only a second floor window and there was a tree outside. It was the work of a moment for Beth to leap through the window, catch hold of the branch and then climb carefully, backwards, down the tree. Now there was shouting from inside the house. They had found Chad and they had found that she was missing. Beth slipped into the shadows and headed for the little building that housed the labs and the small hospital.

"I think we're both warm enough now," said Lily.

"I'm not sure," said Wes. He didn't want to let Lily go. "Maybe we should do that again to make sure."

"Wes! That humming! It's your cell!" "I don't hear it –"

"Of course not. It's in your pants pocket, over there." Tiger hearing again.

Simultaneously, she heard her own cell buzzing.

The two of them struggled into their clothes and tried to answer their cell phones at the same time.

"Lily," said Sandra, "we're here. We're at that motel; we've met Wes' team.

Three big guys. They have one of those new public health warrants that will let them come in, guns blazing, if you find anything, but it's gotta be more than just a lab or a hospital or even some kids in cabins. I want to come in there now, meet up with you. I think I'd have a better chance of finding something -"

"Sandra, you're the only vet we've got, the only one on our side. We can't risk you." Lily had managed to get her pants and boots back on.

"That's what they said. I was hoping you'd say different and help me out here. I don't like this."

"I don't like it, either. But we haven't got much choice. Wes is my onsite backup and you guys are the big guns. I guess, literally."

"Call soon."

"I hope so," said Lily. She hung up and looked at Wes. "Did Clem tell you what Sandra told me?"

"Pretty much, I expect."

They finished dressing and stared at each other in the darkness. Lily could see him clearly, the worry on his face, the determination.

"Lily," said Wes. He held out his arms. It was obvious he couldn't see her nearly as well. "Lily, I love you. I want you to know that. When this is over -"

"Don't say it, Wes, not yet." But she heard it, clear as day: I want you to marry me.

Wes sighed.

"Listen, Wes. I love you, too. I don't think that I've ever loved a man more. I know I haven't. But it's not time, not yet, to talk about anything else.

My daughter's in there." She shivered and put a hand to her forehead. She was hot. And she had a headache and she was feeling nauseous again. A great time to get sick.

"You're right," said Wes. "First things first."

"Wes, I want you to know how much I love you. Whatever else happens, I want you to know. In case -" she didn't finish the sentence.

Wes found her in the dark, coming to the sound of her voice. He put his arms around her and kissed her passionately. "There is no 'in case'. Let's go get Beth." And Stan, he thought, and that SOB John. "Is your phone signal set?"

Lily checked. Her cell phone was set to call Wes' phone if she needed help or found anything that could call in the Specials.

"It's set," she said. "Then let's go."

Beth headed straight for the little hospital and then lurked outside, trying to peer through one of the lit windows. Eventually, she could see shapes moving around inside. She counted four, as best she could tell. After a while two men and a woman came out of the side door and walked away, talking among themselves. They were so busy talking that they neglected to notice that the door had not locked behind them. It was a stroke of luck. That would leave one person on duty. Knowing the way her father had set things up, she assumed it would be a doctor. It was time to go in.

She couldn't get the door open. It wasn't locked, it just required that she turn a knob and her paws just wouldn't do the job. Well, she would need to be in human shape anyway to talk to the doctor. With a sigh, Beth shifted back to human form and then shivered. It was cold, it was raining, and she had no clothes. Quickly, she opened the door and slipped in.

Once inside she stepped back into the shadows. She needed clothes. She headed for the supply lockers and heard whistling. She and the doctor, and whatever occupants of the hospital might be there were not alone. She had someone else to deal with. A young man, a physician's assistant, she thought, turned the corner pushing an IV setup. When he had passed, Beth slipped into the supply room. She found a lab coat, a huge stack of hospital gowns and then, miraculously, a pair of kids' jeans and a pair of sneakers. The jeans were a little too big for her but she rolled up the cuffs, trying not to think about what might have happened to their owner. She stuffed gauze into the toes of the sneakers and laced them on. Then she pulled on a child's hospital gown with a size small lab coat on the top of that. It would have to do.

The corridors of the tiny hospital were empty but the rooms weren't. There were several rooms, most of them with children, often two to a room, children she had met at the cabins. Beth swallowed a lump in her throat. How could her father do this? However good his intentions, could they justify this? She could tell that some of the children were very ill indeed.

When she peeked into one room, however, she drew back in fear and alarm. The occupant of the bed, the only bed in the room, was an adult. It was Stan. He was strapped down and there were tubes running into his arm. Beth stepped back hastily, even as Stan began to pull against his restraints and growl. He was in human form but she knew what was happening: his tiger senses were aroused and he knew she was there. He smelled her. An alarm in the room began to beep. There was the sound of running in the corridor and Beth ducked into one of the other rooms just as the physician's assistant hurried past. As soon as he had gone into Stan's room, Beth headed back toward the lab. She was pretty sure, from the scent of things, that the doctor was back there.

He was. He had his back to her and he was writing up some notes on a laptop computer. Beth tried to think of his name but couldn't. She settled for his title.

"Doctor."

He actually jumped, almost upsetting the computer. He looked both alarmed and afraid, which told Beth a lot. When he saw who it was, he relaxed a little.

"Beth! What are you doing here?"

"I came to ask you a question. A very important question."

"And why are you dressed like that? I heard you were visiting your dad, up at the house, but what -"

"Doctor, if you reach for that alarm button, you will be very sorry."

Beth shifted her eyes from their normal human rounded shape to a cat's eye slit. She moved with the swiftness of a big cat to stand beside the doctor, putting her still human hand over his.

"Oh my God!" The doctor was staring her in shock.

"I'm not going to hurt you," Beth said, and then thought for a second. She needed him to pay attention and believe her. "Not unless I have to, but you aren't going to touch that alarm and you are going to answer some questions."

"Right." The doctor swallowed and his eyes looked slightly glassy. It was Beth's second experience in one night with inciting fear in someone and she didn't like it.

"I want to know how to cure the disease people get from somebody like - like Stan." She didn't want to say, like me. She wasn't like Stan. "The disease like those kids have. And my best friend. My best friend Sarah, back home, is sick."

"She has the shifter's disease?" Despite himself, the doctor looked interested. Beth recognized the flame of academic curiosity when she saw it.

"I don't know," she said. "I don't know what that is. What the, the symptoms are. I do know that Stan, that creep, went to see her. And put her in this coma and she won't wake up!"

"Ah," said the doctor. "That's a bit different. Probably related but different.

We're working on both."

"I know you are. And I know you have a cure for Sarah. I just know it.

And I want it!"

"I would like to help you, Beth, but I can't. What we have farthest along in development right now is a vaccine against what your friend has. It is only about seventy something percent effective - do you know what that means?"

"I'm not an idiot!"

"And it has some bad side effects -"

"I want it. I want it for Sarah and I want it right now!"

"Beth, you don't understand. It's a vaccine. It's not a cure, it's -"

There was a shriek from down the hallway. Both Beth and the doctor froze, and stared. There was another shriek and then a crash and then crying.

"Shut the door!" cried the doctor but it was too late.

A moment later the physician's assistant ran in, or rather, staggered in. He was bleeding from a huge gash down the side of his face.

"He's out!" gasped the man. "He pulled out of the restraints! I thought he was too sick; he looked out of it. I didn't loosen them, I swear, I just went to attach the new bottle to the IV, and he pulled right out of the restraints and he clawed me, oh God -"

"I'm going," said Beth. "He wants me. You'll be safer if I leave." If Stan had wanted the physician's assistant dead, then dead he would have been. She was sure of it. But Stan didn't care about the physician's assistant, who didn't know how lucky he was to escape. Stan wanted her.

"You had better hit that alarm now, doctor. And lock the door. And look after him." She pointed at the wounded physician's assistant. The man was moaning.

"Oh God, I could get it, I could get it! I could get the virus!"

"We've both been vaccinated," the doctor was saying.

Beth frowned. She wished she had time to think about that, but she didn't. "It could be worse. You be could eaten," she said. Both men stared at her in horror.

She needed to get out before Stan found her. She could feel him, feel the force of his searching. He was very sick but he was also very strong. She ran through the door, hearing it slam shut behind her and then she was running down the hall and out the door, the front door this time, which set off an alarm, and into the night.

CHAPTER SIXTEEN

T HE RAIN HAD LET UP, fortunately, although the winds hadn't, but it was a short enough hike through the woods. Lily held out her hand to stop Wes several times, as they waited for John's perimeter guards to go past. She could see Wes' hand go for his gun but she knew he wouldn't shoot unless he had to. He wouldn't have to, not if she heard the guards first, and she would.

The plan was for her to walk right up to the front door of the house and knock. Wes didn't like it, of course, but it was the easiest way for her to get in. Getting out again would be the problem but she wouldn't admit that.

"Just wait in there." Lily guided Wes to a small shed that was really not much more than an overhang on the side of the house. Trash cans were lined up in this little shelter. "You can squeeze in back there," she told him. "It's just household garbage, nothing toxic. It shouldn't take me long. If he's got Beth, it's kidnapping, right? We can call in Clem's guys on that even if we don't find anything else. It doesn't matter whether or not it will stand up in court. And we know she's in there. It'll only take a couple of minutes."

Wes wished she would stop saying that. He knew from experience that these things rarely went as planned.

"You have that number punched in, right?"

"Right." Lily touched her bra. She had stuffed her cell phone down there. It wasn't hard to reach and in the unlikely event that John had her searched, his men wouldn't dare go that far. She waved at Wes, then remembered he couldn't see it in the dark.

"Here we go," she said. She walked up to the front door and raised her hand to knock.

Two men converged on her, one from each side.

"Hold it right there!" said one. He had a drawn gun which took Lily by surprise. It confirmed that something was definitely going on up here.

"Whoa," said the other man, holstering his own weapon even as he shone a flashlight in her face. "It's Dr. Mossberg, the boss' ex."

"Sorry, ma'am."

"What's going on?" Lily noticed they hadn't backed off even though the weapons were now out of sight. Of course they didn't answer her. She knocked on the door.

It was John himself who opened the door.

"Lily!" He didn't seem surprised to see her but then he glanced around outside. "How did you get here? Why didn't you tell me you were coming? I thought we were going to set this up through the lawyers."

"I didn't want to wait for that." "Where's your car?"

"I left it at the motel and took a cab over and walked in. I didn't want to run into problems at the gate. John, where's Beth?"

"What do you mean, 'where's Beth'? Wherever you left her."

"I left her at school. Your guys picked her up and brought her up here." "Lily, no. They didn't. Come on in, don't just stand there in the doorway.

Phil, check her, please."

"What!" Lily feigned surprise and took a step back from the man who moved toward her hesitantly.

"Lily, there are strange things going on. We can't take any chances."

John was upset although he didn't show it. He had no warning. He had guessed she would come when she found Beth missing, but he didn't know she would be there now and he hadn't planned for it. He should have. He was paying his contact in the Specials a small fortune to insure that he knew every move Lily made. Just because Stan was out of the picture - had been out of the picture, didn't mean his contact was off the hook. John tried not to show his concern.

Lily wouldn't have brought her so-called team with her, would she? No, he doubted it. Not from the look of her, disheveled and worried. If they were here, she'd have them with her, wouldn't she? She had certainly done what she claimed: driven straight up, like the proverbial bat out of hell, straight from finding out that Beth was missing from school, and then walked in to avoid being held at the gate. It was bad enough that she had eluded security and she could have run into Stan, now loose out there somewhere on the grounds. Even worse than that was the fact that he really didn't know where Beth was and he was worried sick. He couldn't admit that to Lily. He could only hope that Stan didn't have her. For a moment he wished that he and Lily could join forces.

Lily subjected herself rather less than gracefully to the search. Fortunately, Phil, the searcher, was a bit embarrassed and somewhat less than thorough. He made sure she wasn't armed and he checked only perfunctorily to see if she wore a wire. He certainly did not dare to fish inside her bra.

"She's clean," Phil told his boss.

"Lily, come and sit down, and tell me what's going on." "I don't want to sit down. I want to see Beth."

"She's not here. Lily, you had better tell me what happened."

There was no way around this. She could hardly storm through the house, looking for her daughter. She turned down the offer of tea or something stronger but she let John lead her into the Great Room near the fire. When he heard the story of Beth's disappearance from school he frowned.

"I didn't authorize that. You're sure it was my pilots?" "One hundred percent."

"I'm going to look into this," he said. "Lil, you know that your boyfriend, ex-boyfriend, whatever he is, Stan, was doing some work for me. He's well, he's gotten sick. It's possible he's behind this." John pulled out his cell phone and thumbed it on. "I'll take care of it, don't worry."

For a moment Lily almost believed him.

He thought he was hungry but he wasn't sure. Stan knew it wasn't a good sign that he couldn't distinguish physical from psychic hunger but that wasn't all that important right now. At least he was out of that hospital and away from the doctors. There was business for him to take care of, lots of business.

He knew Lily's cub was here, and he wanted to find her. He needed to find the cub and kill her. This would accomplish two things. It would get rid of the little brat, who was far too smart for her own good, once and for all, and would free Lily up for him. Once she no longer has the cub, she would be more willing to be his mate. She had been his mate before and she would be again, and this time he would take care to guard her more carefully.

She was here, he knew it. She had followed her cub. He had caught a trace of her scent on the wind. He would kill her cub and mate her tonight, whether she was willing or not. Then he would have staked his claim and then he would take care of the males, of the men, the other men in his Lily's life. He would kill them all.

Stan was having a difficult time separating tiger thinking from human thought. He supposed it could be his illness but it was also his power. He needed to kill his rivals and any male who threatened him. That meant that cop who thought he was Lily's mate. And it also meant John. Stan saw no reason why he couldn't kill his employer and take over his enterprise. He had the knowledge, the sheer physical power and he had the research capability. As for John's men, that was simple. He could see them before they could see him and he could smell them before that. He could take them out before they fired a shot.

For a brief second, the drawbacks of this approach flashed across his mind.

Murder with the intent of taking over someone's business empire was not an accepted practice in human society. And The PDC might have something to say about his tiger capabilities, too. That didn't matter. He had his contact within the PDC Specials and he would kill any Specials who came after him tonight, male or female, and eat their essence. It seemed like a good plan and he was too far gone to see the holes in his logic.

Step one was to find the cub. That should be easy. She was only a cub, on the run from him in the night. He was smarter and more powerful than she.

Stan leaned to one side and vomited. For a moment he felt dizzy, but it passed. And there was a bright side to this. His illness only heightened his abilities. He knew where the cub was.

Beth knew Stan was behind her. Now she wished she had stayed in the house, under her father's protection. She, too, had caught the scent of her mother on the winds of the storm. If she had stayed in the house she could be with her mom right now and her mom would protect her. Her mom would have found her no matter how hard her dad tried to keep her hidden. Her mom would have helped her get the vaccine for Sarah. But she couldn't get back to the house. Stan was between her and the house, and he was hunting her. He was very sick, she could tell, but he was also big and he was strong. There was a thicket of some sort of decorative bushes ahead of her. They grew low to the ground and Beth scrunched low and sidled back into their cover. They were scratchy and she closed her eyes as she wriggled back. Maybe that would help if Stan came after her. When Stan came after her. She wished she could reason with him but he was too far gone, she knew it. She wondered if she went back to the doctor if he would give her the vaccine for Stan, but wouldn't they have already tried that? Maybe they wouldn't have. She suppressed a little whimper.

"Nobody here has Beth." John made no attempt to hide his worry and concern now. He had done a good job of suppressing it before but now it was in his interest to let Lily see it. "It is possible that my guys picked her up from school, since I had the Citation down there on business, but then anything is possible, including that the sky might fall. They would have had no reason to pick her up. If they did, they would have brought her to me. But on the off- chance that you're right, I'm having the grounds searched. No one has seen her." That part was strictly true and John looked his ex-wife directly in the eye when he said it.

Lily felt a new wash of alarm. John didn't know where Beth was, he truly didn't.

"Look," John was saying, "I know we've got our differences where Beth is concerned and I know we both have our legal eagles flapping around in attack mode. But I believe, no, I know, that we both want the best for Beth. I know neither of us would ever harm her. Tell me you believe me, Lily."

"I believe you, John. When you say you want the best for her, anyway. Our ideas of what that means are very different."

John sighed. "Look," he said, "if it makes you feel better you can have a look around the house. As I said, I'm having the grounds checked. "

They walked through the house together. Jenna was in the kitchen, having tea.

"Jenna," said Lily, "have you seen Beth?"

The housekeeper took a deep breath and then looked Lily in the eye. "No, I haven't," she said. There was a tightness around her eyes and the corner of her mouth twitched slightly but her voice was steady.

Lily nodded. "Thanks, Jenna." Liar, she thought. So there it was. Her daughter was indeed here.

"After this," she said, "I'm going out to help with the grounds check." John swallowed. Jenna hadn't been all that convincing to him either. "Lily, I don't think that's a good idea. With Stan out there -" John stopped, horrified. It was just like Lily to get him to let his guard down. "What do you mean, 'Stan's out there!' Explain that!"

"He was here." Sometimes it was a good idea to tell the truth, or at least some of it. "We had him locked up in the little hospital but he got out. He's very sick, Lily; I don't expect him to make it far or last long. But it's not a good idea to go out there until we get him back."

"If Beth is out there, I'm going out!"

"We don't even know for certain she's here. I doubt she is. I know my people. If they say they didn't bring her here, they didn't. Come on, Lil, check out her room and then we can talk it over, figure this out."

He wasn't offering to call the cops, she noted. Not that he would do it if he offered. They climbed the stairs to Beth's room, the one she always stayed in when she was here, the one that had been hers ever since she was little, before the divorce.

The room was empty.

"See?" said John. "She's not here. Go in and check it out for yourself."

The bed was made up but there was no luggage, no backpack, nothing to show if her daughter had been there. Lily stepped into the room. She noted the new bars on the window but she said nothing. She glanced in the closet: nothing there but an old jacket of Beth's, one she knew Beth had left on a prior occasion.

Then she saw something from the corner of her eye, something behind the antique trousseau chest in the corner. She knew without looking at it, without examining it any further, what it was. It was Bunny-buns' ear. She gave no indication she had seen anything out of the ordinary. She turned away and made a pretense of going to look further in the closet. Under cover of that move, she reached down into her shirt to press the button to give Wes' cell phone the alert code.

Her arms were grabbed suddenly from behind and twisted. John pulled her around and the cell phone in her hand went flying, landing by his foot. With a vicious motion John stomped it, smashing it.

"Damn it!" he said. He sometimes tended to act precipitously. He should have saved the phone, had the aborted call traced.

"Who were you calling, Lily! Who!"

Lily said nothing. John twisted her arms up harder behind her back, causing her to cry out with pain. John released her suddenly, throwing her down on the bed. Then he scooped up the smashed cell phone and stomped from the room, slamming the door behind him. She heard the locks being turned and outer bolts being shot home.

Lily sat up, slowly massaging her arms. After a moment, when the circulation returned, she got up and went to the chest in the corner. She reached behind it, pulling out Bunny-buns. She put the stuffed animal down carefully on the bed and rubbed her arms some more.

What now? In hindsight it was easy to think that she should have shifted to tiger form as soon as John had grabbed her. She had been too surprised. In all their years together John had never been physically violent with her before.

Manipulative, yes, of course, but not violent. And if she had shifted, then what? She couldn't have killed him, and she wondered if she would have even escaped the house. Well, she needed to escape it now. The question was how.

She went to the window. Even with tiger strength she couldn't break through steel bars. Could she break through a triple-locked door? The door was wood but it was heavy wood, and there would certainly be at least one guard, if not more, outside the door. She had to do something. Unfortunately, the next thing she did was run into the bathroom and throw up.

Wes waited. He waited some more. He glanced at his watch. The numbers glowed faintly, picking up ambient light, rather like Lily's eyes when she shifted. An hour had passed. He waited some more.

He was good at waiting. It was part of his job, although he didn't like it. Another forty minutes passed. That was enough. He should have heard from Lily by now. Wes came out of the trash shed, moving cautiously, alert, keeping to the shadows.

It was a huge house. Obviously Skyline Pharmaceuticals had been good to John Belkner. Wes knew the layout from Lily but he wasn't sure if he should try to get in. He had seen several of John's private security guards and managed to avoid them so far but if he went in there he was afraid it would have to be with a drawn weapon and he could clearly see that wouldn't get him very far. Maybe he could get in through the kitchen entrance a little more easily. He would still be found but he might have a few more minutes and the element of surprise. He moved stealthily toward the back of the huge house. As he went he stared at the windows, noting which were lit and which were not, trying to see if anything looked out of the ordinary.

He put his hand on his cell phone. He should have felt the soundless buzz of Lily's call by now. There was something wrong. He couldn't call in the Specials, not yet, not without evidence. He would have to go in, one way or another. If only Lily were a telepath. He tried reaching out with his mind. He felt nothing. If she felt his touch she could not return it, let alone pass any information that way.

Damn the torpedoes and full speed ahead, he thought.

He waited until the pair of guards had made their rounds past the kitchen door. When they were well past he drew his gun and slipped the safety off. With his other hand he felt in his pocket for the set of keys Lily had given him, and hoped the locks had not been changed. Then he edged forward toward the door.

"Hold it right there! Drop it and don't move!"

The command came out of the darkness. For a moment Wes was tempted to disobey, to throw himself to the ground and fire in the direction of the voice, but he knew better. Cursing his luck, he dropped the Glock to the ground.

"Now kick it away from you."

He did, and then there were three guards surrounding him. If he had given in to temptation, he would almost certainly be dead.

They searched him thoroughly, finding the gun on his ankle, the keys, and his cell phone. They took all of them.

"Okay, buddy, you want inside, let's go inside. You can talk to Dr. Belkner."

CHAPTER SEVENTEEN

Lɪʟʏ ʜᴇᴀʀᴅ Wᴇs. Iᴛ ᴡᴀs more apt, actually, to say that she felt him, the touch of his mind on hers. She wanted to answer him but she couldn't. Why couldn't she be a telepath? Of all the psi "diseases" that one was the most useful. But no, she had to be a shape shifter.

Lily leaned over the toilet bowl and threw up again. The light hurt her eyes. She was most definitely sick; there was no denying it any more. It was the worst timing, except for one thing. In an odd way, she felt more powerful than before.

In human form, it didn't seem to mean much but perhaps in tiger form she could take advantage of this. Lily shifted. She felt her clothes rip around her and didn't care, because now she saw something she hadn't seen, or rather, something she had overlooked in human form.

There was a heating duct. Of course there was heating duct, but this one was well overdue for repair. The wood around it was soft. it was a very, very old farm house and they had never gotten around to having all the repairs made. She and John had discussed this, it now seemed light years ago, but obviously John had never had the repairs made. Maybe because it would require ripping out part of the wall, maybe because he had forgotten about it, maybe because Beth was the only one to use this little suite and Beth didn't know or care. The reason didn't matter. What mattered was that the wood was not only soft but the wall was an exterior one. It would be easy to claw a hole and then smash through.

Lily threw up again. Then she crawled into the tub for an episode of diarrhea. Then it was out of the tub again to lie on the floor panting, with the worst headache possible and her eyes half-closed against the too-bright lights.

She didn't know how long she lay there. She needed to rip through the old soft wood around the heating duct. Rip through it and pull the wall apart, and make her way outside. There was a tree outside that she could leap to and from there to the ground. She just couldn't remember why she was supposed to do these things. It would take so very much effort. She threw up again but not much came out. Nothing left of dinner, she thought. Had she had dinner?

Maybe she needed food.

Yes. She needed food. She felt queasy but food would help. There were two kinds of food here, she could smell them: the usual kind and the psychic kind. She needed both. She would have both. They should not be too hard to find, she just need to find the energy to rip through this flimsy wall. Lily snarled softly.

She was back in the bushes. He could smell her there. She smelled of fear and she also smelled like Beth, Lily's daughter. Lily's daughter, the child he had laughed and played with. For a moment this almost gave Stan pause, but only for a moment. Lily's cub stood in the way of his claiming Lily, of claiming everything that should be his.

The cub was hiding under the scratchy, thorny thicket, hoping he wouldn't go after her. Stan crouched, swishing his tail in anticipation. A little rose thicket wouldn't stop him. His fur was dense and thick, a good protection.

Beth saw him outside her hiding place and she knew had been discovered.

She wriggled back into the thicket, trying to make as little noise as possible, preparing herself to come out on the far side and make a dash for the tree she saw, a big old oak. Stan could climb up after her, of course, but adult tigers were not as spectacular climbers as some other members of the cat family. She was smaller and lighter, and could go higher and with any luck farther out on a thinner branch. After that - she didn't know what, after that. It was as far ahead as she could think.

Beth eased toward the back edge of the rose thicket and prepared herself.

She gauged the distance to the oak tree. And then she broke cover and sprinted.

Stan crashed through the thicket right behind her. The rose thorns unexpectedly scraped his wounded nose and his ear, and he let out a sound, half-growl, half scream. But then he was through the thicket and on the other side, and there was the cub, just in front of him. He reached out with one paw and smashed at the cub, trying to knock her off her feet.

Beth staggered. Stan's paw had knocked her off balance and she rolled.

She knew now she would never make it to the oak tree.

Stan saw the cub roll and he pounced, claws extended, huge jaws open. Beth flipped onto her back and extended her own claws. He was so huge, this adult tiger, and he was going to kill her, but she was not going out without a fight. She was terrified and she was furious. As Stan crashed down on her, she could see that his ear was torn off and the rose thorns had done more damage, and his nose was streaming blood. With the claws on all four feet extended, she went for his wounded nose and ear. She connected.

Stan yowled and then bellowed, the combined growl-threat of an adult tiger. He had been going for the cub's throat, intending to crush her windpipe, to sink his teeth into her jugular. But now the pain caused him to pull back slightly and the cub wriggled free and ran.

Beth ran for the tree and leaped up, grabbing onto the trunk. She could feel the swish of air behind her as Stan swiped again at her. Beth screamed for her mother. It was a terrified and angry sound, the cry of a cub in mortal distress.

Lily heard the screams, both of Stan and the cub. Her cub, Beth.

She was on her feet before she knew it, standing in a puddle of vomit. That didn't matter. Only one thing mattered. Lily hooked a claw into the rotten wood around the air duct and ripped. She hooked all four claws on her right front paw and ripped again. There was a satisfying splintering sound. Then Lily slammed the wall with all the strength of a female Siberian tiger whose cub was in danger.

The wall smashed and there was a hole. Lily rammed through it at speed, leaping for the tree outside the window. As she did, she roared her challenge to whatever endangered her cub. She knew what that was and who it was. She knew where to find him now, how to follow the sounds she had heard. She was going to find him and then she was going to kill him. Stan was finished whether or not he knew it.

"Holy fucking shit!" One of the men holding Wes let go of him and staggered back.

All the men either froze or turned in the direction of the roaring and the animal screams.

"What the fuck was that?" whispered one of them. "You know what it is," said another.

It bespoke good training that only one of his guards had released him, Wes thought. The roaring had certainly taken him by surprise and frozen him in place, temporarily disabling him. Even had he been prepared, he would not have been able to break free of the other two guards, unfortunately. But things got rapidly stranger.

There was a crashing, ripping, tearing sound right above them, coming from the side of the house. Pieces of wooden shingle and siding, insulation and boards began to rain down on them. The men dropped back, one of them still holding Wes.

"Fuckin' A, the house is collapsing!"

From right above them came a deafening, bloodcurdling roar, a challenge that made all of them duck and cower. Then from directly over their heads came another crash. Wes looked up. All of them looked up. In the tree above their heads was an enormous tiger whose eyes shone in the darkness. One of the men screamed, a hoarse, terrified sound.

The tiger leaped to the ground and stared for the briefest of moment at the trembling men. Wes had just enough time to recover and he was ready. He stood up and spun away from the guards. The tiger stared straight at him and then nodded, jerking its head in the direction of the original screams. Then it turned and ran, vanishing into the darkness.

Wes grabbed the flashlight one of the men had dropped, and pulled his own Glock from the unresisting hand of another of the men. Then he turned to follow the tiger. She was gone already.

"Lily!" Wes called. "Wait!"

Of course she didn't. He flicked on the flashlight so he could try to follow her tracks, the giant pugmarks in the soil. Soon he lost them on the packed earth. Simultaneously he came to the realization that leaving the flashlight on was a good way to draw his pursuers to him. He was not only hunter but hunted, but he needed the light to see anything at all in these unfamiliar woods. He compromised by trying to shield the light.

He needed help. It was time to call in the Specials. He reached for his cell phone and then remembered: he had grabbed flashlight and gun but not his cell phone. He had no way to call Clem and no way to get Clem's team in. It didn't matter that he didn't have evidence in hand, he would any minute now if he didn't get shot or eaten.

Another roar echoed through the night and he froze, but only for a second.

Now he could orient on the sound. He slipped the flashlight farther up his sleeve to shield it further, just as the rain began again. Thunder boomed overhead. He shivered.

Maybe after this I could get a desk job, he thought, wryly. At least it wouldn't have me out in the woods at night in a freaking gale with a sick shape shifter and Specials back at their hotel. Lily had looked sick, too, in her tiger shape. Come to think of it, she hadn't looked all that well in human shape, either. One thing he would need, and soon, he just knew it, would be a doctor.

Wes stopped dead. The rain poured down and another roar echoed, much closer now. He had an idea how he just might be able to contact the Specials, waiting warm and dry in their motel. He didn't know if she would hear him.

He didn't have the connection he had with Lily, and he wasn't anywhere in the proximity of the motel. Proximity had always been necessary before. He wasn't even completely certain that she was what he thought she was, but he had to try.

Sandra! he shouted the name mentally, with all the force he could put behind it. He considered trying to give details but simple was better.

Sandra! Help!

He could only hope she would hear.

"I don't like this." Clem was pacing. "We should have heard something by now. I think we have to go in."

"Clem, we can't. You know better. Whatever the media thinks, whatever people say, we need some evidence, even with the new public health warrants." Frank had been working for and with Clem on and off for a long time on field assignments. So far his boss had been a stickler for the rules. This new side of Clem worried him.

"Think," said Clem. "What? Think of what?"

"The media. It's a plural noun. The media think, not thinks."

"Whatever. We can't just go charging in there, boss. Especially not when it's Belkner's place." Unspoken was the relationship between John Belkner and the PDC Specials.

The other member of the team, George, sat on one of the beds with the television remote in his hand. He flipped to another channel where two young women with big muscles and virtually no clothing were attempting to push each other off a tightrope into a swimming pool.

"Look at that!" George said.

Sandra couldn't take it anymore. She had surprised herself by liking Clem but that went only so far. The idiots with him reminded her of why she no longer wanted any connection in any way with the government. One of the reasons, that, and the other thing> the thing which nobody had figured out, for all their supposed capabilities. She pulled on her rain slicker and opened the door.

"Where are you going, Sandra?" Clem had made it clear that no one was to leave the room, go anywhere without his approval.

"Just outside. Not going anywhere. Just need a little air." "Okay, just stay right outside."

The members of the Special team regarded Sandra as a tag-along. She was also pretty sure that they resented the fact that her cell, and not theirs, was set to receive one of the emergency signals from Lily or Wes.

Sandra went down the motel corridor and out the nearest door, only a few yards from the room. It was raining again, coming down in sheets. Thunder boomed, not too far away. Sandra couldn't shake the oppressive sense that something bad was happening, something that wasn't just the storm. She pulled out her cell phone and looked at it for the umpteenth time. No message. She hadn't missed it.

The door opened again and Clem came out, in both rain slicker and poncho. They looked at each other.

"Something's wrong," said Clem. "I know it is. They should have signaled by now, one of them anyway."

"What happens if they both just - disappear?" Sandra finally voiced her fear. The thought of Lily in that place, and little Beth -

"If we don't hear by morning we'll have to come up with another pretext to go in there."

"Let's come up with one now."

"Sandra," Clem sighed, "you know Frank is right. We could all lose our jobs, well, we Specials could -" he broke off. It was clear that the veterinarian was no longer listening to him.

Sandra felt as if she couldn't breathe. The force of the mental shout was so great that she almost staggered. Her ears rang and it took a few moments to realize that the cry had come only to her mind.

"Sandra! What's wrong! What is it?" Clem was half-supporting her. After another moment Sandra pulled away from him.

They were in trouble. Wes had taken a great risk to contact her but they were in trouble and it was obviously dire. Sandra looked at Clem, catching her breath. If she told him, if she said how she knew - no matter how she had come to like him, he was still a member of the Specials, still an agent of the government that could not always be trusted. This was her secret, the part of her life she had guarded from everyone.

"Clem," she said. "We gotta go. Now. They're in trouble."

"Sandra, relax. Don't let it get to you. Your cell phone didn't buzz; mine would have, too," Clem paused. "We can't just go in there - Sandra, where do you think you're going?"

"I'll walk, if I have to, but I thought I might try to call a cab along the way." "Cab is a bad idea. We don't want to leave a record. Wait here; I'll get my gear. Or come in and get anything you need. I've got the keys to the agency car."

"I've got what I need except my vet bag." "I'll get it."

"Hurry!"

When Clem emerged a few moments later, he had her medical bag, night vision goggles, several hand guns and a tranquilizer gun. She took her bag and the trank gun while he threw the rest of the gear into the car.

"What about Frank and George?"

"They're not happy we don't have a call for help, no evidence. I said I'd call 'em once we got it. They'll cover for us later."

Now they were both in the car. "Seat belt," said Clem.

Sandra looked at him incredulously but fastened her seat belt. "Let's go," she said.

Clem floored it.

CHAPTER EIGHTEEN

S HE WAS AS FAR UP the tree as she could go without losing her balance. Stan was behind her and below her, swiping at her. He had ripped through the fur on her hind leg and Beth knew she was bleeding, but it wasn't bad. He kept reaching for her, though, and Beth was afraid he would connect and pull her down. She bunched herself up as tightly as she could on the branch. And then, with a shudder, she changed back to human form. Her center of mass shifted and for a second she almost lost her balance. Then she began to edge farther along the branch she clung to. She hoped to get herself just slightly farther from Stan's reach. It seemed to work and Stan roared with frustration.

Beth shivered. She was momentarily beyond Stan's reach but now she was cold and getting colder. He was shaking the branch she was on, while still trying to reach her with a giant paw. It was only a matter of time before her hands were so numb that she could no longer hold on or before he shook her loose.

"Stop it! Stan! Get away from her! Stan! Listen to me! We'll help you, we'll get you well, you will have a contract with me, be my primary researcher, as long as you want it. Guaranteed! Come down!"

John was at the base of the tree shining a flashlight up at him. Stan glanced down, not directly into the light, and snarled. This was perfect. The cub first, and then the cub's father. The male whose territory should be his. For a brief moment Stan's human side took over and he wondered at himself. Surely he was sick now, just as John said. He really did need help. But then Beth shifted her position on the branch just out of reach above him. And she sobbed. Stan snarled again and pawed for the child, his claws raking her ankle. Beth screamed, a human scream.

There was the loud pop of a gunshot. Something burned in Stan's shoulder, making him almost lose his balance. John had shot him. It hurt like fire. Stan glared down at the human below him, the man for whom he had done so much research, the man who had made it clear that he was not valued as he should be. John aimed again.

Stan made no rational decision. All he knew was that he had to act fast and now his priorities were reversed. The man first, the child later. In one fluid motion he leaped from the tree to the ground. A shot sped by him as he leaped; he could feel its wind. His shoulder burned with painful intensity. He ignored it. Once on the ground, he turned and ran straight for John. He roared.

John saw what Stan was doing and tried his best to aim again. How could he possibly misses the center of mass on a tiger? He had forgotten or had never really known how fast the big cats could be. When Stan hit the ground and came for him, he fumbled the gun, then dropped it as he panicked and turned to run. He slipped on wet leaves and then something huge hit him from behind and he was face down on the ground. An enormous paw raked down his side and pain flared.

"No! Not my Daddy, not my Daddy!" Beth was screaming.

I'm dead, John thought. *And Beth will see it happen.* He waited for the snap of huge teeth in his neck.

The killing bite never came. What came instead was a challenging roar that shook the forest. It came from above and behind him. John stopped breathing from the sheer force of the noise. Then the weight on his back was dragged off. The roars continued above him, along with snarls and hisses. When he could move, John rolled away. He was hurt, badly. One of his legs was twisted and broken and it hurt to breathe, probably a crushed rib, he thought, with an odd clinical dispassion. When he coughed, blood came out of his mouth.

Punctured lung, too. It was not good. Where was his security staff? He had left the house in such a hurry that he had neglected to call anyone for backup but surely they heard the commotion. Surely one his security guards would arrive soon. Help had to be on the way.

John looked up. Beth was still safely above him in the tree but nearby a cat fight was under way, a cat fight between two enormous Siberian tigers. John dragged himself back, painfully, trying to find shelter somehow. Fighting to remain conscious, he looked for his gun but it was lost in the darkness.

The two tigers rolled and snarled, and then John saw his gun. Miraculously, it had landed near him. Barely conscious, he dragged himself toward the weapon, finally managing to close his hand around it. Then he passed out.

Lily saw that John was unconscious. He was not dead, not yet, but he could be soon if he didn't get help. She saw Beth above her, clinging precariously to the branch but she had no time to focus on either her ex-husband or her child. She needed all her concentration for Stan. She had wounded him again, her claws ripping through the fur on his left hind leg. He had rolled and pulled away, freeing himself. He did not fight back as he could have. He snarled and yowled but he wasn't inflicting damage on her, just fighting her off.

And then he moaned. It wasn't the moan of a wounded animal; it was the invitational moan of a tiger who wanted to mate. Stan did not want to kill her, he wanted to mate with her. Lily was startled enough to momentarily break off the fight. She looked into his eyes and saw the tiger he had become but also the human he had been. Stan still had feelings for her. He loved her, in his way.

He moaned again and approached her slowly, blinking his eyes. Surprised and stunned by the friendly gesture, Lily did not attack. Looking into his eyes she could see how much he wanted her. She remembered all the time they had spent together, the movies, the pizza, the lunch breaks on campus. And the sex. The sex had been good. The human man was still somewhere in that tiger body. Perhaps he could be saved. She could not kill him, not if he could be saved.

Stan was still approaching her slowly. She could see now that she had hurt him badly, and also that he was sick, as sick, no sicker, than she was. But he would recover, be well, and so would she. Together they could have anything they wanted, after they had rebuilt their strength by feeding. The two kinds of food they needed were both right here in the form of wounded or helpless humans.

Lily drew back slightly. She did not want the psychic food, the sustenance that Stan desired, that she now felt her body craving. And to actually eat human flesh - the thought repulsed her. She did not want it, yet she did. Her confusion cost her concentration. With a sudden leap, Stan was on her back, but he was not hurting her. He had the scruff of her neck in his jaws, a means of control for a mother with her cubs, but with adults it meant something else entirely. Lily could feel the heat of fever and of lust from Stan as he rubbed himself against her, trying to move her tail aside so he could mate with her. She wanted to roll and to push him off, and claw him but she also wanted to mate.

He pushed down with his powerful torso, forcing her shoulders down and her hips up. Her hind quarters rose to meet his. Stan grunted with anticipation.

No, thought Lily. I will not do this. She knew what Stan wanted, beyond this mating, and knew what he would have, if she let him. She dropped her hips and pushed up with her shoulders, beginning her roll, unsheathing her claws, snarling.

"Lily!" Wes was out of breath but he had found them and now the beam of his powerful stolen flashlight illuminated a confusing and upsetting scene.

There was John Belkner, whom Wes recognized from his photographs, lying unconscious or dead on the ground, with a gun beside his hand. Little Beth, wearing no clothes, clung sobbing to a tree branch overhead. And on the forest floor there was a tiger who had to be Stan holding Lily pinned to the ground, with her neck in his jaws. Wes recognized Lily immediately, somehow. And it looked as though the other tiger, Stan by default, was going to kill her. Wes aimed his Glock.

Stan heard the shout and turned his head, even as Lily shifted beneath him. It was that cop Lily had been seeing, and more than seeing. He could smell Wes on her, which infuriated him. And Wes had a gun drawn and aimed, aimed at Stan. Stan's lust was transmuted to fury. In just another few seconds he would have mated his tigress but now that would have to wait. He released Lily and leaped for Wes.

It was so fast that Wes almost didn't see it happen. One moment there was Stan, with Lily in his jaws. The next moment, Stan was on him, going for his throat. Wes fired, but he didn't think he hit Stan.

It would work out, Stan knew. In a moment, this rival, too, would be dead. He would eat his soul and perhaps later and at his leisure, his body. But eat the soul first, yes, for strength. And then, newly empowered, he would take Lily.

He had felt her begin to resist him but that wouldn't matter, not after he had soul-fed, and he could feed quickly. He would be stronger than she was then and he would overpower her. And then for the cub, who still clung to the tree branch. And then he would eat John Belkner's soul, if the man was still alive.

He pinned Wes beneath him and turned his head to roar at Lily, the roar that immobilized his victims. It should hold Lily in place until he had finished with Wes, and then he would complete his interrupted mating of her.

Lily was not immobilized. She could feel the heat of fever in her and the strengthening of her powers as well as her dreadful hunger. She knew it was the same kind of power Stan had but she knew now what she wanted and it wasn't Stan. It wasn't anything that Stan represented. Stan was not going to kill Wes, not if she had anything to do with it. That Stan tried to immobilize her the way he had his intended victim in the parking garage infuriated her.

Lily sprang. She sank her teeth into what was left of Stan's already mutilated ear and with her right front paw, all claws extended, raked his face, trying to sink a claw into his eye.

Stan screamed and turned. This should not be happening. He went for Lily's stomach with his claws and teeth, and tasted blood. Now Lily screamed, but she fought back.

Wes lay on the ground trying to catch his breath. He felt as if he had been run over by a truck. Something sticky was running down the side of his face, a lot of something sticky. He put his hand up and felt that part of his scalp was loose, a flap of it. *Gives a whole new meaning to the term "scalp wound"*, he thought. He realized he was in shock. A scalp wound wouldn't do that, shouldn't do that, it wasn't serious, even if it was bloody. Worse than the scalp wound, though, was what oozed from beneath the huge tear in his jacket and shirt. Wes put his hand to his stomach and felt something protruding from the long, deep wound there. His intestines? He felt dizzy and slumped back on the ground. As if from far away he heard Beth crying, "Mommy! Mommy!" and there was a crashing through the underbrush, somebody approaching. Maybe one of Belkner's security team, who would shoot everyone but Belkner. He needed his gun but he couldn't seem to find it, couldn't seem to think.

"Holy shit!" breathed Sandra, as she came into the clearing.

Clem was right behind her, both of them with powerful flashlights. Clem gawked. It looked like a battlefield but the snarling, screaming and roaring made it clear that this was this was an animal rampage. Clem drew his weapon but then froze. He had no doubt one of the tigers was Lily and one was Stan, but which was which? He remembered Stan had a wounded ear but there was so much blood now that it was hard to tell, and the two feline combatants kept shifting position.

Then one of the tigers pinned the other one on its back. The tiger on top tried to grab its opponent's muzzle in its jaws.

"Shit," said Sandra.

She had been rummaging in her backpack and Clem saw she had the tranquilizer gun. Perfect, he thought. Why hadn't he thought of that? There needed to be a protocol for dealing with shape shifters.

Sandra was having a hard time getting the dart into the gun. In the meantime, the tiger on top seemed to be trying to roll its opponent over. And then the most amazing thing happened. Afterwards Clem was not certain he had seen it, it happened so fast, and then it was over. He never reported it, afraid he had been hallucinating.

One moment Beth had been clinging, naked, shivering, and sobbing, to the tree branch. The next moment, she wasn't. When one tiger pinned the other, she screamed.

"Not my Mom! No!"

Suddenly there was no longer a human child clinging to a branch. A tiger cub leaped down, somehow landing on its feet. The cub grabbed the top tiger, sinking its powerful little jaws into the tiger's already wounded leg. The tiger roared with pain and turned.

The cub was no longer there. Clem blinked and so did the tiger. When Clem looked around he saw Beth, shivering and naked, beside her father. How had that happened? Was he truly hallucinating? He must be. He had no time to consider the question. Beside him, Sandra fired her tranquilizer dart at the top tiger. The dart hit and the tiger roared but the dart seemed to have zero effect.

Clem had no doubt now as to which tiger was which and he aimed, and fired at Stan, hitting him in the shoulder. Stan charged him, roaring. Clem froze, dropping the gun, incapable of moving. He knew his life was over.

Stan never made it to Clem. It wasn't the bullet which brought him down and it wasn't the tranquilizer. It was Lily. She slammed into him from behind and sank her teeth into his neck.

Stan fell, and then rolled part way. Lily did not release her hold but now she was looking into Stan's eyes. She saw again the man she had known; the man she had thought she could love. She saw the lust, which no longer touched her. And she saw pleading. He was gravely wounded but if she let him go he could escape and perhaps he could heal. She could help him to heal.

"Lily, do not let him go."

The voice was Grandfather Lee's and Lily heard the words clearly. She glanced up aside without releasing her hold. She thought she saw the old man under the trees, near where Beth crouched beside John. His form seemed to shimmer slightly. To the side of his shimmering form, she saw Sandra loading another dart. Even as she looked, Stan made one more try. He reared up, his claws raking down the side of her face. Reflexively, Lily bit down. She felt her canines pierce the jugular and she held on until Stan ceased to thrash.

Then she looked up again. Stan lay motionless beneath her, still bleeding.

The taste of his blood was in her mouth. It wasn't just Choua Lee's form that shimmered. Everything shimmered. Clem and Sandra stared at her in shock, Sandra with her now loaded trank gun dangling loosely from her hand. Wes had pushed himself to a sitting position under a tree but he was barely conscious. And there was Beth, shivering. Why had no one given her child something to wear?

She shook her head and tried to ask but what came out was a tiger's growl. Everyone but Beth and Wes flinched. Lily knew she needed to change back to human form. Or did she? Being a tiger was so much better. And she was hungry. She looked at her fresh kill. Another tiger, true, but fresh meat. The blood tasted so good. And nearby were fresh souls.

"Lily, you must not." It seemed to be the voice of Grandfather Lee, but then he wasn't there, was he?

Lily stared again at her kill. She realized just where that blood came from, the blood whose taste she had been savoring. Lily backed away from Stan's body. She sat on her haunches and heaved until the contents of her stomach were emptied out onto the rain soaked ground. Then the headache crashed back so strongly and painfully that she mewled like a kitten. With the last of her strength she changed again to human form. She was vaguely aware of the cold ground beneath her, of Clem and Sandra leaning over her.

"Beth," she whispered. "Take care of Beth. And get Wes. Don't let him die." Then she passed out.

CHAPTER NINETEEN

Tحسب...

HERE WAS SUNLIGHT STREAMING INTO the room. It was warm. The curtains were open and Monster was curled up beside her in a pool of sunlight. Lily opened her eyes all the way. There was something she should remember, something - she sat up abruptly, almost pulling the IV out of her arm. An alarm began to begin to beep and in a few moment Sandra was by her bed.

"Finally," Sandra said.

Lily swallowed. The memories were coming back now.

"Where's Beth?" she croaked. "Where's Beth! Is she okay! And Wes?

What happened? Is Clem okay? John?" She wanted to ask more questions but her throat was too dry. Sandra handed a glass of water with a straw in it.

"Beth is fine. Drink that. Not so fast! Slowly. Beth is fine. She didn't get sick. Nor did Wes. Or Clem. You're another matter. You've been at death's door and delirious most of the time. It's probably due to this guy here that you survived." She gave Monster a scratch behind one ear.

"What?" Lily handed the glass back.

"Distemper. The new form. That's what you had. It's what made you and St - what made you so sick. Monster must have given you some immunity. The good news is that you won't need a booster for two or three years." Sandra grinned at her. It was a joke. She did not mention that it wasn't just Monster who had saved her. Beth's blood carried the same antibodies and, even though she showed no signs of shape shifting. A transfusion of Beth's blood, performed by Sandra herself, had helped Lily fight off the illness. Sandra decided to save this fact for later, much later. She still wasn't just sure what she had seen Beth do and what was hallucination.

Lily did not smile back. "You had better tell me what happened. And Beth, where is she?" She remembered some sort of dream about Beth, that her daughter was a tiger cub. Surely it had been just a fever hallucination.

"She's over helping out at the clinic, with her friend Sarah. Beth is fine. She told us about sneaking out of the house to find a doctor who could give Sarah the cure for whatever was making her sick and how Stan almost caught her. She was lucky; all she got was a scratched leg and ripped up clothes.

Sarah's fine, too, by the way. Whatever she had was self-limiting. They took her to the hospital and gave her some clinical support but they couldn't find anything. She had some cuts and Stan clawed her a bit but she's okay - really, she's fine. The wounds have healed amazingly fast, just like Beth's. Lily, really, Beth's okay. And Sarah pulled through. Some of those Hmong kids pulled through, too. The word is that they got their wandering souls back, or some such. Lily! Are you listening? Beth is completely fine so you can stop worrying. She stayed at our place most of the time you were sick."

"Thanks, Sandra, I don't know how to thank you."

"That's what friends are for. Beth is a great kid." "How long have I been out of it?"

"A week. Nine days, actually." "And Wes? And Clem? And John?"

"Wes and Clem were in the hospital for a while." "But I was never in the hospital?"

"Not for long. Clem got you pulled out once we figured out what to do. We didn't want to risk it. We thought it was better if we gave you care at home.

Fewer questions. Fewer questions by fewer people. Clem's not all that bad a guy, you know? We've been taking shifts."

"We?"

"Clem and I. At least, Clem and I since we got out of the hospital. They only held us over night."

Wes came in, carrying a mug of steaming coffee.

"Wes! You shouldn't be drinking that stuff! Not yet!" Sandra glared at him. "I know, I know, but I figured a few sips wouldn't hurt."

Sandra went and took the mug firmly from his hands. Lily stared at him. "I know," said Wes. "I look like hell."

"You look," said Sandra, "like Frankenstein's monster. Well, maybe not that bad."

"Meep!" said the cat on the bed, hearing his name.

Both Wes and Sandra laughed but Lily did not. She couldn't stop staring at Wes. Stitches ran down the side of his head, where the hair had been shaved away. Wes saw where her gaze was.

"These come out tomorrow," he said. "They're no big deal. They were going to use staples. It's just scalp wounds. It'll all heal up. What you don't see is what was serious."

"Is still serious," said Sandra. "Show her."

Wes hesitated but then lifted the loose t-shirt he wore. Lily gasped. A long red wound ran down his abdomen, held together with surgical stitches.

"They just let me out a couple days ago because I promised to be good and take care of myself. No showers for another few days. Just sponge baths, if you can believe it." He made a face.

"Oh my God, Wes." Lily leaned over, almost pulling the IV out again. "Oh Wes." She felt tears dribble out of her eyes and was shocked. Furthermore, they stung her face. She reached up and felt the little butterfly stitches down one side of her face.

"Here," said Sandra, "lie back. He's going to be okay if he behaves himself." She gave Wes a glance that said he'd better.

"Lily, I'm fine. I will be fine." Wes came and sat on the edge of the bed and tried to put an arm around her. "Maybe not as stunningly good-looking as I was but fine. The scars will give me a certain dangerous allure."

"The scars will be mostly under your hair when it grows back, and the other scar will be under your shirt and pants," said Sandra.

"When I wear clothes," said Wes.

"Get this IV out of me," said Lily. She knew the banter was at least in part to relax her. It didn't.

"I'm not sure that's wise," said Clem, from the doorway. "You still needs supportive care, Lily. The IV should stay for a bit."

"I'm fine," said Lily.

"Have you seen yourself?" asked Clem. "When you do, you'll know I'm right."

"Clem!" Sandra and Wes spoke together.

Lily stared at them. "Give me a mirror," she said. Her hand went to her face again but she pulled it back.

"Clem," warned Sandra, but Clem picked up the hand mirror from the dresser and gave it to Lily.

A huge scar ran down the left side of her face. It was held together with what seemed like an endless line of tiny stitches.

"We had a hard time keeping you from pulling on those when you were out of it," said Clem. "For a time there we had to tie your hands down to the bedstead. Wes, don't get up. Not unless you're going to move over here and sit in this chair. You shouldn't be walking around much yet."

Lily kept staring at her face.

"You can get plastic surgery," said Sandra.

"The feds will understand if you go for plastic surgery. They're keeping track of you now, since you're one of my team, and feds take care of their own," said Clem, "so don't worry about that."

"Clem, you're a fed yourself." Lily did not put down the mirror.

"Yeah, that's why I can say that. And I'm a pretty high up fed at that. Got promoted. We found out where the leak was. John Belkner had paid somebody to report on your movements and on Stan's.

And on Stan's research. And Stan paid him for the pretty much the same thing in reverse, only he paid more than John Belkner, if you can believe it. Our guy - our ex-guy - chose to collect from both. Somebody in my unit." He looked grim. "He is, shall we say, no longer employed by the Specials."

"Oh God," said Lily. "Stan." It was all coming back. "And John." The mirror slipped from her hand and she felt sick again. "Stan - did I - oh God."

"You killed Stan," said Sandra. "You had to. You saved all our lives.

Including John Belkner's. He's very badly hurt and still in the hospital but he will survive."

"You saved my life, and I'm grateful to you." Clem came to the bedside and took her hand. "I want you to know that."

Lily looked away. She couldn't think of what to say. "You killed him," said Wes, "but that's all you did."

Lily remembered it now. The taste of blood. She felt nauseous. "I didn't -" "No," said Wes and Clem together, "you didn't."

"What you did do was stave off an attack by a shape-shifting, man-killer of a tiger, and you did it by distracting the animal and pulling it off me with your bare hands. It's no wonder you were hurt in the process. It's a miracle you weren't killed yourself, an ordinary human against a tiger. You were very lucky." Clem's face betrayed no hint of expression other than sincere gratitude.

Lily opened her mouth to ask a question, caught the gleam in Clem's eye and didn't ask it.

"I see," was all she said.

"I'm sure it will all come back to you in time," said Clem. "In fact, when it does, the Specials would like to have you as a consultant, full time. Just a consultant, Lily, that's all. On my team. You can keep your university job if you want to, but you know we pay very well for consultation and we would love to have a cultural anthropologist as a resource. It's true that to work with us you have to be tested for psi diseases but you've already been tested many times, including while you were so sick, and you came up clean. No need to do it again.

All you got from those tiger bites was a bad case of septic shock. I'm really glad to see you pulling through."

"Uh. Right. Uh. Thanks."

"By the way," said Clem, "we tested Beth. She's negative for everything, too. Dr. Belkner has been babbling things about several tigers, but he was badly hurt and delirious. He is no longer considered a credible source in the light of events. Anyway, think about the consultation offer. I would love to have someone with such special, um, analytical talent."

"Right," said Lily again. "And Clem. Thanks." "De nada."

"Hey, Clem," said Sandra, "come out here a minute. I need to talk to you.

Wes will look after Lily for a minute."

"In a few minutes, Sandra. I want to tell Lily more about the job-"

"Now, Clem. They may have something to discuss."

"Oh, right."

Sandra followed him and they closed the door. Lily stared at Wes. He looked back.

"Are you really going to be okay?" She heard the catch in her voice but she didn't try to hide it.

"Really am," said Wes.

Lily began to cry and then found she couldn't stop.

"Whoa," said Wes. "Hold on." He came and sat gingerly on the bed beside her. "I'm going to be fine and so are you. You really can get the plastic surgery, you know. The feds will pay for it. Clem said."

"I don't care," Lily began, and then she stopped. She had never really cared before about how she looked. "Am I ugly this way, Wes? I am, aren't I? I'm ugly. Do you think I'm ugly?" It mattered more than she had thought it would.

"Lily, you are the most beautiful woman in the world. Right now. Just as you are. Stitches, IV line and all."

"Oh, Wes." Lily began to cry in earnest. "Are you really going to be okay? I don't know what I'd do without you!"

"Fortunately," said Wes, "that's not something you're not going to have to worry about. Not ever, not if I can help it." He leaned over and kissed her gently.

Lily kissed him back.

Lily stood looking out the kitchen window. It was open, and the smells of early summer wafted through the window. She was marinating tuna steaks for the barbecue and Monster twined around her feet, meeping hopefully. Sandra and Leslie were coming, bringing salad. Wes and Clem were bringing beer and soda, and Wes would undoubtedly be staying after the others left. Lily smiled. This barbecue was in part a celebration of his recovery and hers. The Lees were coming, bringing corn they had grown themselves on the community plot. Deb Lattinger was bringing dessert.

Sarah was already here, and she and Beth had been playing out at the edge of the woods all afternoon. Lily would have to check them for ticks when they got in. They would both be going to summer camp, but the later session, just before school opened again in the fall. Lily no longer needed John's help to afford the camp, not after the amazing bonus the Specials had paid her. She was seriously considering the consulting job. Besides, John would need to focus all his attention and his resources on salvaging his pharmaceutical empire. Custody battles were no longer even remotely on the horizon.

Lily glanced at the clock. People would be arriving before long. She figured she had better call the girls in and get them cleaned up. It was a relief greater than she could express to know that Sarah had pulled through her illness and that Beth was clear of the shape-shifting mutation. Any odd and vague memories from "that night", anything she couldn't reconcile with her own reconstructed outline of events, had been shoved aside as fever dreams, soon to be forgotten, she hoped. It was only fear and fever that had made her think, even for a moment, that Beth could be a tiger. She leaned up close to the window. As she did she caught a reflection of herself in the glass.

Her scar was minimal and still healing. She didn't think she would need to take Clem up on his offer of paying for surgery.

"Beth! Sarah! Come in and get cleaned up!"

Just inside the edge of the woods, the two cubs were playing chase. First the tiger cub chased the cougar cub, then the reverse. When they heard Lily's call they were rolling over and over together in the leaves. They stood up reluctantly and there was a brain-twisting shimmer. Two girls stood naked in the shade of the forest.

"Where's our clothes?" said Sarah.

"Behind that rock. Hey, look, you're getting boobs!" "Am not!"

"Are, too! Lucky!"

"Girls!" Lily's voice was closer.

"Shit!" said Beth. "She came out looking for us! Hurry up and get your clothes on!"

"How come you're a tiger and I'm a cougar?" said Sarah.

"I dunno. We talked about this before. Just get your clothes on before my mom finds us or we're both toast." Beth frowned. She would have to have a talk with her mother some time. Her mother would remember, would figure out for herself that Beth knew she was a tiger, and maybe even that Beth could be a tiger herself. Beth would have to talk to her. Just not today.

"There you are!" Lily looked at the two children. Their shorts were askew and Sarah had her tank top on inside out. Odd, she hadn't remembered that detail from when Deb had dropped her off. It must be some new preteen fashion. Both had leaves in their hair.

"Look at you!" said Lily. "People will be here any minute. Come in and get washed up!"